MOTHERS OF MIST

EMMA SHELFORD

MOTHERS OF MIST

Kinglet Books
Victoria BC, Canada

ISBN: 978-1989677391 (print)
ISBN: 978-1989677346 (ebook)

www.emmashelford.com

First edition: August 2021

DEDICATION

To Wendy, who was there for every story

CHAPTER I

It wasn't so bad, being possessed. Except when the spirit possessing me was in a bad mood.

"I can't believe we didn't find an artifact this trip," Caelus grumbled from his perch on my shoulder. His silvery thread-form swayed with the motion of my steps as we approached my condo building.

"I had high hopes for the Royal Ontario Museum," I said. I walked briskly, but an arctic wind wriggled its way between my coat and scarf and chilled my skin. A January cold spell had hit Vancouver while I was away in Toronto, and I'd arrived this afternoon to steely gray skies and a threat of flurries. "Maybe we'll have better luck in a few weeks when we visit the Smithsonian. That should be stuffed with ancient relics. Surely, at least one of them will be a magical artifact."

"It will probably have nothing." Caelus sighed and glared at a robin perched on a railing, its feathers fluffed against the cold. "Just like the others we've visited in the past month."

I shook my head at Caelus' dramatics and unlocked the door to my condo's lobby. Warmth embraced me like a cozy blanket, and my shoulders relaxed for the first time since I exited the airport. The elevator was parked on the sixth floor, but it swiftly descended when I pressed its button.

"How about a little positivity?" I said to Caelus. "You quickly forgot about the Celtic neckband we liberated from that museum in Montreal. That torc was a genuine, bona fide artifact, infused with excessive elemental threads. That was an unqualified win. And now it's destroyed, and our safety deposit box contains the Leaf artifact, awaiting annihilation."

"One artifact," Caelus said. "One, in over a month of searching. We need to pick up the pace."

"So impatient. We're visiting as many museums as we can."

I glanced at my reflection in the wall mirror when I entered the elevator. My mahogany hair was flat from the plane's dry air, although it was nothing a shower wouldn't solve. A good sleep would cure my tired eyes, although I noted with approval that fatigue didn't detract from my overall beauty. Being in the flush of youth again, after years in my former fifty-something body, had many perks. I'd discovered a few downsides, notably my unexpected and unwelcome monthly visitor, but on the balance my younger body was treating me well.

"I just want to complete my mission in good time," Caelus said quietly.

I glanced at him in surprise. His tone was wistful with a hint of hopelessness, which was a far cry from his usual pep. I was about to probe further, but the elevator doors opened. Caelus' eyes focused on the entrance to my suite.

"Someone tried to open your door." He pointed. "Look at the handle."

My eyes followed his finger. Because Caelus shared my body, I could see the world through his eyes, and it was a magical sight. The threads of the world—as Caelus called them—surrounded everything with energy or life. Every person was wrapped in threads, and every animal, plant, and inanimate object with inherent energy showcased a different color of strand. Even the elements of nature were represented: air, fire, earth, and water. Every shade imaginable created a layer of shifting, glimmering color over my vision.

It had taken some getting used to, but the wealth of information it provided was worth the learning curve. I focused on the threads hanging from my door handle. They were all the same color, a dusty salmon-red, and they shivered with movement.

"Strange," I said at last. "I don't know anybody with that thread color. Maybe it was visitors to another apartment that had their directions wrong."

"Maybe." Caelus didn't sound convinced.

I wasn't convinced either, but I shook myself and reached for my key. No stranger had a reason to visit me at my home, but I also had no reason to expect trouble. My natural caution made me slide my key into the keyhole with as little noise as possible.

The door was already unlocked.

"Be ready," I whispered to Caelus, then pushed the door open wide.

Every drawer in my kitchen gaped open, and utensils and bowls littered the floor. My couch's cushions teetered in a pile on the rug, and my hall closet's door disgorged a sweater and my running shoes into the hall. The same salmon-red threads from the door handle draped over many of the items.

A rummaging sound floated out of my bedroom. I tiptoed forward, hands up and fingers tense, ready to grab the nearest air threads. I wasn't defenseless—far from it, with Caelus' elemental abilities at my fingertips—and I was confident I could handle this home invasion in ways I couldn't have dreamed of before my body-switch and co-habitation with Caelus.

I peeked into the bedroom. A figure dressed in clichéd black faced away from me and rummaged in my night table drawer. My ire, already raised from the ransack of my condo, rose even higher. The figure was slight, and her form-fitting clothes told me she was a woman, but a black balaclava hid her features.

I raised my hands and yanked at nearby air threads. With a shriek, the woman's feet slid toward me, and her head smacked the night table's edge with a solid thud.

I barely had time to smile in satisfaction before she whipped her arm toward me. Her fingers gripped a short chain, unremarkable except for copious threads that swirled around it. Instantly, vertigo took over. I staggered into the doorframe and crumpled to the floor. Everything spun with nauseating color, and the meager lunch I'd bought on the plane threatened to make an encore.

I squeezed my eyes shut, but it didn't help. Rage flooded my body and blood pounded in my ears, but I didn't fight my body's reaction. To be attacked in my own home? Any anger I felt was entirely justified.

The woman stumbled past me, and I thrust my hand out blindly. It hit hard shinbone, and the woman tripped with a gasp.

My head stopped reenacting a fairground ride, and I opened my eyes with relief. The woman scrambled to rise from her position sprawled on my carpet. With a twist and a flick, I crafted an air blade and tossed it toward her.

She hissed in pain, and I used her hesitation to crawl toward her. I grabbed her ankle, but she kicked me aside and leaped to her feet. I joined her—thanking my youthful body again for its nimbleness—but before I could prepare a further air blade, she pulled another amulet from her pocket.

My arms froze in place. I tried to step forward, but my legs weren't listening to my brain. Even my eyelids wouldn't blink. Whatever the woman had done, it had paralyzed me.

"Move, Morgan!" Caelus shouted. He dived into my body, then came back out with a look of terror. "What did she do to us?"

The woman huffed with a mixture of mirth and pain then rushed to the front door, her hand clutching her bleeding side. I wanted to shout for her to stop my paralysis, but my vocal cords were similarly frozen. My unresponsive lungs added to my mounting panic. Was I going to die here?

"I don't know what to do." Caelus wavered back and forth in front of my face. "I can try to give you some air, but it won't be the same."

I couldn't answer him, not even to give him an expression of consent, but Caelus went to work anyway. He dissolved his humanoid thread-form, and his silvery strands flowed into my nose and mouth and then out again, in and out. Fresh air entered my beleaguered lungs with every movement, and the terrible ache in my chest lessened slightly. Every few breaths, he wafted a draft of humid air toward my drying eyeballs.

A full minute passed—the longest of my life, as I fought in vain to breathe or move—before the paralysis passed. I dropped to the carpet, heaving in sweet gasps of air on my own and blinking furiously.

Caelus reformed and hovered near my head until I caught my breath.

"We need to work on defensive thread-armor," I said weakly. "I know they say the best defense is a good offense, but I like being prepared."

"We can do that." Caelus nodded vigorously. "Humans are so fragile. We haven't encountered any danger since the dustup with Starr and the sisters, and we got complacent."

I leaned against the wall, drained from my ordeal. I briefly considered running after the woman, but too much time had passed. She would be long gone.

"Who was she?" I said. "Who would be going through my things? What did she want?"

"You don't have much." Caelus looked thoughtful. "The only thing you do have is an artifact. Could she have been after that?"

"How does anyone know about that? Although, I agree she must be connected to the sisters and their order. Who else has amulets of power? Every drawer, every cupboard was systematically searched. She wasn't a garden-variety thief. You're right, the only thing of interest I possess is that artifact. But how did she know, and why does she want it?"

The sisters didn't know I'd relieved them of their artifact last month, and I had no intention of telling them that they were no longer the caretakers of their precious Leaf. Who else would know or care about artifacts?

I had no answers, but I had a condo to straighten. It was best to focus on the tasks I could complete. No sense in spinning my wheels in fruitless pondering.

After my condo was somewhat orderly once more, daylight had faded, and I was ravenous. My cupboards contained only a jar of jam, olive oil, and spices, and my fridge was similarly unequipped.

A tapping on my patio door distracted me from my examination of the kitchen. I turned my head. Beaky, the rust-colored pigeon who had strutted in front of my security camera last month like a runway model entranced with her own image, gazed at me through the window. Her beady eyes stared at me with expectation.

"The cupboard is bare, my friend," I said aloud to the bird. "You'll have to wait until I visit the bakery. I know you're as addicted to sourdough as I am."

Beaky cooed with a strident tone. When I didn't respond, she turned with a disdainful air and walked away, her head bobbing. I chuckled at her antics. She had claimed my balcony for her own, but I didn't mind. She was welcome company in my quiet life.

What day was it? I checked my phone. Saturday, which meant that the sisters were training tonight. After the debacle with their youngest sister Starr, the sisters had ramped up their training schedule. As their former security guard, I had a standing invitation to join them. As a friend, they held me in high esteem for my part in saving them and their artifact from their wayward sister.

Guilt prevented me from growing a savior complex, since I had stolen their Leaf. I couldn't pass up their offer of training, though. It wasn't in my nature to ignore opportunities when they arrived on a golden platter, and my physical talents were underdeveloped. I might have the power of the wind, thanks to Caelus, but as this afternoon's encounter had shown, I needed to sharpen my skills. Combined with physical strength, increasing my magic abilities would make me truly formidable. And with greater power, my options only grew. I wouldn't need to worry about wandering down dark streets at night. I could continue my quest to find ways to help the disadvantaged with more power.

I looked forward to these sessions that trained my body as well as my magic abilities. I had been given a priceless opportunity with this younger body and Caelus' magic, an opportunity to be more than I was. I wanted to plumb the depths and stretch myself to be as powerful as I could be.

Nothing came for free, but training three times a week seemed like a small price to pay for greater abilities. The company was pleasant, too. I was not currently rich in friends. I'd never had many, if I were being honest with myself. My friend Anna Green was the best I had, and the rest were merely acquaintances or hangers-on.

The sisters, while not my bosom buddies, were pleasant people who didn't want anything from me. I enjoyed their company.

I pulled on stretchy exercise pants and a pair of runners before exiting my condo with a spring in my step. The rain was thick and heavy, wanting to turn into snow but without the wherewithal to take the final plunge. I avoided puddles in my porous running shoes and shook my umbrella off vigorously at the door of the neighborhood bakery, Upper Crust. I needed a bun to satiate my growling stomach, since I had muscles to build and magic to hone.

No lineup slowed me at the closing bakery, and I walked with purposeful strides to Rosemary's salon. The door of Cut Right was unlocked, and I slipped inside and quietly paced to the back entrance. My feet took me through the hall and down the stairs. Chattering female voices beckoned me from a brightly lit doorway, and I stepped inside.

CHAPTER II

"Morgan!"

A chorus of voices greeted me inside the sisterhood's basement gym. I smiled. After I'd saved them from their wayward sister Starr, popular opinion in the group had classified me as a hero and a welcome member into their society. Even Denise and Shu, stalwart skeptics, now waved at me with friendly expressions. Joy, her frothy blond curls bouncing as she jogged on the treadmill, waved me over.

"Come warm up with a run," she panted. "Shu's not ready for sparring yet."

"That's fine." I climbed onto the track and touched buttons with practiced fingers. The conveyor belt jerked into motion and I picked up my pace. "I've been on a plane all day. I need to work out the kinks before Shu gets a hold of me."

"How was your trip?" Joy glanced at me. The sisters wondered about the purpose of my travels, but I hadn't told them about my artifact goals. All they knew was that I liked to visit new places.

"It was great. I mean, the weather in Toronto this time of year is terrible, but the museums and restaurants were worth visiting." I changed the subject before Joy could pry more. "I meant to ask last week. How is Starr doing? I know she's not in the sisterhood anymore."

"She's back at school, according to Jasmine." Joy nodded at a dark-haired girl in the center of the room trading kicks with slender Amanda, whose fiery red ponytail flicked with her motions. "She seems fine. Subdued but content. Jasmine says she visits with the school counsellor Thea frequently, so that's positive. Thea Diamanto is the leader of the motherhood, the next level of our order."

"Is Starr visiting for counseling or for whatever punishment the mothers promised to hand out?"

Rosemary had hinted that Starr would be punished for her role in last month's incident, but she hadn't known the details. As misguided as Starr's actions were, and as terrible as the consequences would have been without my intervention, I still worried for her. Her actions could have been my own, if I hadn't had the benefit of age, experience, and a little soul-searching to back me up. I hoped she was receiving counseling from Thea and not punishment.

Joy shrugged, her face unusually somber.

"I don't know. I hope she sees the error of her ways. She could never come back to the sisterhood, but it's not the same around here without her."

"Good riddance," Denise said when she passed in front of our machines on her way to the free weights. Her dark skin glowed from exertion. "I'm glad she's gone. I want to know I can trust my sisters, not have them stab me in the back."

Joy glanced at me.

"Everyone has their own opinions about Starr. Some are stronger than others. She's left a hole in our sisterhood, though, one way or another." Joy's face softened into her usual cheery smile as she looked across the room at a scrawny fourteen-year-old girl on a stationary bike. Her face was red from effort, but she laughed at something Wanda said to her. "And Sarah is doing so well. She's young, but I think she was a good choice for our newest sister. She's Amanda's cousin, did you know? We all thought that Sarah would take Miranda's place because of her heart condition, but ever since you fixed her up, Miranda's been as right as rain."

"It's not a permanent solution," I said. "I have to heal her again every week. It's not a replacement for surgery."

Joy waved my comment away.

"But she can live, and train, and be a full sister! It's huge, and don't you forget it."

"It's hard to," I said with a smile. "Miranda treats me well."

Every week during our healing, Miranda brought me a treat.

One week it was a bouquet of flowers, last week it was a box of baklava from the Lebanese grocer down the road. I tried to discourage her—she was only nineteen with a job at a hair salon and rent to pay—but she insisted.

"Where's Rosemary?" I asked before Joy could launch into her next monologue. She loved to talk. Normally I didn't mind listening, but sometimes I needed to get a word in edgewise.

"She'll be along soon. Oh, look. Speak of the devil."

Rosemary entered the door wearing mid-calf yoga pants, her wavy brown hair in a ponytail that made her look younger than her twenty-five years, and a frown. She looked tired, like she hadn't slept well, but she brightened when she saw me.

I pressed a button to stop the treadmill and hopped off to greet her. She tossed her purse against a nearby wall and wandered to the free weights section. Denise moved to a rowing machine across the room to give us space.

"Good to see you, Morgan," Rosemary said. She picked up a dumbbell with a sigh and curled it into her chest in a repetitive motion. "I'm glad you decided to train with us lately. The others enjoy having you here. Brings up morale, I think."

"After the Starr debacle?"

Rosemary winced. I picked up a kettle ball to pretend I hadn't seen her reaction and started swinging it like Wanda had taught me.

"After all you've done for us, you're a beacon of hope. It's good they have you, because I don't know how much longer I'll be here."

I stared at the younger woman.

"Why? Where are you going?"

"My hearing is sometime next week. The mothers are gathering to decide whether I'm worthy to lead the sisterhood." Rosemary laughed bitterly. "I'll be blamed for the whole thing, just watch. I know I should have done more to stop the attacks sooner—I probably should have called the motherhood right away—but you don't know what they're like. They would have taken over, and this was a chance to prove myself. Not everyone is promoted to the motherhood, you know. They are carefully selected, and I thought—" Rosemary took a deep breath to compose herself. "I really thought I had a chance, that I was on the right track. Now, I have no idea if they will let this incident slide, or if that's it for my dreams."

I didn't know what to say. Rosemary was probably right—she should have contacted others in her order for help instead of letting the attacks continue—and I couldn't relate to her passion for joining the mysterious motherhood. The sisters had all been raised reading the Book of Souls, a selection of ancient legends that outlined the entrapment of the Spirit elemental and the steps to release her to the world and create a utopia on Earth. It was all a bit hand-wavy and idyllic for my no-nonsense brain to buy into, but Rosemary was certain of the rightness of her path.

"We'll find out next week, I suppose," I answered. It wasn't much of a consolation, but I didn't have anything else to offer.

"I'm running a tight ship around here, just in case that improves my odds," Rosemary said with a straightening of her shoulders. "Training is now three times a week for all sisters, and the amulet library is locked down. Only one amulet allowed out at a time per sister, and they must have it back the next day. They have to say what they want it for, too. No more helping themselves to our riches. I don't want another Starr on my hands."

That would put a crimp on Amanda, Denise, and Miranda's questionable dating strategies, and Shu's ease of gaining tips as a hairdresser. Many of the sisters used amulets to control the minds of those around them. I hesitated to use the word unscrupulous, but it wasn't an inaccurate description.

Joy wandered over—her previous companion Jasmine must have been too engrossed in her magazine for engaging conversation—and picked up a dumbbell. She lifted it carelessly, but soon enough her mouth opened with her real purpose in joining us.

"Rosemary, any word on the Seed?"

I glanced sharply at Joy. "What's the Seed, again?"

I vaguely recalled something in the Book of Souls that Rosemary had shown me last month, but I wanted to hear the full story from another source. Within me, I felt Caelus stir with his interest.

"The Seed is another artifact that our order is searching for," Rosemary answered for Joy. "Bringing the Leaf and the Thorn together with the Seed will create the Tree of Life. That, in turn, will bring Spirit to Earth and complete our mission."

"And the others are getting so close to finding it," Joy interrupted. "There's currently a dig in Turkey, and all the signs are there. Inscriptions carved in the rocks, a secret chamber under the ground—any progress on the dig?"

Rosemary pulled out her phone and tapped it, looking for something. Her eyes were bright after her moroseness of earlier. No matter what she thought of her prospects, she was still indoctrinated enough to yearn for the completion of the order's mission. They believed that all living creatures would unite, wars would cease, and cruelty would die a merciful death, all because every lifeform would sense the feelings of the others.

I had a hard time imagining the end of all wars. All it took was a little imagination to understand what your opposition was experiencing, and humans had excellent imaginations. The real trick was making others care.

But the sisters believed, and that fueled their quest.

"There's a hidden chamber at the dig site," Rosemary said. "They can tell with radar or something—I don't know the details—and they'll be excavating soon. Check out the markings on the chamber's door."

Joy and I drew closer to Rosemary's phone, and Shu wandered over for a look. On the tiny screen was a picture of a dusty stone tablet, maybe the length of my torso. Carved onto it was a tree surrounded by the same swirling threads that I saw everywhere with Caelus' elemental vision.

"It's just like in the Book of Souls," Joy said with reverence, and Shu nodded fervently.

"Fascinating," I murmured, my eyes raking over the picture. It was clearly something elemental, given the threads. I had no idea if the order's precious Seed were underneath, but I wouldn't doubt that an artifact was buried deep in the soil of Turkey. Inside, Caelus stirred with excitement.

It might be an artifact, I thought at him. *But it's on the other side of the world. Let's focus on the artifacts within our reach right now.*

His wriggling subsided with a sensation of grumbling and annoyance.

"How is your order digging at historical monuments without getting in trouble with the authorities?" I asked.

"Two are archaeologists," Rosemary said. "Our leader was one as well, that's how she found the Leaf in the first place, back in the forties. They applied for permits and are working with local researchers, everything is above board. Of course, when they break through to the actual Seed—"

"Assuming it's there," Joy said.

"Assuming it's there, they will have to sneak in at night and take it into safekeeping." Rosemary shrugged. "I don't know, I never went down the archaeology path. Didn't have the grades for it. I was doing the people management stream instead—it's important in a secret organization."

"True enough." I had enough experience with secret organizations to recognize the truth of Rosemary's words. I shook my head in puzzlement and set the kettle ball on the ground with aching arms. With all the talk of archaeological digs and ancient artifacts, I had been holding the heavy ball without thinking. "So, some people in the organization specialize in archaeology to better find these artifacts?"

"Absolutely," Joy said with enthusiasm. "I didn't get into

the program—I'm taking online courses in accounting instead, focusing on the financial end of things—but Miranda is taking university classes, and I know Jasmine is thinking about it."

I fell silent for a moment, digesting the news that the sisters centered their whole lives and livelihoods around this nebulous idea of a future utopia. I couldn't decide if their dedication was admirable or foolish. My thoughts drifted with guilt to the Leaf in my safety deposit box, which led me to recall the burglar in my condo.

"I spooked a burglar when I got home today," I said. Anger boiled inside me at the memory, but I tamped it down. This body was so unruly at times.

Joy and Rosemary looked at me sharply.

"Are you okay?" Rosemary said. "What happened?"

"I'm fine. I don't think she took anything. It looked like she was searching for something, but I don't know what. She did use an amulet on me, though."

Rosemary looked horrified.

"It wasn't us, I swear," she blurted out. "The amulets are tightly locked away. I can check the inventory if you like. What did the amulet do to you?"

"It wasn't one of you," I said. The woman's threads had been a rusty salmon-red, and none of the sister's threads came close in color. "The amulet completely paralyzed me. I couldn't even breathe for a minute."

Joy frowned.

"I don't remember one of ours doing that," she said. "Do we have one of those, Rosemary?"

Rosemary shook her head sharply.

"No, we don't. Who else has amulets, besides us and the rest of the order?" She bit her lip. "I don't know, Morgan. I wouldn't swear that it wasn't a mother, but I don't know why they would be searching your condo."

My stomach dropped. I had one theory, and it shook me to my core. If a mother from their order was searching my condo, then they must suspect me of something. Since my only possible wrongdoing was stealing their most precious artifact…

How did they find out? I had the irrational impulse to rush to my safety deposit box to check the Leaf. That would be foolish, though. If they were searching my condo, then they might be watching me. If I did check on the Leaf, I needed to do so without being followed.

My consternation must have been written on my face, for Rosemary's expression changed from concern to determination.

"I'll get you an amulet," she said firmly. "A protection one. I know you have your own powers, but it never hurts to be over-armed. Give me a minute to grab it."

Rosemary carefully placed her dumbbell on its rack and jogged to the door. When I met Joy's glance, she shrugged.

"Lucky you," she said. "We have to beg for amulets these days. But if anyone should get one, it's you. Goodness knows you've earned one."

I smiled my gratitude to Joy and pointed to the central mats.

"Are you up for some sparring? With powers?"

Joy's eyes lit up.

"Yes, definitely. It's our one chance to use amulets at will." She raced to an open briefcase on the floor that contained an assortment of trinkets. Swirling threads surrounding each inanimate object indicated its amulet status. Joy hovered over the case, fingers poised, then she swooped down to select three. One was a ring, one a necklace, and one a keychain with the image of a startled moose. I raised my eyebrow at the last one, and Joy laughed with she saw the focus of my gaze.

"Misdirection," she said. "Sometimes it helps to have an amulet that no one would want to steal."

"What do these amulets do?"

Joy clicked her tongue with a grin.

"That would spoil the surprise, wouldn't it? Come on, let's

find out.”

I walked to the center of the room and gathered air threads in my hands in preparation. Joy faced me across the mat with eyes narrowed in concentration. Wanda stepped forward with her arm extended, and the other sisters paused their activities to watch our bout.

“On my count,” Wanda said. “And stop when I give the signal. Ready in three, two, one. Go!”

Joy threw out the hand with a ring on it and shouted something in Latin. I didn’t wait to find out what she had in store for me. My own hand flashed upward, and I tossed crafted balls of condensed air toward her. The other hand threw up a shield of air that would hopefully deflect whatever Joy had thrown my way.

The air balls were a new trick Caelus and I had developed. With the right twisting, each ball would explode upon impact with different sensations. Some brought a blast of cold, some brought heat, some a terrible itching. This one was my favorite.

“Make it stop!” Joy wheezed between gasps of laughter. She wriggled and writhed with the ticklish sensation that covered her entire body. I grinned, but Joy wasn’t out of the running yet. With a breathless incantation, she grasped the necklace around her throat.

I didn’t raise my hand quickly enough. My limbs moved with excruciating slowness, like I had been dropped in a vat of cold molasses. I tried to grasp air threads, but the motion took forever.

Caelus whooshed out of my arm and regarded me.

“Hi, slowpoke,” he said.

I tried to roll my eyes, but it took far too long. Instead, I directed my frustrated thoughts toward him. He winced.

“A little more gratitude. I came out to help. You might be slow, but small finger twitches can cause damage just like huge sweeps of your arms.”

My frustration retreated as I considered Caelus’ words.

Slowly, so slowly, I crooked the fingers of my left hand. I trapped a few smooth threads in my grip.

Joy stood up once the tickling air slowed, her eyes streaming from involuntary laughter. She raised the moose keychain with determination.

As she tossed the keychain toward me, I drew the threads in my hands backward and poured my intention into them. Miraculously, the keychain slowed its arc of movement and dropped to the ground. When it hit, black powder exploded from nowhere to cover the mat between us.

The other sisters laughed, and Joy chuckled as she released me from my slowness. I stretched my arms over my head, relieved to be free of the restraint.

"What were you trying to do, get me to run to the showers in despair?" I asked Joy.

She laughed.

"Ink works for squid. This is similar. While you're dealing with the dirty darkness, I swoop in to take you down."

I nodded. It was a clever trick, one that I should remember for my own powers. What if I could create a thick fog to obscure my movements from others?

"I hope you know where the broom lives."

Rosemary's displeased voice carried over the chatter of the sisters from her position near the entrance. Joy drooped.

"Yeah, yeah, I'll clean it up," she muttered.

Rosemary nodded tightly and walked toward me. She thrust out an amulet, this one a bracelet of silver chain.

"Here," she said. "Wear this, and attacks of the mind won't stick quite as well. They'll still work, but you can fight them if you stay alert."

"Thanks, Rosemary," I said. "I appreciate it."

"You're welcome." She gave me a sad half-smile that didn't reach her eyes. Her upcoming hearing must have been weighing on her heavily. "Without you, we wouldn't have a sisterhood. It's the least I can do."

CHAPTER III

I slept in, and only woke when the January sun streaming in my windows became too bright to bear.

"Mmnph," I groaned and flipped over to face the closet.

Caelus slithered out of my arm and shoved his face into mine. I jerked back in surprise, my heart pounding with the sudden movement.

"Good morning," Caelus said in a voice that was too upbeat for my mood. I swatted him before I could control myself, and he ducked. "Hey, is that any way to treat your body partner? For shame."

"Sorry." I withdrew my wayward hand and wiggled it like I could shake sense into the digits.

"I've been waiting forever for you to wake up," Caelus said.

"Why?" I yawned and pulled myself into a seated position. My clock told me it was later than I'd expected. Jetlag and heavy exercise would do that to a body. I wished my coffee would make itself.

"Because," Caelus said in the sort of slow, patient voice one used with toddlers. "We need to plan our next artifact search. Where are we going, and when? Sooner is better than later. Today would be best."

"What is the rush?" I said. "We returned from a trip only yesterday."

"A failed trip. We didn't find any artifacts."

"Not every expedition will result in an artifact."

"Most don't," Caelus muttered.

"Look." I ran my hands through my hair, trying to marshal my thoughts into coherent sentences. It wasn't easy so soon after waking. "Trips to other cities takes money and time. Time is something I have, but money is short and growing shorter every day. The funds from my offshore account that I transferred to my cover business Sweet Thing are not inexhaustible. I need to find a job to fuel our artifact searches."

At the thought of a job, my stomach shrank into a ball of dismay. I had no idea what to do about that, despite my half-hearted searches to date. As Morgan Leigh Feynman, I had no experience and no proof of education. My options were limited, and I didn't know where to begin looking. I'd avoided asking at the local shops and stores, but I would have to swallow my pride soon enough and beg for a chance to prove myself.

I hadn't yet put aside the idea of starting my own business—it was what my former self was best at, after all—but the right idea hadn't presented itself. In the meantime, my bank account was dwindling rapidly. I couldn't replenish it from my offshore account now that March Feynman's assets were frozen. There was enough for a while longer, but I liked contingency plans. I never wanted to reach a point of desperation. It was an uncomfortably familiar feeling, and one I would avoid at all costs.

"A job will take time away from our artifact search," Caelus said with a grumpy expression. "I don't understand why you don't simply steal the money you need. You certainly have the abilities to do so. In fact, we walked by the bank yesterday, and I was planning exactly how to—"

"Stop." I held up my hand. "I am not turning into a bank robber just because I can. I do have some standards, some morals."

"I don't understand morals. What's the point?"

I turned his sincere question over in my mind. This was all too philosophical for still being in pajamas.

"Morals are a code of conduct," I said at last. "They help humans get along while living in groups. We all promise to follow similar guidelines for living, and then we rub along more comfortably together. Without morals, everyone would do whatever they wanted without thought of how they hurt others. If I steal from the bank, that's someone else's money that they earned. It's up to me to work for my own money."

"I still think it would be easier to just grab some. Those armored trucks are stuffed with bags of money. I bet they wouldn't miss one."

"Of course it would be easier." I stretched my arms above my head, and my spine cracked. "But life isn't made to be easy. Usually, the easy way out is not the best way."

Caelus subsided into a grumpy yet quiet swirl of silver at my abdomen. I wandered into the bathroom, but my own words came back to taunt me. Was I ready to follow up my big talk with action? Was I ready to ask for a job at a local shop?

I sighed with heartfelt abandon. Yes, I suppose I was. It would be better than running out of money. I had standards, and not simply ones that stopped me robbing a bank. I needed my morning coffee, my decent clothes, my condo. Purchases such as a car dangled tantalizingly out of reach in my current state. And lemon tarts. Those were a necessity these days, not a luxury.

It was time to get a job.

I stepped out from the copy shop with a warm stack of resumés under my arm and took a deep breath to bolster myself for the task ahead. It had been many decades since I'd looked for a job with a resumé. My current document, awkwardly crafted on my phone and sent to a copy shop to be printed, was a necessary mix of holes and fabrications. I would have to rely on the strength of my personality to find a job.

Still, the sun was attempting to shine through thin clouds, and the resumés sat solidly under my arm with thick promise. I strode down Cormorant Drive, looking for a likely candidate to start my job search.

Caelus blossomed from my arm.

"How long will you be looking for a job today?"

"As long as it takes," I said. "We've been through this. I need money to hunt for artifacts. This is a necessary step."

"I know, I know." Caelus sighed and his face took on a mopey expression. Then he brightened. "Wait, isn't there an artifact in this city? You mentioned something about a grail, whatever that is. That wouldn't take any money to find."

I didn't reply to Caelus immediately. My mind drifted to the grail's current owner, Merry Lytton. Or, as I knew him in the foggy memories of my past lives, Merlin.

Re-introducing myself to Merry was the last thing I wanted. I had a fresh start with Morgan, and with the sole exception of my friend Anna Green and an almost-incident with my ex-husband, I'd been successful in relegating my life as March to the past. If I contacted Merry and demanded he hand over the grail, I would surely have to explain who I was and why I wanted it. I shied away from that mess.

"It's in a safe place," I said vaguely. "We can get it anytime. Let's focus on finding new artifacts."

"But it could be in our grasp today! Why aren't we picking the low-hanging fruit?" Caelus closed his eyes in concentration, then his eyebrows raised. "You have history with the guy who has it. Really? That's your reason? It's a terrible one. We should get the grail right now."

"Fine!" I exhaled sharply. Sometimes I forgot that Caelus could enter my mind and see the louder thoughts there. "We'll get the grail soon. But I really do need to find a job first."

Caelus subsided with inaudible grumbling and sank into my arm once more. I stopped before a women's clothing boutique and took a deep breath.

"Here we go," I whispered to myself and pushed the door open.

An unknown number called me the next morning. I answered after placing my coffee on the table.

"Hello?"

"Is this Morgan Feynman?" An unfamiliar voice spoke softly into my ear.

"Speaking."

"My name is Thea Diamanto. I am the leader of the motherhood. I was informed that you're acquainted with the sisterhood."

I blinked in astonishment. Why would the leader of the motherhood be calling me? Had Rosemary given her my number? A chill ran down my spine when I recalled the burglary of a few days ago, and I resolved to speak carefully.

"Yes, I am. What can I do for you?"

"Actually, I was hoping to invite you for tea. I would love to thank you properly for exposing the corruption in the sisterhood. We're grateful for your efforts, and I'm only sorry that I took so long to reach out. Would you do me the honor of coming to my house this afternoon, say at four o'clock? If you're available, of course."

As I didn't have a job yet to occupy my time, and I wasn't due to volunteer today, I had no real excuse to decline. Was it wise to meet with Thea? Part of me wanted to run away as fast as possible from the potential burglars, but the other half wanted to know more. The mothers were the ones searching for the Seed, after all, and any news I could gain about another artifact was another step closer in helping Caelus with his mission.

"That sounds lovely," I said. "Text me your address, and I'll be there."

My stomach growled as I entered Upper Crust, the bakery near my condo. Warm air scented with freshly baked bread and luscious lunch smells hit my nose when I opened the door, and I breathed in deeply to enjoy the scents.

The lineup was long, but it gave me time to consider my options. Maybe a panini. An order of lemon tarts went without saying. I nodded my head and spoke my order firmly to the attendant when it was my turn.

A large figure caught my eye when he emerged from a back room, his arms dusty with flour. My mouth curled upward in a smile, and I waved at Jerome.

He noticed my motion, and a grin broke out on his face. He mouthed the words "five minutes," and I nodded. I grabbed a table, my heart lighter than a minute ago. Yes, I would be ready for a dubious meeting with the leader of the motherhood, after lunch with a good friend and a healthy helping of his delicious lemon tarts.

The server delivered my panini, and I inhaled scents of cheese and toasted bread before sinking my teeth into the sandwich. Raised voices from the kitchen caught my attention.

A short man with a rotund stomach and oval glasses peered with owl-like intensity at Jerome. He brandished a long spatula that I recognized as one of Jerome's cake-decorating tools. Jerome stared at the utensil with dismay.

"You have to clean up better after yourself," the man hissed. He was clearly trying to keep his volume down but wasn't entirely succeeding. The server at the front ignored the scene behind her and smiled too brightly at her next customer. The woman making sandwiches for lunches glanced up with raised eyebrows but kept working at her counter.

"I'm sorry," Jerome said quietly. "It won't happen again."

"This is a working bakery," the man continued, his tirade not nearly finished. "We are under strict scrutiny by the Canadian Food Inspection Agency to keep a sanitary workspace. Anything you do after hours can jeopardize our certifications. You had a deal with the last manager of Upper Crust, but I'm this close to reneging. I can't have a dirty bakery."

"I promise, it won't happen again." Jerome's threads were coiled tightly with anger, but his eyes strayed to the ground. His body language was an odd mix of tense resentment, boiling fury, and despondency. I didn't know what to make of it. It looked like the other man's tirade was angering Jerome beyond endurance, but he was reining in his reaction. As someone trying to keep her own unruly reactions in check, I was impressed by his restraint.

However, there was a time for mollification, and there was a time to stand up for oneself. Jerome was clearly avoiding conflict at all costs, but his restraint appeared to only feed the other man's self-righteous rant.

"It'd better not," the manager growled. He slammed the spatula against Jerome's chest. Jerome clutched the utensil before it fell. "One more screw-up, and you can kiss your after-hours activities goodbye. And your job. I don't want unreliable workers in my bakery."

Jerome opened his mouth—presumably to defend himself—then closed it again with a thunderous look that nevertheless didn't make eye contact with the manager.

"Understood," he choked out, and the manager left with what I could only classify as a flounce.

Jerome took a moment to collect himself. The kitchen worker slid a sandwich on a plate toward him.

"Take your break now," she said in a kind but firm voice. "It's time."

He nodded tightly and took the offered sandwich then walked with jerky steps to my table. I gestured at the other chair, and he lowered himself into it. His lips were tight and his face hard.

"I've never known you to take a sick day," I said quietly. "Nor come into work late. You're hardly unreliable. Why didn't you speak up?"

Jerome sighed a huge whoosh of air, and he sank his head

into his hands with a release of all tension in his body.

"If I can't use the kitchen after hours, my cake decorating business Butter and Scotch is dead in the water. If I lose my job, there are no guarantees I'll get another one, not with—" He sat up and took a deep breath. "I can't afford to lose what I have. He's got me over a barrel, and I can't jeopardize this."

I took a thoughtful bite of my panini. When Jerome stared at the table, lost in his gloomy thoughts, I gently nudged his leg with my foot.

"Eat your sandwich. Food helps."

Jerome huffed in disbelief, but he picked up his sandwich anyway and took a bite.

"I understand not wanting to rock the boat," I said. "When you have no fallback, all you want to do is avoid conflict in the situation you're in. But there's a fine line between being aggressive and assertive. I suspect your manager would respond well to assertiveness. He seems the type to feed on submission."

"I can't risk it."

"I get that." I sighed and took another bite. "Well, here's hoping he settles down after a few days of exemplary behavior on your part. The problem is, you're too much man for him to handle."

Jerome choked on his sandwich with a burst of laughter. When he emerged from his coughing fit with streaming eyes and a grin, I smiled back. As I'd hoped, my words had jolted him out of his doldrums.

"Too much man?" he said finally with another snort of laughter. "I aim to please."

His expression changed, and his mouth opened. I was worried about what he would say, so I beat him to it.

"Speaking of cakes, any new clients lately?"

Jerome's distraction as he detailed the three new brides-to-be who had contacted him for their wedding cakes made me sigh in relief. In the past week, I'd had the sense that Jerome was steeling himself to ask me something. I had the shrewd guess that he wanted to take me on a date.

I didn't understand my reluctance. Jerome and I got on well, very well, and during our frequent coffee visits, lunches, and business meetings, we clicked in every way. He had come to my rescue last month with Starr, and I was grateful for his unquestioning help. And, last but not least, his handsome face and well-muscled physique made my new body's stomach squirm with pleasure.

What was stopping me? Heavens knew I was no blushing maiden. I'd had fifty-five years of living before this body, and I'd seen every type of man many times before. Jerome was one of the good ones, I could tell, but my mind balked at dating him.

Part of my problem was that he was just so young, and I didn't know how old I was. My body was attracted to his, of course, because both were in their late twenties. My mind enjoyed Jerome's company, but his lack of life experience would surely build a barrier between us eventually. How could we ever be anything more than a fling, a passing fancy? What was age, anyway?

I mentally shook my head and resolved to ponder this dilemma in private. For today, I had successfully distracted Jerome.

CHAPTER IV

Thea Diamanto lived a fair distance from Cormorant Drive, but the sky was clear, and the crisp winter's air begged to be walked in. I had plenty of time before my tea with the head mother, so I bundled myself into my coat and pulled a toque on my head then struck out for a nearby park to practice using the amulet Rosemary had given me.

"How are you going to do this?" Caelus said when he blossomed from my arm at the small patch of trees near my condo. The park was empty, despite the sun, although it didn't matter if it were full. The only ones who could see the threads of the world were Caelus and me, and manipulated wind was invisible. The worst that could happen would be someone thinking I was crazy, and I was too old to concern myself with the opinions of strangers. I tapped my foot in thought.

"Let's activate it then see how it feels," I said. "I don't suppose you can attack me from the outside?"

"We share the same body. I'm not truly separate from you, not without another body to inhabit. If I leave, I'd have to go back to the elemental plane, and I'm not ready to do that without plenty of artifacts destroyed."

"Activate it is, then."

I pushed back my sleeve to reveal the silver chain bracelet Rosemary had given me. Multicolored threads swirled gently around the silver.

"I think it's already activated," Caelus said. "Try prodding it with my magic to get a better sense of how it works. I'll help guide you."

He melted into my arm, and his silver threads flowed toward the bracelet. I concentrated my intention on examining the bracelet and allowed Caelus to direct my thoughts. A welcome sense of strength and clarity infused my mind. We lingered in the sensation for a moment, then I pulled away.

"That's a potent mix to defend against mind manipulation," I said once Caelus re-emerged from my arm. "I feel better having that bracelet around my wrist."

"It will do nicely," Caelus said with approval. "I very much dislike when order members wielding amulets get the jump on you."

I chuckled.

"Me, too. Come on, let's meet the infamous Thea."

My path led directly past the private high school that Jasmine and Starr attended. It was midafternoon, and as I approached, a buzzer signified the end of school. Students disgorged from the main doors and streamed to their next destinations.

With a start, I recognized one of the students. Starr had transformed her untidy green hair into a neat blond bob. She walked sedately beside two other girls, unusual considering her former loner status.

I was astonished at Starr's change. Hairstyles came and went—that wasn't a surprise in a teenage girl—but her chumminess with other students was a welcome difference. Despite Starr's unforgiveable actions against her sisters and me, I still harbored sympathy for the lonely girl she had been. If she'd found friends, then I was glad for her.

Two boys skirted the slower girls and walked with lanky steps toward a bus stop. I recognized one as Trent, Starr's boyfriend. I glanced at Starr, but beyond a casual flick of her eyes, she didn't react to his presence. I wondered if their relationship had been as fleeting as many that age were. Although to not react at all? Starr's strands swirled calmly around her body, unlike the expected turmoil of attraction or angst.

My eyes turned to the other students, and I frowned. Most of their strands were calm, far calmer than I would expect for people their age. I had made it my mission to study the threads of others to learn how I could interpret motion into emotion.

Youths, with their heightened reactions, often had highly reactive threads.

I shrugged and continued along my path. Maybe after a long day at school, reactions were dampened. I hadn't encountered endless teenagers on the sidewalks, after all.

I approached Starr and her companions and waited for a flicker of recognition in Starr's eyes. It didn't come. Her gaze slid over me without a glimmer of interest or a jolt of threads.

Impulsively, I reached out and touched her arm.

"Starr," I said. "How are you?"

The girl shook my hand away, but she didn't appear alarmed.

"Good, thanks," she said vaguely. "I'm late for the bus. See you."

My feet were planted on the ground in shock. I didn't know why I had reached out to her—my body taking control again, I guessed—but Starr's reaction astonished me. I could understand her not wanting to acknowledge me, given that we only knew each other through the order, and our last meeting hadn't ended well, but her control over her threads was astounding.

I shook my head and continued walking. Her lack of reaction surprised me, but I was relieved that she was unhurt. After Rosemary's ominous comments of punishment from the mothers, I had been worried for the girl's wellbeing. Starr was whole and well, and that was all I needed to know.

CHAPTER V

I walked for a few more blocks in the winter chill then checked the street number on my text message. My eyes glanced at the numbers on the nearest house. A large cedar shrub, carefully trimmed into a ball but still almost as tall as the eyebrow roof, partially obscured the metal number. With a quick step to my left, the rest slid into view.

I nodded and briskly strode down the paved walkway. The spacious house, painted a calming sand color and trimmed with fresh white, was innocuous in this development of similarly designed abodes. Steep roofs lent the dwelling some style, but all in all it blended into comfortable unobtrusiveness. The only dash of stronger color were tiny pink blossoms of a winter heather in the front.

I didn't know why Thea wanted to speak with me, but after the attack at my condo, I couldn't be too careful. I pulled out the protection amulet Rosemary had lent me and examined it. Strength and clarity pulsed from the amulet when I prodded it with my intention, and relief swept through me. An extra layer of protection was always welcome. I tucked the bracelet into my sleeve and strode up the cement walkway, neatly edged by grass.

A mat on the threshold spelled "home", and the doorbell jingled with a pleasant chime from inside the house. Footsteps approached, and I straightened my coat. The door clicked and swung open to reveal a heavyset woman, her dark hair cut in a smooth bob and her eyes sharp with intelligence. Navy blue threads swirled calmly around her body.

"You must be Morgan," the woman said with a smile. She held the door open wide and gestured me inside. "Please, come in. I'm Thea."

I accepted her offer to take my coat and glanced around the interior without restraint. Everything inside was tasteful and understated. Indeed, the style was almost of no-style. Abstract paintings in muted colors lined the walls, a smooth, creamy white vase sat on a side table in the hall, and beige carpeting led upstairs.

I followed Thea into a well-appointed living room, bright with pale walls and cream couches. The only splash of color came from muted burgundy throw pillows. I stifled a chuckle at the angst that Thea must have gone through in choosing such a wild color.

"Let me get the tea," Thea said. She glided through an opening to what must be a kitchen beyond and called over her shoulder, "Make yourself comfortable."

I wandered to the mantlepiece, where family photos graced the polished wood mantle. Prominent were two young adults, a boy and a girl, likely Thea's children. The girl beamed out of a graduation picture, dark hair smooth and expression confident. In a different photo, the boy had his arm around Thea in the woods, maybe on a hike. His eyes stared at the camera with intensity.

Thea drifted into the living room. I pointed at the photos.

"Are these your children? They look just like you."

Thea pasted on a smile, but her navy-blue threads spasmed and then coiled around her torso tightly.

"Yes, that's Joey and Filippa." Another spasm passed over her threads at Joey's name. "Joey isn't with us anymore."

"I'm so sorry." My heart squeezed for Thea's loss, and I felt bad about my inner mocking of her color scheme. It really was very beige in here, though.

"Yes, well." Thea placed the tea tray on her coffee table next to a decorative metal vase strangely covered with glowing threads. "Filippa is doing very well. She's at university studying archaeology. She's a credit to her training, and I expect she'll follow in my footsteps one day."

At my frown of confusion, Thea laughed lightly.

"Not as a school guidance counsellor," she continued. "No,

as a member of the order. She is so bright, and she's well-versed in our lore. Mark my words, she'll join the motherhood when she's old enough. Hopefully by then we will have found the Seed and be well on our way to retrieving the Thorn. I hope she can see the day they are united. I hope I can too, for that matter."

She smiled at me with a we're-all-in-this-together grin of conspiracy, and I returned it with hesitation as we sat on the pristine couches. I still didn't know what Thea's purpose for inviting me here today was, and I wanted to stay on my guard until I found out.

"She looks the right age to be a sister of the order," I said. "I'm surprised I haven't met her yet. There are only nine lockets for the Leaf, right?"

Thea made a noise that in a less-ladylike person I would have classified as a scoff.

"The sisters are a wonderful group, and they do a superb job keeping the Leaf safe." Thea sniffed. "Usually. But their skills are limited. I didn't want to waste Filippa's potential on guard-dog duties. With her brains and ambition, she is destined for greater things. Very few of the sisters manage to join the motherhood. There are only five of us mothers, after all. I might have to make an exception with Filippa shortly, but that's a topic for another time."

Thea poured tea into a bone china cup with a simple gold rim and passed it to me. I accepted the cup and took a sip while I thought about Rosemary's ambitions. She wanted to join the motherhood so badly that it had almost cost her sister's lives last month. Did she know her chance of success was so small?

"Tell me." Thea shuffled back in her seat and brought her tea to her lap. "How did you learn about the order? Rosemary gave me a very abbreviated version earlier, but I would love to hear it from you."

At Thea's words, the multicolored threads surrounding the metal vase darted toward me. I jumped in surprise, but a boiling of strands from the protection bracelet from Rosemary instantly built a barrier that the vase's tendrils could not penetrate. I glanced sharply at Thea.

"What is that metal vase?"

Thea looked at the coffee table and gave an unconvincing start of surprise.

"I forgot I had left that there. Let me remove it." She swiped it off the table and glided into the kitchen. When she returned, her hands were empty. "I'm so sorry. It's an amulet that encourages truthful speech. Sometimes I bring it out during counseling visits. Secrets that are meant to stay hidden will be, but if the person wishes to unburden themselves, the amulet will help them find the words and the courage. I meant to put it away before our visit. I apologize."

"Apology accepted." Caelus' suspicion filtered into my mind and mirrored my own pounding anger at Thea's obvious lies, but I decided to squash it for the moment. Thea's actions would bear pondering later. "As for your question, I stopped two attacks on sisters, simply by being in the right place at the right time." I shrugged, not wanting to delve into more details than I needed to. "I used my special abilities, and the sisters noticed. Rosemary offered me a job as security guard for the sisterhood, and I agreed. That's the extent of the story."

"But your abilities." Thea set her cup on the table and leaned forward. Her eyes scanned my face. "Where do they come from? Where did you get your amulets? It's intriguing to discover another group of people making amulets. You understand my interest."

A frown creased my face before I could school my expression. Starr, the youngest sister who had been behind the attacks last month, had figured out that I was paired with an air elemental. I guess she hadn't passed on her suspicions to her fellows, and Thea hadn't seen my abilities in person to gather any clues herself.

"I would rather not divulge that information. Their secrets

are not mine to confess."

Caelus' mirth bubbled inside me, but I kept my face impassive. Thea's strands twitched, and she fought her irritation by smiling calmly.

"Of course. I understand the need for secrecy. After all, the order is built on secrets. I'm told your abilities are well-developed, however you came by them. If you are interested in joining the order, I am sure we could speak further about that possibility."

I shook my head before Thea could finish her last sentence. I had no desire to join another secret society. This one, especially, held no interest for me. Not only did I not believe in their mission of releasing the Spirit elemental, I'd already stolen one of their precious artifacts and planned to destroy it. I doubt I would be welcome in the fold if Thea knew that.

But I wasn't certain she didn't. Why was she inviting me into the order? Did she want to keep a closer eye on me, maybe manufacture a chance to snatch the Leaf back? I didn't know what she knew, and the lack of certainty grated on me.

"I appreciate the offer," I said finally. "I find the legend of the Leaf, Seed, and Thorn intriguing, but I don't know if I'm ready to devote my life to it." I cast around for another topic to distract her. "You said you are a guidance counsellor at a school?"

"Yes, I am." Thea sat more comfortably against her couch cushions. "At the same private school that Jasmine and Starr attend. It's a lovely institution, and the students are so well-behaved. It's a pleasure working there."

"How did you join the order?" I was curious about the structure of this organization. Rosemary said they rarely recruited, but if sisters didn't become mothers, how did it all work?

"My mother is one of the current elders," she said. "I didn't have an interest in archaeology like Filippa, but there are other necessary skills for inclusion in the order. People management is where I excel—hence my guidance counsellor career—and my mother groomed me from an early age. The Book of Souls is very much part of our family's tradition, and it was natural for me to join when I was ready."

"Fascinating," I said quietly. Thea was indoctrinated from childhood by one of the elusive elders, and now carried on the tradition with her daughter. I didn't get fanatic vibes from her, not like from some of the sisters with their starry-eyed hope of a utopic future, and I wondered what Thea really thought about the Book of Souls. She seemed too level-headed to be whisked away by a dream of interconnectedness of all living things.

A thought struck me.

"Your children's father, what does he think of the order?" I was curious about the men excluded from this all-girls' club. Were they the supporting cast?

"He never knew," Thea said calmly. "It wasn't his secret to keep. We've been separated for years, now."

Another strike against joining the order. Was it forbidden to tell loved ones about the mission, or was Thea simply too reserved for her own good?

My tea was gone, and I couldn't think of other questions to ask. Suddenly, I wanted to escape Thea's piercing gaze and her barely held-back questions about Caelus. Someone in the motherhood had broken into my condo and searched for something. The longer I stayed with Thea, the greater chance I had of exposing my secrets.

My fingernails squeezed into my palms. What if the motherhood was using this opportunity to search my condo while I was occupied? The Leaf was safe in my pocket, but I still didn't like the thought of strangers rummaging through my possessions again. I wanted to leave Thea's bland yet cloying presence.

"Thank you so much for the tea." I set my cup down and stood. "But I have an appointment to get to. It was lovely meeting you, Thea."

Thea stood with a look of disappointment, carefully smoothed over.

"You too, Morgan. I appreciate everything you've done for the order."

Caelus emerged from my arm once Thea shut the door behind me.

"What did you think of her?" I muttered without moving my lips much. A young mother pushed her baby in a stroller on the sidewalk past the house, and I didn't want her wondering to whom I spoke.

"I don't know." Caelus shrugged his thready shoulders. "Humans are your thing. There were some interesting threads in her house, though."

"What kind of interesting?"

I was annoyed with myself for missing them. Seeing the threads of the world might be new to me, but so much information was stored in the constantly shifting strands that I'd taught myself to pay attention. Apparently, I hadn't noticed enough.

"That house is loaded with amulets." Caelus glanced at me expressively. "Loaded. It makes Rosemary's stash look like a child's collection."

"It's another level, this motherhood. Having more amulets doesn't surprise me. I wonder what they do."

"I couldn't tell without closer examination. But that wasn't the only thing I saw."

Caelus paused for effect, and I sighed explosively.

"Spit it out, Caelus. Don't keep me in suspense."

"Red threads," he said with deliberation. When I didn't respond with exaggerated alarm, he scowled. "The same threads of the woman who burgled our condo. Honestly."

"So, the motherhood was behind it," I breathed. "I knew it.

But it wasn't Thea. Her threads were navy blue."

"Not Thea. But it was someone she knows well. Someone who comes to her house frequently."

"I knew Thea was too pleasant to be believed."

I turned a corner onto a busier street and scanned the sidewalk for the nearest bus stop. I had toyed with getting myself a car, but with funds growing scarcer by the day and no job in sight, the bus seemed prudent.

"But do they know I have the Leaf?" I continued. "Or are they just suspicious?"

"Hard to say." Caelus scowled in the direction of Thea's house. "But watch your back, either way."

CHAPTER VI

To my intense relief, no one had entered my condo while I was gone. The next morning, I volunteered for Grandview Women's Center, this time sorting donations of clothing and children's toys for women in need to take home. When I held up a woman's cream-colored blouse to check for rips or stains, a brilliant thought shot into my mind like a bolt of lightning.

"Caelus," I hissed after my head swiveled to check that I was alone. "Get out here."

"Your whole mind jolted," he said after he emerged from my arm with a grumpy expression. "It was disconcerting."

"Could I imbue our magic into clothes?" I shook the blouse for emphasis. "Maybe I've been thinking too small, trying magics that are too immediate. Can I store magic like I do with my air balls?"

"I suppose. What kind of things?"

I smoothed the blouse over my lap in thought.

"If I could build in a trigger for the magic, then it could release an effect. Say, if someone threatened the person wearing this blouse, a blast of itching magic could distract the attacker in time for the person to get away."

"I'm no expert on human psychology, but would itching diffuse an attacker's anger?" Caelus raised an eyebrow. "Maybe sending the attacker to sleep would be better, or releasing a draft of calmness."

"Yes." My mind whirled. "Yes. Oh, or even infuse the clothing with calm or peace or clear-thinking for the person wearing it. Everyone could use that. I wonder how long the effect could last for."

"Without renewing the thread manipulation, a few weeks, at most."

"That's still helpful." I grabbed a pile of clothes from the donation bag. "Here, help me figure out what to do."

For an hour, Caelus and I sorted clothes from the donation bags and matched effects to each article. To the children's clothing, we infused calming magic. For the women's clothing, we twisted a tricky little mix of strength, peace, and clear-thinking. We attached a draft of calmness to three of the shirts, triggered by a raised voice, but fashioning the trigger was complex, and Greta wandered to the back before I could complete any more. I left the Center tired but buoyed by my use of magic for good.

"Those twists would last longer if we had more power," Caelus mused as we exited the Center after my shift. "I'm powerful, but what you're trying to achieve is difficult. Maybe another artifact would boost your skills. Too bad we need to destroy them when we find them. Our best will have to be good enough."

I tucked Caelus' pronouncement away for future thought. Maybe if we found another artifact, I could come back to the women's center before destroying it. More power could bring more peace and contentment to the lives of the people who needed it.

In the afternoon, I spent a few hours walking down Cormorant Drive and passing out resumés to any shop owners who would take one. It grated my pride—I had been a CEO of multiple companies in my previous life as March—but money was money, and a lack of provable experience was a tough hurdle to vault. I didn't have a portfolio of reference letters, only a single note from Rosemary.

Anger simmered below the surface every time a manager waved away my resumé without a glance—or worse, took it like it was something smelly—but I bottled up my ire. My body's volatility was not helpful while job hunting. My mind's cooler sensibilities needed to take the reins to improve my chance of success.

After a few hours, I directed my steps to Sacred Grounds for a pre-arranged meeting. I bought a drink then slid into a chair across from Rosemary. Her leg jiggled under the table, but I sipped my coffee without commenting on her nerves. I was curious, certainly, but she would tell me when she was ready. Besides, I was certain I knew the source. Rosemary was waiting for her hearing with the motherhood about her actions with Starr the previous month, and it was sometime today.

After my talk with Thea, I didn't hold high hopes for Rosemary's future in the order. Rosemary desperately wanted to ascend the ranks into the motherhood, but Thea's dismissal of the sisters didn't bode well. I didn't bother mentioning my revelations. It looked like Rosemary had enough to worry about today.

Joy slid into the chair next to me with a sigh and unzipped her jacket. Her blond curls were still bouncy despite the rain, and I reminded myself to ask her what product she used. Although, I wouldn't put it past the sisters to have an amulet that dealt with great-looking hair.

"Hi, Morgan," she said with cheer. "So nice to see you. How's the job hunt going?"

I gave her a wry smile and ignored the flutter of concern in my stomach. My bank account, while still reasonable, was the smallest I'd seen for decades. I wasn't used to living on the edge of a paycheck, much less not even having a paycheck to live on the edge of.

"It's going. I've handed out plenty of resumés. Too bad my experience is so limited." I smiled at Rosemary. "Your referral was glowing, though."

Rosemary's answering smile was fleeting.

"Happy to help."

Her forlorn sigh was interrupted by a ping from her pocket. She extracted her phone and listlessly checked her notifications. Joy opened her mouth to say something to me, but we were both distracted by Rosemary's sudden straightening. Her body was so tense with excitement it almost quivered.

"It's from the motherhood," Rosemary breathed.

"What is it?" Joy said. "Is it your summons?"

"No." Rosemary shook her head so violently that her hair whipped her face. She was normally so calm and collected that this display of agitation startled me. "No, it's the Seed. They found it."

Joy's eyes widened, and her hand gripped the edge of the table.

"Seriously?" she whispered. "For real?"

"What's up?" Denise stood over us, her eyes fixed on Rosemary's face. She must have seen the excitement and rushed over from her place at the coffee counter. Amanda glared her way, but she was stuck at the cash register and couldn't abandon her post.

"They found the Seed," Joy said for Rosemary, who skimmed her message without acknowledging Denise's presence. "They actually found it."

Denise flopped onto the chair beside Rosemary's and nudged her.

"Come on, what else do they say? This is huge."

"They opened the chamber with the signs on it. The Seed was inside. They're working on taking it away from the dig site without alerting suspicion among the other archaeologists who aren't in the order."

Rosemary finished reading the message then put her phone down on the table. We leaned in to look at the photo. A small box with a rounded lid glowed golden on a folding table. Designs of rudimentary leaves and flowers had been hammered into the chased gold. The picture was bright, as if it were a sunny day, but the box was shaded. The lid was open, and inside was a seed no larger than a grain of rice.

Caelus stirred within me, and my stomach clenched with anticipation. The Seed was another artifact for Caelus' mission. But, more than that, it was the promise of more power. After my infusion of magic into the donated clothing, I yearned to examine the Seed for its power. What abilities hid in that innocuous package of unborn plant?

"There it is." Denise whistled and shook her head. "I can't believe they finally found it."

"Then it's just the Thorn." Joy stared at Denise. "Just the Thorn, then the three will be together. The Book of Souls will come true."

"Just the Thorn." Rosemary laughed bitterly and retrieved her phone. "They took decades to find the Seed. You think the Thorn will be next week?"

"Weren't there clues—" Joy began. Rosemary interrupted.

"I'm just saying, don't hold your breath. Don't get me wrong, this is amazing, but keep it in perspective. Don't relax your vigilance with the Leaf, and don't celebrate just yet. We have a long way to go."

"Okay, Debbie Downer," Denise muttered. "This is only the biggest thing to happen in the order since before we were born, but sure, we don't need to celebrate."

Rosemary sighed and passed a hand over her face.

"I'm sorry," she said. "This hearing is weighing on me. Of course, you should be happy. You know what?" She pulled out her wallet and passed Joy a credit card. "Organize a party. Put it on the sisterhood expense card. I would do it, but I'm not really in the mood right now. You'll do it justice."

Joy and Denise flashed grins at each other.

"We certainly will," Joy said.

"Denise!" Amanda's sweet but sharp voice carried across the room. A line had formed at the till, and Amanda's gaze threw daggers at her sister. Denise jumped up.

"Got to go. But we'll go shopping after work, right?"

"Got it," Joy said, and Denise jogged behind the counter.

"Congrats," I said to Rosemary. "I know you're distracted today, but it's still big news. I'm pleased for you all."

Rosemary gave me a wan smile.

"Thanks. I'll celebrate once this hearing is over. I can't

wait."

"Speaking of the motherhood," I said. "I had tea with Thea yesterday."

Rosemary frowned at me, and Joy looked puzzled.

"Why?" Joy said. "Aside from our monthly meetings, she rarely contacts the sisters. And you're kind of an honorary sister."

"She wanted to meet me, after last month's events." I shrugged and took another sip of coffee. "Honestly, I think she was curious about my abilities."

Joy chuckled.

"You won't even tell us that. Funny that she thought you would open up to her."

I hadn't told the sisters about Caelus. Starr had figured it out by the end, from watching my powers and putting together clues from the Book of Souls, but none of the others had.

"It's not my secret to tell, unfortunately." I held my coffee mug in both hands to stay warm. I could tell them about Caelus, but I liked keeping my cards close to my chest.

Caelus' longing for the artifact pulsed in my gut, and I sighed. The Seed was on the other side of the world. Maybe I should focus on booking a flight to another museum to find artifacts for Caelus until the Seed was more readily available.

Another ping emanated from Rosemary's phone, and she snatched it up. Her face grew pale.

"I have an hour," she whispered. "Until my hearing. I have to get changed, prepare…"

"Go!" Joy made a shooing motion with her hands. "Then come back and help us plan the party. It will all be fine, I know it."

I wasn't as convinced as Joy about the outcome of Rosemary's hearing, but I gave the head sister a warm parting smile for courage.

"Good luck."

After a dinner of hearty lasagna, I was relaxing with my feet on the couch and a glass of Chardonnay in my hand when the door buzzer rang. I frowned and switched off my Gershwin playlist. Who would visit me at this hour without warning? Did anyone know where I lived? I hadn't invited anyone to my condo before, preferring to meet Jerome and the sisters in public locations. I wasn't sure what I was afraid of, but my condo felt like a retreat where I could be myself. Inviting others into its sanctity felt like a step that I wasn't yet willing to take.

I pressed the button with hesitation.

"Hello?"

"Morgan?" Rosemary's voice crackled to life. "I know it's late, but can I come up? I have something important to tell you."

I sighed. Rosemary must have my address from the contract I'd signed for my previous security job. I wondered what could be so important that a phone call wouldn't suffice. Then I chastised myself. I wasn't exactly flush with friends, so why was I debating whether to allow Rosemary in?

"Of course. Come on up."

Rosemary appeared at my open door a minute later. Her peach threads sparked and snapped around her in an angry cloud. I took one look and retreated to the kitchen, returning with another wine glass. Without comment, I poured a glass and handed it to her. She took it with a choked laugh and downed half the glass in one.

"Do I look that bad?" she said.

I waved her toward the couch, and she sank into it as if bricks weighed on her shoulders. I sat on the other end and tucked my feet under me.

"You look like you could use it, yes. Tell me. What happened?"

Rosemary heaved in a breath and released it with a whoosh of air.

"I'm not the head sister anymore," she said in a rush. "In fact, I'm not a sister anymore. They kicked me out."

My heart squeezed at the pain on Rosemary's face.

"The hearing didn't go well, then?"

The younger woman screwed up her face.

"Terribly. Thea rabbited on and on about how I'd failed my duties, how I should have contacted them from the start of the Starr debacle, how I put my own ambitions over the mission, and if I did that, I clearly didn't understand the importance of what I was taking care of."

I nodded and tried to look sympathetic, although I couldn't disagree with Thea's points. Rosemary had put her own ambitions over the safety of the Leaf and her sisters. Rosemary didn't need to hear that from me right now, though, so I held my tongue and poured more wine into her glass.

"I made a mistake," she continued, the wine sloshing with her agitation. "I admit that. But to cut me out completely? What about forgiveness, allowing room to grow? Why did they kick me out of the sisterhood entirely, not just as head sister?" Her eyes welled with tears, and she dashed them away with an angry swipe. "Then at least I would have been a part of it all. I know I was about to age out of the sisterhood, but still."

I opened my mouth to offer condolences, but Rosemary sat up straight and continued to rant.

"The whole order is a mess, from start to finish. Yeah, we have two artifacts, but it's taken decades. And the decision to place the Leaf around the sisters' necks? What an insane way to keep something safe. I think it's a testament to my leadership that everyone still has a necklace. Our leader was crazy to begin with—her finding the Leaf in that archaeological dig in the forties was the beginning of the end for her, I think, she hasn't handled the responsibility well— and now that she's ancient, she shouldn't be allowed to make any decisions. If I were in charge, things would be done right. I remember when I first became head sister. The amulet room was a total mess. Who organized and catalogued everything? Me. Who devised a system to check out amulets to keep accountability? Me!"

Rosemary was red-faced at this point. A cold shiver crawled down my spine. Did Thea know that the Leaf was no longer in their possession? Worse still, had I been burgled and questioned at tea-point because Thea suspected my involvement? Thea's reaction to Rosemary's crimes could be explained at face value, but maybe the loss of the Leaf was driving the head sister's dismissal, even if Rosemary didn't know the reason. The loss of an artifact on her watch was surely an unforgivable crime.

Rosemary took a swig of wine and visibly tried to calm down.

"But it's done," she said. "I'm officially out of the order. They will carry on without me, and when the Thorn is found and the artifacts joined, I won't be a part of it."

"You're in good company," I said and raised my glass for a toast.

Rosemary's mouth twitched with the hint of a smile, and she clinked my glass. Silence reigned for a long moment as we both contemplated the events of the evening.

"I'm not part of the order anymore," Rosemary murmured, half to herself. "But what is the order, but a human-made institution? Nothing states that the artifacts can't be joined by anyone. The order was only created to help that goal along. They're clearly incompetent and corrupt. They can't even see a dedicated sister if she stands before them." Rosemary drummed her fingers on her knee.

I let her ruminate, curious where she was going with her comments. There was a time for stern proclamations, and there was a time for listening. Both tactics had their place in the board room and in life. It was often enlightening to let another speak their mind without interruption.

"Maybe they aren't worthy to fulfill this scheme," Rosemary continued. She gazed at the far wall, her mind clearly elsewhere. "This is an opportunity. Why shouldn't it be me who is meant bring the artifacts together?" Rosemary's brows contracted with anger and resolve. "Maybe I had to fail to stay humble, but the only difference between those gatekeepers and me is their lack of worthiness. Screw them. How can they cut me out like that? I've given everything to the cause. I have the purest motives of anyone. I think it's time I took over the destined path."

I raised my eyebrows, impressed by the speed at which Rosemary had pivoted from dejected outsider to self-proclaimed chosen one. I was about to temper her delusions of grandeur when she faced me, her eyes shining with passion.

"Morgan. I need to get the mothers' Book of Souls."

"Explain."

"The sisters have only a portion of the real book," Rosemary said in a rush. "A photocopy of the main stories. The mothers have more, and the elders have the original book. I have no idea where the elders keep the main version, but I know Thea has the mothers' copy in her house. It has so much more information about the artifacts, where they can be found, about how to make amulets, stuff that I don't even know about. It's a treasure trove, and it's crucial to finding the Thorn. I need to read it if I'm to carry out my plan."

"And the plan is?"

Rosemary's eyes widened further in her doll-like face.

"I'm going to unite the Leaf, Seed, and Thorn."

CHAPTER VII

"The order isn't trustworthy," Rosemary said after a gulp of wine. She pressed her hand into my couch cushion as if to steady herself. "Why should they oversee the greatest find in history? I am far more suited, and my motives are purer. It's time I found out what's in the mothers' book. But I can't do it alone."

Rosemary placed her glass on the table and took my hand in both her own. I looked at it in surprise then up at Rosemary's beseeching face.

"What are you planning?"

"Help me steal the mothers' Book of Souls," she whispered. "I have no amulets anymore, and all I have is my knowledge of Thea and her house. But you have abilities that would make stealing the Book laughably simple. I know it's a lot to ask, but would you help me? I promise, when the fateful day comes and the artifacts are united, I'll make sure you are honored above all."

I searched Rosemary's face. She was so earnest it almost hurt. Caelus stirred with interest, and I shared his sentiment. The Book of Souls—the little I'd read of it—was a fascinating compendium of elemental lore, and even Caelus hadn't known of its contents. What more could we discover about the role of his world in mine?

And the Thorn—would there be clues for finding it in the pages of the Book of Souls? If I could find the last artifact before the order, Caelus would be one step closer to avoiding dormancy. As much as we teased each other, I wanted no harm to come to him. If finding the Thorn meant the difference between his freedom and dormancy, then I would try my hardest to find the artifact.

Rosemary's hints about how to make amulets also intrigued me. I would never say no to an increase of power, and a recipe book to gain more was tantalizing.

"You aren't a sister," Rosemary said, pressing her advantage at the hesitation in my face. "And you took no vows. We don't have to steal the Book, even, just take pictures of its pages. We could sneak in, click-click-click, and get out. Nobody gets hurt, nothing is lost, everything is gained. What do you say?"

Slowly, I nodded. Caelus flopped over at my stomach with his approval. Rosemary stared at me with burning, hopeful eyes.

"Good," she said. "Now, when do we start?"

For the second time that week, I found myself staring at Thea's neat suburban house. This time, the sand color was gray in the dimness with orange trim from streetlights. Rosemary took a deep breath.

"Okay, what's the plan?" she said. "Can you get us in with your abilities, or do I have to try picking the lock? I used to be good at it as a teenager, but I'm pretty rusty now."

"I can do it. Let's do a back door, though. Out of sight of the street."

Rosemary led me through a side gate that creaked ominously when opened. A harsh wind gusted in our faces, and a fat raindrop splattered on my cheek with the threat of sleet. I shivered and hurried after the ex-sister.

At a back door with its top half-windowed, I set to work. Rosemary jiggled her leg beside me, but I turned my body to avoid looking at the distraction. Caelus blossomed out of my arm.

"This is becoming quite a habit for you," he said in a conversational tone. "Isn't breaking and entering considered against human rules? You rebel, you."

I grimaced and ignored my elemental. He chuckled.

"I love talking to you when you can't talk back. You could always tell Rosemary about me, you know. I wonder what she would say. Oh, the drama. I love the insight peering into your mind gives me on human behavior. You're a fascinating species."

The lock mercifully clicked open. I dissolved my air pick and stood with relief then waved Rosemary forward.

"After you."

She gave the open door a fearful look then squared her shoulders and tiptoed past me. She led me through a kitchen gleaming with stainless steel appliances and a carefully cultivated row of cow figurines on the windowsill. Floorboards in the hall creaked with minute noises that sounded thunderous to my overwrought ears, and Rosemary's shoulders rose with her unease. She flitted through a door on the other side of the stairs, and I followed as quietly as I could manage.

Something brushed against my leg. I leaped into the air and released a stifled scream. When I looked down, a fluffy white cat's yellow eyes gazed at me with reproach. I placed a hand over my palpitating heart and listened with held breath. Had anybody upstairs heard my cry?

Silence greeted my waiting ears, and I let out a sigh of relief. My fingers twisted air strands with intention. Gradually, air flowed from downstairs into the hall. Thumps and bumps wouldn't be muffled, but other sounds we might make would now have a harder time traveling upstairs.

I tiptoed into the room Rosemary had disappeared into. She stood in front of an antique writing desk lit by bright streetlights filtering through a nearby window. Its spindly legs held up a boxy mahogany top with drawers below and an angled cupboard that clearly folded down. This room was as neat as the rest of Thea's house, and I despaired of finding the Book of Souls in this magazine-worthy room where clutter was a dirty word.

"Over here," Rosemary whispered. "I need you to pick a

lock again."

I moved closer. There was indeed a lock on the drawer, and the desk around it was hung with copious dark blue strands the exact shade of Thea's. She must have used this drawer recently. I fashioned another serrated blade out of air and inserted it into the opening. This lock sprang open easily, and Rosemary tugged at the drawer with eager fingers. It didn't budge.

Caelus emerged from my arm and peered at the drawer.

"It's locked with threads as well," he said to me. It was jarring to hear his voice so loud in the silent house, and I winced at the sound. "Unpick it."

"Let me try something," I whispered to Rosemary.

She moved aside, and I kneeled in front of the desk. Now that Caelus had pointed it out, the threads of the lock were faint but present. Multicolored swirls peeked out from the keyhole and wriggled below the drawer. It must be an amulet keeping the drawer shut.

I picked at the strands, wary of provoking the amulet, but all was still except for Rosemary jiggling silently beside me. I ignored her and concentrated on my task. After two minutes of painstaking pulling, the final thread was gone. I sighed with relief and stood.

"It's all yours," I whispered to Rosemary.

She didn't need a second invitation. With eager fingers, she slid the drawer open with ease. Inside lay a day planner, a stack of books, and papers in file folders. Rosemary shuffled through them until she pulled out a book bound in plain black cloth. Embossed in printed gold on the front were the words "Book of Souls—Mothers".

"Yes," Rosemary hissed. "Here it is." She opened it up and flipped through the pages with trembling hands. Halfway through the slender volume, she paused and pulled out her phone. "Let me grab pictures of the pages I don't have, then we can go."

She clicked away, and I flipped through the day planner for something to do. This week had a few items, but most prominent was the word "ceremony" circled three times. Was that the intended day of the Seed's incarceration? I didn't have long to find it, if so. On the day before, it said, "take Seed to location".

I nudged Rosemary and pointed at the relevant entries. Her eyes widened, and she nodded vigorously then continued to take pictures of the book with frantic motions.

I put the day planner back and rustled through the drawer some more.

"Anything interesting?" Caelus asked. "Too bad Thea doesn't have a stash of artifacts here. I wonder if she has anything interesting in this house. Amulets are boring. I want artifacts."

I shook my head and raked my eyes over the contents of the drawer. The file folders contained information on the sisters and mothers—as head mother, Thea must keep track of her underlings—but under the folders was another copy of the Book of Souls. I frowned. Would Thea really miss a copy? Even if she did, what would she do about it?

Caelus must have had the same idea I had, because he said, "Let's take it. I want to know more about the Spirit elemental. I can't believe I've never heard anything about her before."

I nodded and slid the book free of the papers, then tucked it inside my coat and into the back of my jeans. Rosemary was absorbed in her task and didn't noticed my antics.

"Got it," she finally whispered, long after I had stopped feeling anxious and was merely bored with waiting. "Let's go."

She slid the book under the file folders and closed the drawer quietly. We tiptoed to the door.

A creak from upstairs froze us both. Rosemary stared at me with eyes as round as coins. I didn't breathe.

Another creak, as if someone were walking toward the

stairs. It was no good—we'd have to run. We couldn't be cornered in this office, especially if Thea wielded any of the amulets Caelus had sensed that were lying around. I gestured to the kitchen. Rosemary shook her head violently, then a footstep changed her mind. She bit her lip then broke into a sprint across the front hall. I followed, grateful once again for my youthful limberness.

"Stop!" Thea's voice carried down the staircase. "Thieves!"

I didn't wait to hear more, nor to test my theory that Thea was armed with more than a frying pan or baseball bat. Part of me surged with terror-fueled anger, and I nearly turned around to face Thea's unformed threat.

Then my mind asserted its dominance and forced my body to dash after the fleeing Rosemary. It might want to fight, but flight was the safest course of action now. A flash of light burst against the wall behind me, accompanied by a burning smell, and I jumped in surprise. What sort of amulets did Thea keep on her bedside table at night?

Steps clattered down the stairs, then Thea shouted again. I dodged around a kitchen island and slipped on tiles underfoot. Another flash of light exploded on the counter next to my steadying hand, and I snatched it away. Rosemary burst through the back door with me on her tail, and we fled the house.

We ran to Rosemary's tiny hatchback parked a few blocks away. She unlocked the car, and I flung the passenger door open and threw myself inside. Rosemary turned the key in the ignition and cursed when the car coughed. The engine finally turned over, and Rosemary gunned it down the street. I didn't want to be anywhere near Thea's house when the police arrived.

In front of my condo building, Rosemary pulled over and shut off the car. She dropped her head to the steering wheel, her shoulders shaking. I leaned against the headrest and released a huge sigh. The book pressed into my back, but I ignored the discomfort.

"We did it." Rosemary spoke into the steering wheel, then she lifted her head and gave me a shaky smile. "Thanks, Morgan. I couldn't have done it without you. You have some serious skills."

"I do, don't I?" I let out a breathy laugh, still winded from the chase and adrenaline. "Happy to help."

Rosemary pulled out her phone and flicked through the pictures. She stopped at one that caught her attention. Her eyes flicked over the Latin words, and her face gradually darkened.

"What did you find?" I asked.

Rosemary silently read the words with one finger raised for me to wait, then she looked at me with narrowed eyes.

"The sisters took vows to protect the Leaf because we believe in the cause. One day, when the artifacts are united, Spirit will be released and every living creature will be connected. We think this vision of paradise is a worthy goal in and of itself."

"But…"

"But the motherhood, apparently, needed more incentive." Rosemary's fist clenched. "It says here that a chosen few will receive power beyond their imagining, in gratitude for releasing Spirit from her bonds. And guess who didn't get those pages to read?" She thumped her hand on her chest. "The sisters, that's who. Why weren't we included? We do all this because we believe we're bringing a better life to the world. Is there anything more selfless than that? I ask you, shouldn't the people getting power be those who are worthy? The mothers are nothing but power snatchers in it for all the wrong reasons. They are all unworthy."

She leaned back in her seat, her breath coming in short bursts. Her peach threads were sharp and moved with jagged thrusts outward.

I stared out the window. Our discovery tonight certainly

soured my perception of the order and their goals. I remembered Starr's warning of the controlling consequences of too much power in the hands of those unworthy. Maybe she had been onto something. Maybe the utopia the sisters' Book of Souls described was simply a way to get young idealists on board with protecting the Leaf. The real goal wasn't paradise for all, but power for a select few. Suddenly, I felt much less guilty about stealing the Leaf.

"What will you do now?" I asked when it was clear Rosemary was trapped in her own thoughts.

"I can't let them do this," she said in a low voice. "They aren't worthy to have that sort of power. I can't let them keep the Seed. They need to be stopped. Someone worthy needs to unite the artifacts, and that isn't the motherhood. I need to stop them."

"You want to steal the Seed and Leaf from the order." I wanted to make sure she stated her goal clearly before I spoke further.

"Yes." Rosemary nodded slowly then with firmer motions. "Yes, exactly."

"I can help," I said quietly.

Rosemary's head whipped around to stare at me with disbelief and hope.

"Really? Oh, Morgan, your abilities would make this so much easier. By myself, it would be a faint hope. With you, I'll have a fighting chance. But why would you help?"

"Maybe I don't want to see that much power in the hands of the unscrupulous."

Rosemary nodded with a smile and sighed happily. My words were true enough, but my real reason was far more self-serving. An ally in my quest to steal an artifact wouldn't hurt, and if Rosemary managed to get her hands on the Seed before me, I was confident that I could wrest it away from her. Caelus was on my side, after all, and he wanted the artifact more than I did.

“We can do this,” I said. “We will do this.”

CHAPTER VIII

Once Rosemary drove away and I was ensconced on my couch with a cozy blanket once more, I extracted the book from behind my back and laid it on my lap. Caelus formed out of my arm, and we stared at the cover.

"Come on, open it," he said. "I want to know what the mothers are hiding. What is this Spirit elemental? Why is there a tree involved?"

"It's all in Latin," I warned, but I flipped the cover eagerly.

The title page was the same as the sisters' copy, as was the first half. While I was interested in what the first half said, I was more concerned with the new content. When I didn't recognize the pages, I slowed, and Caelus and I gazed at the pictures.

The first one was of three women dancing in a circle. The faces were crudely drawn, but from their figures, it was clear that one was a girl, one a woman, and the last a wizened elder.

"Are you sure you can't read just a little bit?" Caelus said finally. I snorted.

"It doesn't work like that. I don't know how to read Latin. I used to, in another lifetime, but my memories of those years are so fuzzy that I can't make out more than a twentieth of the words on this page. Trust me, I'm as frustrated about it as you are."

"Why didn't you get Rosemary to read it for us?"

"I don't want her to know how interested I am in the Seed. She thinks I'm helping her for her sake." I twisted my lips in guilt at my deception. Rosemary, for all her quirks, had been good to me. If Caelus' needs hadn't taken precedence, I wouldn't be double-crossing Rosemary. I shook my head to clear it. "It's best if we find another way to translate the book so she'll keep us in the loop for her Seed-stealing antics."

I flipped the pages until another picture stopped my hand.

This one clearly depicted the three artifacts—Leaf, Seed, and Thorn—but this time, the image was reminiscent of a how-to guide. The Leaf crumbled into a small pile at the bottom of the image, the Seed burst open with a small shoot rising from its innards, and the Thorn dripped liquid onto both. Colorful strands of purple, green, yellow, and red surrounded a seedling.

"What does this page say?" Caelus leaned toward the paper until his nose almost brushed the page.

"Remember? No Latin. But it looks to me like an instruction manual. The Seed grows in soil made by the Leaf and watered by the Thorn." I drummed my fingers. "I need someone to translate this for me."

"Why don't you get one of the other sisters to do it?"

"I don't want them to know I stole a book. They might start questioning my motives. No one can know we have the Leaf, or that we're planning to get the Seed. I don't want any barriers to information. No, we need an outsider, someone who can read Latin."

My brain immediately jumped to Merry Lytton. As someone who had lived since Dark Ages Britain, he was uniquely qualified to read medieval Latin. He probably read it better than English after centuries of practice.

I rejected the notion. If I started asking him for translation favors and seeing him regularly, he would piece together the clues about my identity. He wasn't a fool.

"We live in a university town," I said aloud. "There has to be a professor who can read medieval Latin for us. I'll look one up."

The next morning found me on a bus halfway across the city. I had taken care with my clothing—form-fitting yet classy pants, a blouse that was presentable yet hinted at my youthful curves—and carried a box of Jerome-baked goodies with two takeaway coffees. I wanted my translation done promptly, and the sort of clout I used to possess was gone with my old body. I had to appeal to the professor in other ways. Food and youthful charm were often winners, especially since money was tight.

I caught sight of myself in the window's reflection and practiced my best beguiling smile. It took a few tries to get one that was pleasantly innocent yet with enough suggestion to be interesting. A man standing in the aisle caught my eye and grinned hopefully at me. It looked like my smiles worked.

At the history department's office, I asked for directions to Dr. Yevgeny Romanoff's office. I navigated the busy hallways until I found a closed door with Yevgeny Romanoff engraved on a plastic label. No one answered, so I leaned against the wall and settled in to wait. Hopefully, the coffee would stay warm until he arrived.

A few minutes later, a tall man with trim salt-and-pepper hair and a pair of gold rimmed glasses tucked firmly on the bridge of his nose wandered toward the door. His head was down as he skimmed papers in his hand, which gave me time to stand straight and compose my face into a friendly expression.

"Dr. Romanoff?" I said. I tried to pitch my voice lower— my body's natural tone was too high for either professionalism or sultriness—but wasn't sure how well I'd succeeded. No matter. The coffee and smile would have to do.

Yevgeny Romanoff's head snapped up and he focused his deep brown eyes on me. I couldn't help thinking how March would have admired his clear gaze and distinguished brow. My current body preferred Jerome's muscles, but I could remember well my earlier desires.

"That's me," he said easily. I gave him a warm smile and stepped aside from his door.

"I was hoping to speak to you for a moment, if you aren't

too busy." I held up the coffee and box. "I brought refreshments to convince you."

He chuckled and unlocked the door.

"I don't need bribes to answer questions from students, but I won't deny gifts freely offered."

He waved me inside, and I stepped into his cramped office. Books and binders filled an entire wall of the small space, but the large wooden desk held only a monitor, a notepad, and a pen. Diplomas hung on the wall next to a child's drawing of a gray and brown cat. I sat in a molded plastic chair and set the coffees on his desk. Yevgeny placed his papers on the clear space and sank into his office chair with a sigh.

"I'm not a student," I said. "So feel free to help yourself to the treats without fear of bribery. I'm in need of a translator for an old Latin text, and I hoped you could lead me in the right direction."

Yevgeny's eyes brightened with interest. He took a sip of one of the coffees then set it aside.

"What sort of old Latin text? If you have it here, I can take a quick glance and see what sort of challenge we're facing."

I slid the Book of Souls out of my backpack and placed it gently before Yevgeny. He hastily swiveled to put his coffee on the windowsill to avoid spills, then he ran his fingers over the gold embossed title.

"Where did you say you got this book from?" he asked without looking at me.

"I didn't."

He raised his eyes to meet mine, but I maintained a pleasant smile that didn't reveal anything. He huffed through his nose and resumed his exploration of the book. His fingers flipped open the front cover and gently thumbed through the pages. He stopped at a central page, one that wasn't in the sisters' version, and paused. The image was of a spreading tree surrounded by threads. His eyes flicked back and forth across the page, and I tried not to fidget with impatience.

"This is fascinating," he murmured. "Do you know what this says?"

"That's what I was hoping you could tell me." Why else did Yevgeny think I had come?

"Of course. I don't know what the whole book is about—a more thorough examination is needed for that—but this page tells a story about a spirit in a tree. Some folklore I haven't heard of. It's a recipe of sorts, I suppose one could say."

"A recipe for what?"

"To grow this spirit-tree. Important trees are a common motif in many cultures, most famously Yggdrasil of Norse mythology, or the tree of the knowledge of good and evil from Judeo-Christian belief. The Tree can represent a spiritual realm, or a connection between heaven and the underworld. Sometimes the fruit produced can bestow power, health, or even immortality, depending on the legend. It's a pervasive symbol in world religions."

"How does one grow a tree using a recipe?"

Yevgeny spread his hand over the page and traced the tree.

"That was the best way I thought of to describe it. It's an imperfect analogy. The text states that a new tree can only grow in soil infused with the remains of the old tree. Old bark mulch or leaf matter, from what I gather."

I sat up straighter. The Leaf fit that bill.

"It must grow from a seed of the old tree, of course," he continued. "But the text also states that it must be watered with the blood of the faithful, drawn by a cut from the old tree's thorn." Yevgeny chuckled. "It's quite the process. It's no wonder that these magical trees from legends are not as prolific as maples and firs."

I leaned back, digesting this information. Leaf, Seed, and Thorn, all had a vital part to play in growing this so-called spirit tree. This wasn't entirely news—Rosemary had said as much before—but I had labored under the impression that the three objects were one-of-a-kind artifacts, not pieces of a once-mighty tree. And did the Leaf, Seed, and Thorn have magical properties of their own, as legend suggested?

"The rest of the text on this page details the powers available to those who complete the recipe," Yevgeny said, echoing my own conclusions. "It says something about power without limits to the faithful. This is quite the tale. Do you have any idea what culture it is from?"

"Not a clue," I said briskly. "But I would be indebted to you if you could help me translate it or point me in the direction of someone who can."

Yevgeny drummed his fingers on the desk.

"I don't have time, myself," he said finally. "Although it intrigues me enough to wish I did. But I have a new graduate student who could use some translation practice. I'll set him up with it as a directed studies project. Would that suffice?"

I smiled broadly. That was better than I'd dreamed. No charge on my depleted bank account, no further inquiries needed… I thrust my hand out toward Yevgeny and he shook it.

"That would be splendid."

I held my hand out for the book, and Yevgeny passed it back with a regretful look. He was fascinated by the mysterious text, as expected, but he would have to be content with the tidbits I passed along.

"I'll email you the pages I hope to have translated," I said. "And I'll do my best to find out more details about the text's history for your interest."

"Please do." Yevgeny looked at the book with a hungry eye. "I do love a good mystery."

CHAPTER IX

I felt buoyed by my success at the university. I hoped Yevgeny's graduate student would deliver on his new task quickly. Caelus' excitement was palpable as a low-grade buzzing in my torso, and I was curious myself. We needed clues about the location of the Thorn if we were to find it before the order did.

I had promised Grandview Women's Center that I would volunteer that afternoon. Once I returned to Cormorant Drive, I grabbed a souvlaki from a Greek restaurant—imagine me getting takeaway—and walked to the center. A few hours in their employ—another few bags of clothing donations had arrived, and I spent a happy shift preparing them with our magic—and I emerged satisfied and ready for a change of pace.

Caelus emerged from my arm once I exited the center into the chill of a steel-gray afternoon.

"Finally, you're alone," he grumbled. "You're always surrounded by people. Well? What did you think of the book?"

"They're trying to collect the pieces they need to grow a tree. This tree will release the Spirit elemental."

"And what is that?" Caelus said. His strands twitched with his excitement. "I have no idea, and I really want to know."

"Hopefully, we'll find out soon." I sidestepped an elderly man and continued to stride along the pavement toward Cormorant Drive. "What really intrigued me was the power infused in this tree and its parts. Are these three artifacts powerful in ways beyond summoning the Spirit elemental? The Leaf didn't do anything, but maybe we needed to activate it. Maybe the Seed also has magic of its own. If we can harness their powers, think of how helpful they could be in finding artifacts for you. Nothing could stand in our way. We need to get that Seed, Caelus."

"Yes," he said with narrowed eyes. "Because it's an artifact we need to destroy."

"Once we find the Thorn," I said. "Just in case the Seed and Leaf are helpful in finding it. Then, yes, we'll get rid of them all and please your superiors."

I wasn't keen on destroying the Leaf, let alone whatever artifacts came our way. The power they supposedly contained held so much potential. What couldn't I do with a little more power? My busy brain had already been crafting new ways to help at the women's center—creating amulets, maybe, that women could use for self-defense without realizing they were using magic—but Caelus wasn't sure if his magic held enough strength for that. But discovering the Thorn was a task with a very distant payoff, so I felt comfortable promising artifact destruction.

"You haven't practiced your powers for a while," Caelus said in a change of topic. "I have an idea for a new trick."

I brightened. More ways to use our abilities were always welcome.

"There's a park right around the corner. Show me there."

We practiced for an hour in the cover of a thick stand of laurels. Caelus wanted to play with different types of air balls, including a new one that pricked the recipient's skin with painful needle pokes, and I wanted to work on lifting my body with air currents.

"Pull everything you've got," Caelus said with his trademark helpfulness.

I scowled at him. "The last time I tried that, my feet flew out from under me. I'll be nursing that bruise on my bottom for days."

"Air is everywhere," he said with crossed arms. "If you find yourself flipping over, pull the other way."

I took a deep breath to calm my frustrated heartbeat. I was tenacious, but learning to lift my body with air needed every drop of determination I possessed.

I bent my knees in preparation, gathered air threads from every side, and steadily tugged upward. Within the cover of a drooping cedar, I managed to rise ten feet off the ground.

"Finally," Caelus said after I fell to the earth in astonishment. "I knew you'd get there eventually."

I glowed with pride at my accomplishment as I walked to Cut Right to help close the shop. How many people could say they could fly? My efforts were little more than a suspended jump, but I would take the win.

Rosemary wasn't paying me much to tidy at the salon, but every little bit helped. I didn't mind. It was a chance to chat with Joy and the others. Despite Caelus' constant presence, more friends were welcome.

When the bell tinkled to announce my presence in the salon, Joy and Shu glanced at me with doleful eyes.

"Did you hear the news?" Joy asked. She fidgeted with a comb in her hand. "Rosemary isn't a sister anymore. They kicked her out."

"She had her quirks," Shu said in a low voice. "But she didn't deserve this. No one was more dedicated to the cause than Rosemary."

Joy gave a sniff and plunked her comb in a container of disinfecting solution. I grabbed a broom and started to sweep.

"I'm sorry to hear that." There was no reason to tell these two about the late-night shenanigans that Rosemary and I had endured together. If she wanted them to know, she could tell them. "What happens to the sisterhood now?"

"Someone will come to training tomorrow night," said Joy. She pushed her hands through her thick blond hair to fluff it out and sighed. "We need a new head sister. I guess they'll pick one of us, but then we'll need another sister to make the nine, and none of the other daughters of order members is old enough yet. I don't know what will happen."

"You should come," Shu said unexpectedly. "You always come to training, anyway, so you're practically one of us. You should know what's going on."

Shu was always pleasant to me, especially after I saved her life during Starr's attack, but we weren't close. Her invitation to tonight's training surprised me. I must have been more trusted than I'd thought.

My stomach squirmed, since I currently owned their precious Leaf, but then I recalled the mothers' power-hungry intentions once the tree was planted and Spirit released. The utopia the sisters longed for was in question, and the truth might be more sinister. I would keep the Leaf for now and think no more about guilt.

"I'd be happy to," I said. "I could use some exercise, anyway."

Caelus woke me the next morning by yawning obnoxiously next to my ear. It was an affectation since he didn't breathe air or tire in any human way. I glared at him as soon as my eyes could open wide enough to see.

"What was that for?"

"You're always sleeping," he said. "We have artifacts to find. Time is wasting. Get a job, get some money, buy us a plane ticket to the Smithsonian. Chop, chop."

I flopped from my side to my back and stared at the ceiling.

"It's not that simple," I said. "I'm trying. I never thought I'd be back trolling the streets, resumé in hand. I feel like a teenager."

"I hear a lot of moping and self-pity, and not a lot of action. Why are you still in bed?"

"Wow." I swatted at Caelus' thread-torso, but he dodged out of the way. "You are extremely annoying this morning. What's eating you?"

"I need more artifacts. We've only found two, and there's a whole world of them out there."

He looked unusually somber. I frowned but didn't push him further. Something was bothering him, but he would tell me when he was ready.

"Also," he continued. "I want to check in with the Leaf. I know you trust this 'safety deposit box', but it's a human contraption. I'd like to lay eyes on it again, maybe strengthen the elemental barriers around it."

"That, we can do."

I hopped on the Skytrain a half-hour later, pushing onto the crowded carriage with other commuters this early in the morning. As I swayed with the motion of the train high above the road, clutching a bar above my head, I reflected on the changes I had undergone. Yes, I had a whole new body, magical powers, and a new name. But taking public transit? That was a big step for me.

I strode briskly down a sidewalk after exiting the train station. The streets were busy with harried-looking pedestrians on their way to work, and cars and buses clogged the streets. It was lively, that was certain. I pushed through a throng of people at a bus stop and walked into a store at random. The clothing boutique held two customers and a bored-looking attendant folding clothes at the back. I strode to her with furtive glances over my shoulder for effect.

"Excuse me," I said quietly. "I think I'm being followed. Do you have a back exit I can leave through? I'm nervous."

The woman's eyes widened, and she glanced to the front. When she was satisfied that no one was charging inside, she nodded and waved me forward.

"Of course. Come this way."

After assuring her that I didn't want to phone the police, I followed her through a back hallway and to a fire door that led to an alley smelling faintly of urine. She watched me go with a worried expression, so I waved my thanks and disappeared around the corner.

That little subterfuge should have put any watchers off the scent. I couldn't be sure that the order wasn't following me, and the last thing I wanted them to know was where I kept the Leaf.

I strode out of the alley, down the street, and to the front of an imposing building set back from the road by an expanse of architecturally interesting concrete slabs and two fountains, neither of which were operational in this cold stretch.

The bank was blissfully warm after the chill of outdoors, and I strode to the front desk.

"I'd like to see my safety deposit box, please," I said with confidence.

The teller glanced at me with polite distrust—my age working against me for once—but when I slid my new identification across the counter for verification, his expression cleared. The unreasonable anger that threatened to flare up in my body subsided.

"Of course," he said. "Right this way."

I followed him through a narrow corridor with tasteful watercolors on the walls. He opened a door and stepped back to allow me to enter. Inside was a small wooden table and two chairs in a style that was functional yet spoke of wealth. The walls were painted a deep wine-red, and a security camera blinked in the corner.

"I'll return shortly with your box, Ms. Feynman," he said and closed the door.

Caelus popped out of my arm when I sat down with a sigh.

"Where's the box? That guy is taking a long time. He'd better not be snooping through it."

"Calm down, Caelus," I said. "I have the key right here. No one is doing any snooping."

Caelus sniffed and floated around the room, examining the camera with interest. He jolted when the door opened again, and his surprise along with the sound of the clicking latch startled me. Caelus' jumpy mood was infectious.

The man entered and carefully placed my box on the table.

"Please, ring the bell when you are finished." He pointed at a small button beside the doorframe. "Someone will be along to take your box away."

At my nod, he slid out of the room and closed the door. I shoved the key into the lock and twisted. Caelus peered so closely that I could scarcely see the box through his threads.

"Back off, Caelus. I can't see what I'm doing."

When he backed away the minimum distance that he could get away with without me snapping at him, I opened the lid. A bundle of tightly woven silver threads lay inside.

"Looks like it's there," I said. "Happy?"

"Let's check it out. Unwrap the threads. Carefully, though."

"Yes, dear," I muttered and reached out my fingers.

It was the work of a minute to unravel the strands. I wondered what the watchers behind the security camera thought of my finger-waving. It probably wasn't the strangest thing they had seen in these rooms.

When the rolled Leaf lay on the table before us, looking dry and innocuous, Caelus swooped closer.

"I never really got a good look at it," he said. "Everything was such a rush when we stole it, and then we tucked it away here. I wonder what it does."

"Do you mean if it has special powers?" I asked. "Besides being a key that joins with the Seed and Thorn to unlock the prison of this Spirit elemental, whatever that is."

"All artifacts have innate power," he said absently, peering at the Leaf from one angle and then another. "Remember what the Book of Souls said? The Leaf might also do something when combined with other artifacts, but that doesn't mean that it doesn't do anything by itself. I wonder how to trigger it."

I gazed at the Leaf. It looked like a light breeze would cause it to crumble, but it had somehow stood the test of time, hidden until discovered in an archaeological dig. Rosemary hadn't told me much about how the Leaf had been found. The more I heard about the Seed, the more I wanted to know about the Leaf's origins. If what Caelus and the Book of Souls said was true, the Leaf was far more than simple fertilizer.

"What do you mean by trigger? Like the words that sometimes turn on amulets' powers?"

"Yes. But it's usually not a word. Sometimes just touching the artifact will unleash its power."

"Like the grail," I breathed. I had found a small cup in a shipwreck, reputed to be the drinking vessel of the legendary King Arthur. I knew that wasn't true, because when I had touched the grail, memories of my past lives had flooded back to me. In my earliest lifetime, I had been Morgan, sister of Arthur. He hadn't been a king, and I couldn't remember him drinking from that cup.

"Yes." Caelus swung around and pierced me with an intense look. "The grail. That artifact you promised we would get. The only other artifact that we know the location of. When are we going to get it?"

I sighed. It was true. The grail was the only artifact that we had a lead on currently. The problem was that Merry Lytton—Merlin in my previous lives—had the grail. I didn't want to get involved with him or his friends. I wanted to leave that side of my life far behind, and revisiting him would entangle me in a life I wanted no part of.

But I owed it to Caelus to pursue the only artifact we knew for certain was in this city. He allowed me to have full control of this body we shared in exchange for my cooperation in hunting for artifacts. I couldn't let him down.

"We'll go after it soon," I said. "I promise. I'm sorry I've been dragging my heels on this. I know how important finding artifacts is to you."

"Well." Caelus looked taken aback by my apology. "Good. Soon, it is. Now, try touching the Leaf."

I reached out my hand and gingerly placed a fingertip on the dusty Leaf.

"I touched it when I took it out of its locket. Nothing happened then, either."

"Hmm." Caelus leaned in closer. "Don't forget intention is key. Try thinking different things."

"That's wonderfully specific. Thank you for your guidance."

Caelus rolled his thread-formed eyes at me.

"Try to move something. Think angry thoughts. Try pushing your will into it, to force its latent power to wake up. Experiment."

I stared at the fragile Leaf and narrowed my eyes in concentration. My mind willed it to create sparks in the air. Nothing happened. I glared at the Leaf and channeled frustration and anger through my fingertip, not difficult emotions to access in this body. Nothing. I gathered my intentions, braced myself, then poured my will into the Leaf. It would show me its power if it were the last thing I tried.

CHAPTER X

With a pulse of its sluggish threads, the Leaf wriggled. Before my astonished eyes, the dusty brown of parchment-dry vegetation blossomed with verdant life. Threads from the Leaf twisted and curled over my hand, up my arm, and around my body. With the creeping strands, a sensation of power and strength enveloped me like armor. I felt powerful and invincible in a way I'd never felt before. Even the discovery of Caelus' abilities in my body hadn't given me the confidence the Leaf now imbued in me.

With my astonishment, the strands halted and slithered back to the Leaf. Before long, every thread wrapped around the artifact once more, and the Leaf slowly changed from a vibrant green to its dusty brown.

"What happened?" I whispered.

"It gave you protection," Caelus whispered back.

"But why did it stop?"

"You lost concentration. It must need constant intention to maintain its bond with you." Caelus leaned back, his face thoughtful. "We should take it with us."

"What?" I was taken aback by Caelus' change of heart. "I thought you wanted it safe until we could destroy it, and that we wouldn't destroy it until the Seed and Thorn were found, in case it was important that they be together first."

"No, not in case of that. In case we needed the Leaf to find the other two artifacts," Caelus said. "And if the Leaf gives you protection, that can only help. Your human body is so fragile. It keeps me up at night worrying about it."

"You're always up at night," I said with a twitch of my mouth. As an elemental only partly connected to a human body, Caelus didn't need to sleep.

"It's a figure of speech," he said in exasperation. "You're the human, I thought you would appreciate it. But with more invulnerability, you can take greater risks when finding artifacts."

I stared at the Leaf on the table. It was such a tiny thing to hold such power. What sort of tree had it been plucked from, and how long ago? Had the tree been powerful somehow—a true Tree of Life—or had the Leaf been imbued with elemental power after harvesting? If so, why use a leaf that was prone to rot and destruction?

I couldn't deny the draw of greater power. Feeling helpless was the one thing I hated more than anything else. Having Caelus' abilities greatly lessened my fears, but even with them, I had been in tight scrapes that I only just managed to wriggle out of. Could my fears disappear with more power?

"I thought you wanted the Leaf kept safe until we destroyed it," I said. "Are you sure we should take it out of here?"

"Yes," he said with decision. "You need protection. And, this way, I can keep an eye on the only artifact we have."

Misgivings fluttered in my mind, but I squashed them down firmly. Artifacts were Caelus' game. If he felt better about having this one near, than who was I to gainsay him?

"Okay," I said. "Let's take it."

I stopped at a souvenir shop once I left the bank. Enough tourists visited Vancouver, even in this weather, that these shops maintained a brisk business. A quick rifle through their racks, and I left holding a keychain emblazoned with a beaver wearing a red and white sweater. Normally, I wouldn't have considered buying a piece of tourist tat like this, but the trinket had one redeeming feature.

"Put the Leaf in," Caelus said as soon as the door to the souvenir shop swung shut behind me. "Let's see if it fits."

"I hope so. Otherwise, what am I going to do with this hunk of metal?"

"It's not that bad. It certainly doesn't warrant the disdain I can feel dripping through your mind."

"I'm Morgan now," I chanted to myself under my breath. "There's no one to impress. Fresh start, new me."

"If you're quite done with the self-affirmations, I want to see the Leaf in that keychain."

I glared at Caelus but pulled the keychain out of its paper bag. With a push of my thumb, the beaver faceplate swung to the side, exposing a cavity for storing who-knew-what. Secret notes? A single coin? Jellybeans for children? I couldn't fathom.

The Leaf fit perfectly inside. Caelus smiled widely.

"Yes. Now, tie it up with threads so it doesn't slip open."

A few twists of my now-practiced fingers, and the keychain securely enclosed the Leaf. I attached it to my keyring and slipped the offending oversized rodent into my pocket.

"There. Now, back to Cormorant Drive." A desire to further explore the Leaf's powers struck me. "On second thought, I could use a stroll in Stanley Park."

I walked briskly to downtown Vancouver's large park. It was too cold and damp to enjoy the walk, but trees would provide some privacy for my testing. The cold would keep others away, although the park was never completely empty of die-hard runners and cyclists.

I pulled out the keychain, grimacing at the beaver that hid such a valuable artifact. The sisters would have my hide if they knew how I was treating their precious possession. Luckily, they didn't know. Caelus ballooned out of my arm.

"Try using it without taking it out of the keychain," he instructed. "It would be best to leave it undisturbed. The air threads we wove around it should help, but still. It's a leaf, and it looks so fragile."

"It must have some powers of preservation, or it wouldn't have lasted this long. But, I agree, no point in testing that theory if we don't need to. Here we go."

I closed my eyes to better concentrate, and I pushed my intention and will into the keychain.

A moment passed during which I felt nothing. Then, something clicked. My eyes popped open, and green threads slithered out of the keychain. They paused, then slunk back.

"Keep concentrating," Caelus hissed. "You need to focus."

I desperately wanted to retort to Caelus' instructions, but I didn't have attention to spare. I narrowed my eyes and willed the Leaf to release its powers. Threads twisted around my wrist and up my arm, and that feeling of invincibility stole over me. It was intoxicating, and I poured more intention into the Leaf to keep the sensation coming.

"I don't think anything can hurt me," I breathed. "This is incredible."

A fat raindrop from an overhead branch dripped onto my nose. I blinked, startled, and my concentration disappeared. Green strands whipped away from my body and hid inside the keychain. I cursed.

"I'm not sure how helpful the Leaf will be in an altercation," Caelus said with a dubious glance at the beaver. "You can't ask your opponent to pause while you gather your concentration."

"I'll have to practice, that's all." I shoved the keychain into my pocket, the memory of my invulnerable state haunting me. "I can do that at home, now that I know the room won't blow up around me. I need to master this. I'm sure it can be done. Can you imagine the edge both your control over the air and this defensive power would give me? I would be untouchable."

"It might help you get the Seed." Caelus sounded dubious. "As long as you can figure out how to multitask. But don't forget we need to destroy the Leaf eventually. Don't get too used to it."

"Yes, yes, I know the mission."

Caelus' reminder rankled, and I was self-aware enough to know that I disliked the thought of giving up that defensive power. He was right, though—the Leaf was a temporary acquisition. One day I would help Caelus destroy it. Was it wrong that a part of me hoped that day would be far in the future?

When I arrived back on Cormorant Drive, most shops were open. It was past time to hand out a few resumés. Once I'd made a solid effort job-hunting, I would reward myself with a coffee and lemon tarts. I smiled as I strolled toward the main street. Hopefully, Jerome would have a few minutes to say hello. It felt like ages since I'd seen him last.

I passed the alley behind the row of shops where the bakery resided. A shout alerted me to a scuffle beside the dumpster, and my heart leaped. This was a chance to use my newly honed abilities to help someone. All the training with the sisters would now pay off.

I leaped out from behind the dumpster. A woman and two men paused their action like a frozen tableau entitled, "Muggers Assaulting a Young Woman, in oils." The woman was dressed in heels and designer jeans, and she wore diamond earrings and a ring with a rock the size of her fingernail. She was dressed to impress, and I wondered where she had been going before her day had been interrupted by these would-be thieves.

The halt didn't last. The woman kicked her closest attacker in the knee, snatched her purse away from him, and darted past me toward the road. The other two stumbled to follow her.

CHAPTER XI

Rage boiled in my gut, but my mind was laser focused. I'd been practicing for this moment for weeks. Finally, I could use my powers to gain the upper hand over assaulters and help a woman in need. I lifted my arms, and a quick blast of wind from my ready fingers swept the would-be muggers off their feet. The woman darted around me and disappeared.

"Hey!" A voice shouted. I looked up in surprise. Jerome stood at a back door that led into the shop row. He crossed his arms and glared at the two men.

"Back off," he said. His face was hard and unyielding, and his entire body exuded menace. "The girl is gone. She jumped into a car and phoned the police. They'll be here soon, I'll bet."

The two men shifted. One glanced at me with a frown, and the other stared at Jerome, his brow furrowed with worry.

"Come on, man, let's get out of here," said the man looking at me. "I don't know what this chick has, but it's messed up. Easier pickings elsewhere."

"You don't need to do this," Jerome said. "There are easier and better ways to make some cash. The hardware store down on Magnolia Street is hiring. Go ask there, say Jerome sent you. Chances are they'll give you some work."

I raised my eyebrow. By rights, I should have called the police right then and detained these muggers until they arrived. But something in Jerome's bearing stopped me. Beneath the menace, he was trying so hard to turn these criminals around. It felt like a wasted effort to me, especially when I could easily wrap them in air threads to stop them.

The man previously looking at me laughed loudly.

"Yeah, whatever," he said. "Get a job, you bum, that's what you're saying." He hit the other man's shoulder. "Come on, let's get out of here before the cops come."

I raised my hand, but Jerome shook his head with a

pleading look at me. The other man still stared at Jerome, indecision playing on his face. Did Jerome really want to let them go? Instead of throwing air strands at the duo, as the angry blood pounding in my ears wanted me to do, I pulled my phone out of my pocket and took a picture of the pair.

"Back off, bitch," the first man snarled and darted away.

"I've got your number," I called after him. "I'll be watching out for you."

"Seriously," Jerome told the other man, who was still hovering between us. "Go see Tom at the hardware store. He's a good guy. He'll find you something if you're serious."

The man gave a jerky nod then raced after the first man. Jerome sighed and ran his hands through his hair.

"What the hell was that about?" I walked toward him and stood with my hands planted on my hips. "Why didn't you want me to keep them here until the cops arrived?"

I didn't really want to interact with the police—my identity was precarious enough without intensive record checks—but Jerome didn't know that. It galled me to let the men escape without some retribution. I had all this power available to me. Why shouldn't I use it for justice?

"They were desperate. I know because—" Jerome sighed again. "Thanks for holding back. I'll check in with Tom tomorrow, see if that guy turns up. It's just—it's tough to break out of bad spots. Sometimes people need strength in compassion. But if it happens again, and you're there to witness, pull out your magic tricks. They can only have so many strikes before they're out."

I nodded slowly.

"Okay. I'll be watching." I rolled my shoulders. "Too bad, I was looking forward to a dust-up. I've been practicing my moves."

Jerome chuckled, and the tension of the moment broke.

"I'd like to see them. Care to demonstrate for me sometime?"

The corners of my lips twitched upward. I wasn't an overly prideful person, but it was pleasant to show off my new talents in front of an appreciative audience.

"Yes. Sometime soon."

I zipped up my coat and pulled the hood over my head to protect my hair from rain that threatened to turn into sleet. It was a miserable day, weather-wise, and I wanted to preserve my professional look as long as possible. First impressions went a long way when hunting for a job.

None of my resumé drop-offs had resulted in callbacks yet, but I was determined to persevere. Not only did my pride forbid defeat, but so did my dwindling bank account. There had to be one business in this neighborhood that didn't mind a sparse experience section.

I pulled open the glass door of the Lebanese grocer, and the briny-sweet scent of olives and honey filled my nose with warmth. My stomach gave an enthusiastic grumble. This body loved its food, and with my new age and training regime, I had to feed it far more frequently than I was used to.

The store was packed with tall shelving filled with imported olive oils, grape molasses, boxes of dates, and jars of red peppers. A refrigerated unit that served as a counter contained large vats of feta cheeses and prepared baba ghanoush and hummus. A self-serve kiosk in the center glistened with mounds of olive varieties.

The grocer, a forty-something man with a head of curly black hair and glasses half-obscuring bright, friendly eyes, was doing brisk business. A line snaked around the wall with customers to be helped at the deli. A teenage boy with a matching set of glasses quietly worked the till near the door.

I didn't want to disturb the grocer more than I had to—I couldn't imagine that barging in front of his customers would endear him to me—so I joined the deli line and watched the proceedings. The grocer greeted every customer with a brilliant smile and frequently asked after their children or pets.

My mouth watered as container after container of creamy cheese passed hands. Since I was here, I might as well buy myself dinner for tonight. Best not make this a wasted trip.

I shook my head in irritation. Hopelessness was not a winning mindset. I would find a job because I was persistent and capable. I could do this.

"Good morning," the grocer said when it was my turn. "Welcome to my store. Are you looking for some cheese? Maybe hosting a party tonight?"

I smiled at the thought. My guest list at such an event would be small, indeed. Although, if I included the sisters, maybe I could fill the living room of my little condo.

"No, just for me. Some of the sheep's feta, please, and a small container of hummus." While he filled my containers, happily humming to himself, I pulled out my resumé. "I noticed you're very busy. If you're looking for help, I'm in the market for a job. Full-time, part-time, whatever you need."

The grocer's eyes flicked to my resumé where it lay on the countertop. He continued to fill my hummus container with a large spoon, but he glanced at my face.

"Okay, thank you. I'll think about it."

My heart sank. That was a no if I'd ever heard one. A thought lanced into my brain, and I leaned forward.

"I also have experience consulting for businesses, including improving online presences." Morgan's only experience was for Jerome's cake-decorating business, but March had plenty of knowledge in that sector. "I'd be happy to go through your business plan and suggest improvements, for free, of course. If you think I'm helpful, we can talk further employment."

The grocer nodded, his eyes thoughtful. He slid my containers toward me and picked up the resumé then glanced at the top.

"Okay, Morgan. That's an interesting suggestion. I think I will call you tomorrow."

I smiled broadly at him.

"I look forward to it."

I grabbed a bag of pita bread and a box of baklava on my way to the till. The teenage boy mumbled his responses to my purchases, but I hardly noticed. Consulting was something I could do and do well. My mind raced over what I would need to set up for my own business—cards, website, name—then I laughed at myself. If I could prove my worth to the grocer, that was the first step. After that, the city was my oyster.

And if I got an employee discount for baklava, I wouldn't say no. Nothing would replace lemon tarts in my heart, but variety was the spice of life.

I sauntered to Upper Crust bakery, unable and unwilling to remove the smile from my face. Others on the sidewalk were hunched into their coats against the winter chill, but my head was high. I had very little—no job, no permanent abode, very few friends—but promise sizzled in the air with an electric zing. Caelus and I were a magic team, artifacts were cropping up, and I had the kernel of a business plan. Things were looking up.

When I entered the bakery, it was heavenly warm and ethereally scented. The mugging had pushed the need for treats clean out of my mind, and then job-hunting had distracted me, but now the desire was back. One day, if I earned a happy afterlife after my second death, I hoped it would smell like this bakery.

I'd timed my visit perfectly. As I stood in line for lunch, Jerome emerged from behind the counter, shrugging on his coat. His eyes looked sad, but they lit when he saw me.

"Morgan." He stood next to me in line. "I wasn't expecting you back. I'm just starting my break. Want to walk around the block with me?"

I smiled back at him, my betraying stomach flopping

around like an untrained seal. I sternly told it to behave. Caelus' amusement floated into my mind, and I inwardly scowled at the meddlesome elemental.

"I'll get my sandwich to go."

Jerome held the door open for me once I'd received my order, and we exited the bakery into the January chill. I took a huge bite of my warm panini, unwilling to let the sandwich grow cold through slow eating. March wouldn't have been seen dead eating while she walked. I took perverse pleasure in taking another large bite.

Jerome sighed deeply and shoved his hands into his pockets. I eyed him sideways and swallowed my mouthful.

"That was heartfelt," I said. "What's up?"

He stared at the sidewalk, but his attention was far away.

"It's the anniversary of my parents' death." He shot me an apologetic glance. "I didn't want to be a downer, but you asked."

I bumped his solid frame with my own small shoulder.

"You're allowed to be sad today. It's a tough day, I understand. My parents are gone, too."

I failed to mention that they'd both lived long lives and died of natural causes. Unless Jerome had been a late surprise to his parents, I suspected his loss had been quite different from mine.

Jerome gave me a swift smile, then his face fell into sorrowful lines again. I had the impulse to throw my arms around him in an embrace to make him smile again, but I resisted. This body's swings of emotion were far more than I was prepared to act on.

"Thanks." He sighed again. "It was a car crash when I was thirteen. I walked away with only a concussion, but they didn't even make it to the hospital."

I couldn't resist my body's impulses—I didn't want to after that revelation—and I tucked my hand into the crook of Jerome's arm. He tightened his arm against his side to squeeze my hand in recognition.

"I'm sorry. What happened to you then?"

Jerome was silent for a moment, and I let him take his time answering.

"My uncle took me in," he said finally. "I didn't have any other family close by, and my parents hadn't made arrangements for guardianship. My uncle offered, and there was no reason for the courts to say no."

Some of Jerome's threads wove around himself, and the rest prickled outward like a hedgehog. I scanned them with interest. What did his reaction mean?

"I gather his guardianship wasn't to your liking."

Jerome shrugged tightly.

"He put a roof over my head and was good to me in his own way. It could have been worse."

His threads told a different story, but I didn't want to pry. I had plenty of secrets of my own that I wasn't willing to share yet. Jerome would tell me when he was ready, not before.

I squeezed his arm.

"Thanks for sharing."

He smiled briefly, then his eyes traveled to my lips. Our steps slowed.

My body flushed with pleasurable heat, and my own eyes fluttered closed of their own accord. I wanted this. I needed to feel closer to Jerome.

Wait, what was I doing? This stubborn body was always trying to break free, but my mind was in control. Wasn't my mind the real me? If that were true, then I was fifty-five, and I was practically robbing the cradle.

I stepped back and squeezed Jerome's arm again, half in warning and half to get him moving. He inhaled sharply and stepped in the direction of the bakery, then pulled out his phone and checked the time.

"I need to get back. I still have an hour on the clock, and I need to plan my next cake. I'm meeting with the bride tomorrow for design sign-off. But are you around later?"

My brain sent out an alert, and my stomach clenched. That sounded like the prelude to a being asked on a date, and—as was clear from my reaction to our almost-kiss—I wasn't ready for that.

"I have training with the sisters tonight," I said in a regretful tone. My brain scrambled for an alternative that was not date-like to head him off. "But maybe I can stop by the bakery tomorrow again?"

"I'll make sure there are fresh lemon tarts for you," he promised.

"You are so strange," Caelus said. I had waved Jerome into Upper Crust a minute ago, and now I marched toward my condo.

"Says the elemental coming out of my arm," I muttered. "Why am I strange?"

"I feel sorry for Jerome. You like him, but you're frightened of moving forward with him—"

"I'm not frightened."

"Sure feels like it from here. You're friendly—and touch him when you can—then you head him off whenever he thinks about asking you on a date or kissing you. Make up your mind."

"I'm not taking relationship advice from a growth on my arm. Don't you have anything else to think about?"

"Yes, actually. When are we hunting for another artifact?" Caelus said, his voice plaintive.

"We have the Leaf," I reminded him. "We destroyed the torc from Montreal, we'll get the grail soon, and the Seed is on its way here. We're doing well."

Caelus' form shivered with emotion. What sort, I wasn't sure.

"I need more," he said.

I frowned and scanned his thread face. His usual mischievous demeanor had been replaced by a desperate worry.

"How many do you need to find? How will you know when you're done?"

"I need as many as I can get." He shrugged with an attempt at nonchalance. "The more, the better. I've been here for almost two months. I don't know how much longer I'll be allowed to stay."

"What exactly happens if you don't collect enough artifacts?" Caelus' mission seemed vague and difficult to measure, and I didn't understand why. It could be that elementals thought differently from humans—although Caelus was usually easy enough to understand—but something felt fishy about the scenario.

"I'll be sent to dormancy." Caelus infused the word with a doom-laden gravitas that sent a tingle down my spine.

"And that means…"

Caelus sighed with a hint of his former exasperation. I hid a smile.

"Dormancy is the lowest level of existence for an elemental. It's not truly existing, not really. More like a bear hibernating or a frog overwintering in a pond. You don't feel, you don't move, you don't think. You simply persist in a state of unknowing until you are chosen to ascend to an active level. But elementals in dormancy can't jump as high as I am now. They have to work their way up the ranks. The lowest levels follow tiny puffs of wind, then sink into dormancy again, then reanimate when another puff of wind materializes. Only when the levels reshuffle—maybe a higher elemental is sent to dormancy and the levels rearrange—can a low-level elemental rise into a more stable position and begin to think again." Caelus shuddered. "I don't want to go back there. I worked hard to achieve this level. Who knows if I would ever rise this high again after my rebirth?"

A lot of things in Caelus' explanation didn't make sense to me, but I focused on the relevant part.

"You need some large but unspecified number of artifacts to prove to your superiors that you are worthy to remain at the level you are, correct?" When Caelus nodded, I continued. "What did you do to earn this punishment?"

Caelus swelled with indignation.

"This is a sacred mission, not punishment."

I stared him down as if he were a stubborn board member. As always, the recipient of my stern gaze deflated.

"I neglected my duties," he muttered. "Once. A water elemental invited me to ride waves off the coast. I was only gone for a day, but in that time an episodic tangling happened in my region. I should have been there to deal with it. Since I wasn't, it grew big enough that the air fundamental—the head of my element—had to come fix it."

"There it is." I nodded. "I knew there was something. Well, we all make mistakes. I suppose it was a great boon that this fundamental allowed you to take this mission to pay for your crimes, rather than be sentenced to dormancy immediately?"

Caelus nodded fervently.

"Most don't get a chance like this. I can't blow it." His shoulders slumped. "But finding artifacts in this wide world of yours is complex and time-consuming, and I don't know how long I have left."

I tapped my fingers on my thigh as I walked past a pharmacy, its bright interior rivaling light filtering through gloomy clouds above. An artifact was in Vancouver, and I knew who had it. I didn't want to stir up my past, not with the present treating me so well, but Caelus' need was greater than mine.

"Maybe it's time to get the grail," I said.

Caelus stared at me with wide, hopeful eyes.

"Yes," he breathed. "Finally. Let's do it. When?"

I stood and brushed off my jeans.

"There's no time like the present. Come on, I want to say hello to my friend Anna anyway. She'll know how best to get the grail."

CHAPTER XII

Caelus melted into my arm and swirled around my stomach. His relief and anticipation pulsed inside me, and I smiled with the sensation. His happiness almost eclipsed the unease I felt at approaching Merry Lytton, the immortal thorn in my side. I had hoped that I could leave that world behind, but there was nothing for it. Morgan Leigh Feynman had to revisit her long and varied past. Hopefully, I could relieve Merry of his artifact quickly and painlessly without entangling myself in his life.

I ran to a bus that pulled up a half-block away. When I settled in the first empty seat, I thought of Anna Green. I hadn't seen her often since my body switch—she kept me a secret from her boyfriend Wayne which didn't allow for many visits, and I'd been busy traveling in search of artifacts—and a chat over coffee was long overdue. Jerome popped into my head, unbidden, and I nodded. I would like Anna's opinion on him and my reasons for hesitancy. Yes, a chat with a kindred spirit was just what I needed.

She was also in Merry's inner circle and would know best where he kept the grail and how to get it. At this thought, Caelus' silver threads shivered on my torso.

It took one bus, a chilly wait on a side street with my hood up against the drizzle, and another bus to finally arrive near Anna's suite. I marched down a quiet street flanked by tall trees devoid of leaves this time of year. Sirens started to wail in the distance, and I wondered vaguely if the police were rushing to a traffic accident. I supposed that was another benefit of the bus: it would win any accident it was in.

Anna rented a basement suite in a large house divided into apartments, and her entrance was around the back. I rounded the corner, walked down three steps, and knocked swiftly on her door.

No one answered, and I sighed. It was a dim hope that she would be home. She was probably at the coffeeshop where she worked. Maybe I should visit her there. I could use a cup of coffee.

A rustling alerted me to the presence of another, and my heartrate picked up. Had Anna arrived home? That would be fortunate timing, indeed. I ran up the steps and peeked around the corner.

A man with dark hair and a leather jacket adjusted the leaves of a massive rhododendron bush in the front yard to hide his motorcycle underneath. My heartbeat, already elevated, thundered in my chest, and my body's ever-eager rage kindled. I squashed it down and focused on the questions his presence raised. Why was Merry Lytton hiding his motorcycle in Anna's front yard? The sirens permeated my consciousness. Was the wailing for him?

Caelus whooshed out of my arm.

"He has an artifact in his pocket," he hissed at me. "It has to be the grail. Look."

Swirls of multicolored threads spilled out of the pocket of Merry's scuffed and dirt-smeared jacket. My fingernails squeezed into my palms. Maybe this was an opportunity, my chance to steal the grail from Merry. I could surprise him, grab the artifact, and run, no further interaction necessary. My past could remain behind me where it belonged.

And I owed it to Caelus to try.

I swiped my hand through the air to gather silver strands, then I rolled them into a ball and tossed it at Merry's turning torso before he saw me. My aim was true, and the blast of gale-force wind slammed him backward onto muddy grass. I didn't let him fully regain his feet before I released another ball of wind.

Somehow, Merry's quick reflexes allowed him to dodge my second attack. My eyes narrowed in dislike, and my hands rolled another ball of air to keep myself on the offensive. Our eyes met, and confusion flickered in his before I threw my third air ball. He rolled to the side in a move that would have made a gymnast proud.

"Who the hell are you?" he shouted. "Why are you attacking me?"

He was full of tricks, and as he yelled, he pulled brown threads until a wall of earth separated us. Caelus emerged from my arm.

"Time to fly," he said, his voice thick with excitement.

I pulled air threads until a cloud of them lifted my feet off the ground. I rose with dizzying swiftness and sailed over the earthen wall to land in front of a surprised Merry. My mouth twisted in satisfaction. Now he knew what it felt like to be the one watching power instead of wielding it.

My hands weren't idle while I flew. By the time I reached the ground, a knife of threads was clasped in each of my hands. Merry eyed them without his usual confidence.

"I want the grail." I tried to sound menacing, but I didn't think I succeeded. "I need it."

"You tell him," Caelus crowed beside me.

Merry's demeanor shifted from wary to angry in a heartbeat. His eyes flashed.

"Too bad," he said. "It's mine."

My chance at surprising Merry was lost, but I had other resources. Without telegraphing my moves, I lashed out with the knife in my right hand. Merry reacted with surprising swiftness, and somehow his hand wrapped around my wrist. I slashed with my left hand, but Merry did something to harden his skin, and the blade barely raised blood.

Knives weren't working, but even Merry couldn't survive without air. I reached with my free hand toward his jaw. With a yank, I pulled air threads that flowed out of his mouth and nose. His eyes bulged at the lack of air, but he pushed his body into mine.

I lost my balance and fell backward, landing heavily on the

muddy grass. Before I could move, Merry had a hand on each of my wrists and fingers, and I couldn't manipulate threads. I twisted to break free, allowing my body's rage at my entrapment to fuel my actions. How had this attack gone so awry?

"I need to keep the balance," I yelled. "Artifacts are made with elemental power, and elementals don't belong in the physical world."

"Then what the hell are you doing here?"

I hadn't told anyone about Caelus yet, but I needed to convince Merry to give me the grail. He was one of the few people in this world who understood elementals.

"Caelus is the elemental in my body. He's on a mission to collect all artifacts and destroy them then return to his plane. This arrangement is only temporary."

Merry looked taken aback, but he didn't relinquish his hold on my wrists.

"Your elemental's mission is to separate the elemental and physical worlds?"

"Yes."

Finally, Merry let go of my hands and stood back. I scrambled to my feet and rubbed my sore wrists. Now, what? Should I attack again? Should I try to convince him to hand over the grail? Merry gazed at me with a familiar expression of pondering.

"I know that look," I said. How many times had I seen it over the centuries? My memories might have been fragmented and fuzzy, but enough remained in my mind to recognize it. "What are you thinking?"

He gave me a perplexed look then shook his head as if to clear it.

"It seems to me we're on the same side," he said. "I agree, the worlds should be far more separate than they are, and I'm in the process of transferring some of my elemental power to the other side, as well as cleaning up after another troublesome half-elemental."

"Is there any other kind?" I said under my breath. Merry gained his power from his half-elemental nature, and he tended to get in my way more often than not. Louder, I said, "Then you will give me the grail to destroy. It's a powerful elemental artifact."

"No. I will not."

I gritted my teeth. Negotiation was out, then. I raised my hands in preparation.

"Then we are at an impasse."

"Take him down," Caelus said with a shake of his fist at Merry. "You can do it."

Merry held up his hand to stop me. His jaw worked.

"Wait," he said. "Let me finish. I will not give you the grail yet."

"Yet?"

"I need it for now. Someone is promised to return to me, but in a different body. Without the grail, I can't wake her past memories of me, and we will be forever sundered. I can't let that happen." He took a deep breath and drummed his fingers against his leg. "If I promise to give you the grail once I find her, will that suffice? I want it for no other purpose."

I gazed at Merry, his face for once earnest and pleading. As little as I cared for Merry's wellbeing, I couldn't help but be moved by his plight. Anna had tried to tell me about some loss that Merry had suffered in the elemental battle last month—the same battle in which March had died and Morgan had been born—but I hadn't wanted to hear the details.

"What are you thinking?" Caelus hissed at me. "Forget the human's sob story. Grab the grail and run."

I tightened my lips. Merry's chocolate-brown threads were motionless with tension and tight against his body as if for protection. My answer mattered more than he could express. A vein of sympathy wriggled through my psyche. As much as I loved to hate Merlin for forever thwarting my plans over my many lives, I'd loved him once, long ago. It had been with the infatuation of youth, but still, the lingering emotion remained as a sweet echo from a distant past.

"That will suffice," I said. I ignored Caelus' howl of dismay. "If you swear."

"I swear on my life that you will receive the grail once I find who I'm looking for."

I nodded and held out my hand. My fingers had to pass through Caelus' threads as he pressed his face into mine to shout his displeasure.

"Then give me your phone," I said over Caelus' noise.

I entered my contact details into Merry's phone. It was a gesture only. Anna could tell me where to find him when it was time. I hid a smile as I typed the name "Morgan." It was delicious having a secret that others could guess if they only put their minds to it. A shadow of doubt crossed Merry's face when he read the name, and my stomach clenched in fear. Was the name too blatant? I didn't want him to know my true identity. I spat out my next words quickly to distract him.

"I'll be waiting. Don't forget, or I'll come after you again. I know how to find you."

I spun around and strode away. I couldn't carry on a conversation with Merry any longer, not with Caelus screaming in my ears.

"The artifact was right there!" he yelled. His threads spasmed with his rage. "Why are we walking away? I need that artifact. I thought you understood, but you don't, not at all!"

Caelus sounded like an overwrought teenager, so I tried to infuse some logic into the situation.

"We know exactly where it is—"

Caelus melted into my arm. My brow contracted with confusion, but a stabbing pain in my gut soon told me what was going on. Caelus was trying to take over our body to get the grail.

I chanted the containment spell I had mastered last month

when our arrangement was new and volatile. I had a moment of panic when Caelus wriggled into my strands deeply, but the chant eventually drove him out. He popped out of my arm, and I leaned over, my hands on my thighs and my chest heaving for breath.

"You promised," I panted. "You promised you wouldn't try to take over our body."

"In exchange for you getting artifacts," he hissed. His eyes were bright with betrayal. "You aren't holding up your end of our bargain. Why should I hold up mine?"

I stood up straight and sucked in a deep breath. It was hard to argue with Caelus' point. An artifact had been in his grasp, and I'd walked away.

"We know exactly where it is," I said. "Merry will keep it with him, I'm sure of it. Wherever he goes, the grail will go too. And we can always find Merry by staying in touch with Anna. I just—" I heaved another sigh. "I felt sorry for him, okay? It's rough to lose someone. Death is like going into dormancy. Most people never get out again, but a few escape and want to be reunited with their loved ones. Do elementals bond with each other?"

Caelus had calmed down enough to consider my question.

"Not like you humans do," he said. "We have allies, not friends or lovers or children. Your bonds seem stronger."

"Yes. I didn't want to take that hope away from Merry. It would either break him, or he would break me when he retaliated against our body. Then you wouldn't have a chance of finding more artifacts. But I promise you this." I reached out my hand until it rested on top of Caelus' cool thread one. "If your fundamental comes calling before we collect the grail, and you don't have enough artifacts to avoid dormancy, I will personally steal the grail from Merry with no hesitation. Deal?"

Caelus searched my face then slowly nodded.

"Deal."

I sighed with relief and continued walking toward the bus stop. A thought made me frown.

"Why couldn't Merry see you? He can see the threads of the world."

"I can hide myself when I want to." Caelus shrugged. "I didn't make it to my elemental level without learning a thing or two. It seemed prudent to mask my signal, given my mission. Who knows who I'll come across?"

I nodded and continue to walk. Caelus floated beside me, clearly lost in thought.

"I want to book another flight tonight," he said after a long silence. "I have a good feeling about that silver bowl in the Copenhagen museum. If that's not an artifact, call me a fire elemental."

I grinned. I didn't know where I would get the money for a trans-Atlantic flight, but I would figure it out just to hear that enthusiasm in my elemental friend's voice.

"Consider it done."

The late January sun was setting by the time I arrived back at Cormorant Drive, chilled from the damp air with a hint of Arctic cold. Cut Right, the salon where some of the sisters worked, was still open when I passed by, and on a whim, I entered. If I were to steal the Seed from the order, I needed more information about it. But apart from that, I wanted to greet my friends, especially after missing Anna. A tinkling bell made Joy and Shu look up from their closing tasks. Shu wielded a broom, and Joy rinsed sinks.

"Morgan," Joy said, her unctuous voice warm and welcoming. "Good to see you."

"I was passing by and thought I'd say a quick hello."

I smiled at the notion that I could pop in and greet friends in this way. As March, I had been too important and too busy to drop in on others. Besides, I hadn't had many casual friends where that would have been appropriate, none except for Anna. March's appearance at an acquaintance's door would have sparked confusion and embarrassment. Morgan's arrival was natural and welcomed.

"We're just cleaning up for the day." Joy waved at the room. Towels draped over chairs, empty shampoo bottles littered the sinks, and a hair dryer haphazardly dangled from the corner of a mirror. "Ever since Miranda started at the university a few weeks ago, we've missed her help. She still takes a few shifts, but nowhere near the number of hours she used to."

"And we're left to pick up the slack," Shu muttered. She grinned apologetically. "Don't mind me. It's been a long day. Rosemary did give us a Christmas bonus, so I shouldn't complain too much."

"I can help right now," I said. "I'll mark it on my timesheet. What's Miranda taking at university?"

I asked my question with genuine curiosity. After my conversation with Thea, I wondered about the career paths of the sisters. Did most of them realize they had little chance of a future in the order?

"Archaeology," Joy replied. "For the order, you know. We're always on the hunt for our artifacts."

I nodded. Miranda must have similar goals to Rosemary. Shu picked up a pile of towels.

"I'll put the laundry on," she said to Joy then disappeared behind a wall at the back of the salon.

"Speaking of artifacts," I said after a prod from Caelus' silver threads at my stomach. "What's the plan for the Seed, now that it's been found?"

Joy's eyes brightened at my mention of the Seed. She leaned against the sink she was cleaning, her task forgotten. To cover my own interest, I took Shu's broom from its perch against the wall and started to sweep where Shu had missed.

"The order members involved in the dig are transporting the Seed in the next few days. It's coming directly to Vancouver. I'm so excited to see it. I'm sure it won't look like much, but the power it must contain!" Joy looked dreamily out the window. "The ability to bring all life together in one glorious, connected way. How amazing is that? And, to think, we only have to find the Thorn, and then our task is complete." She sighed happily.

I already knew that the Seed was coming to Vancouver. I wanted more information than that. How would I make plans to steal it if I didn't know anything?

"So amazing," I agreed. My broom made soft scraping noises on the floor. "Incredible. But what will you do with the Seed once it's here? Will the mothers wear lockets like the sisters do?"

Joy chuckled richly.

"No, thank goodness. It's such a ridiculous system. If our leader didn't insist on it, we would have changed it years ago, I'm sure. She's very old, though, and quite doddery. The other order members figure it's best to humor her until—well, you know."

I nodded, but inwardly I sighed. Normally, I couldn't get Joy to stop talking. When would she get to the point?

"I did wonder about the locket approach. I'm glad to hear you won't entrust the next artifact to a rotating system of necklaces. But what, if not that? Safety deposit box?"

Joy looked scandalized.

"That's not nearly special enough for the Seed," she said with a shake of her head. I considered the Leaf, previously encased in my own safety deposit box, and suppressed a smile. "The artifacts are sacred. They deserve a far more glorious treatment. No, the Seed is destined for a special place. Honestly, I'm not sure where yet. There will be a ceremony to inter it. I hope the sisters are invited. I think we will be. It's such a momentous occasion, I don't know how we could be left out.”

“I’m sure you’ll be included. Will the ceremony take place as soon as the Seed gets to Vancouver? I can’t imagine you’ll want it hanging around on someone’s kitchen table while waiting for the ceremony.”

Joy shuddered at the thought and resumed rinsing her sink.

“Yeah, exactly. I’m sure it will happen right away.”

I leaned my broom against the wall.

“Keep me up-to-date on the exciting news. I know I’m not in the order, but I’m so happy for you. Maybe after the Seed is interred, I could buy you all a drink to celebrate.”

Joy beamed.

“What a lovely offer! I’ll tell you everything.”

Once we closed the salon, I walked home to my condo, my coat zipped up tightly against the driving rain. Dinner tonight was leftover Thai from last night’s meal, and I wondered at myself when the microwave beeped and I pulled out the steaming dish. Takeout, and leftovers to boot? March had definitely left the building.

After dinner, I changed into my exercise gear, slipped on running shoes, and jogged back to Cut Right. The rain had mercifully eased, and my shoes were mostly dry when I ran down the stairs to the basement.

The sisters’ gym was oddly subdued. Usually, chatter and laughter floated into the hallway along with the whir of exercise machines and the thud of feet smacking into floor mats. I entered with trepidation, but all I encountered were long faces. The sisters were taking Rosemary’s absence hard.

“Hi, Morgan,” Miranda said from a stationary bike without her usual bright verve.

I greeted her and the others then hopped on a treadmill next to Jasmine and started to jog. Jasmine nodded but didn’t remove her earbuds. That was fine by me. I had plenty to think about, what with news of the Seed's power, Rosemary's plans to steal it, and Caelus' desire to see it destroyed.

I didn't have long to ponder before the energy in the room sharpened with an almost electric zing. I turned my head. In the doorway was a familiar woman in her early twenties who surveyed the room with assessing eyes that missed nothing. Her dark brown hair was carefully coiffed to cascade down her back in loose waves, and her leather jacket was fashionable if completely impractical in Vancouver's rain.

"Filippa?" Joy said with astonishment leaking from her rich voice. "What are you doing here?"

My eyes narrowed. Filippa was the name of Thea's daughter, the archaeology student.

"Hello, Joy," Filippa said with a smile. "And everyone. It's good to see you all again. After Rosemary's unfortunate demotion, the position of head sister is vacant. I'm here to fill it."

CHAPTER XIII

The silence in the room lasted forever, broken only by the whir of machines. When Jasmine pressed a button to stop her treadmill, I followed suit. The sisters stared at Filippa and each other.

"But you're not a sister," Joy said finally, her voice loud in the silence. "You never have been, Filippa."

"That's true," Filippa said. "I chose a different path. But I'm still in the order, and you've all known me since we were children together. It was a difficult decision for my mother—goodness knows that I have important work elsewhere, what with the Seed arriving and the Thorn still at large—but I am needed here."

"One of us could have been head sister," Shu muttered loudly enough for Filippa to hear.

"And one day you will be," Filippa said with a smile at grim-faced Shu. "But we are short of candidates for the sisterhood. I am qualified, trained for years under Thea's tutelage for all aspects of sister- and motherhood. It was a natural choice." She smiled genially. "But don't worry, this is a chance to get to know you all better—it's been too long since we've hung out together—and I'll train the next candidate to replace me."

More glances exchanged between the sisters, but Filippa's speech appeared to mollify most of them. Only Denise and Shu sported tight lips and narrowed eyes. Joy gave a great sigh of relief and crossed the room to Filippa. She hugged her tightly.

"It's good to see you. You're right, it's been too long. Come in. Did you bring your workout gear? I bet I can still beat you on the mats."

Jasmine started her treadmill again but didn't put in her earbuds. For once, the activity outside her music was more interesting to her. I started my own machine, but only on a brisk walk setting. My ears strained to hear every snippet of conversation around me.

Before I could gather anything, Filippa approached me. I raised my hand to turn off the treadmill, but she waved at me to continue.

"Please, don't let me interrupt you. I wanted to introduce myself. I'm Filippa Diamanto, daughter of Thea Diamanto and now head sister to the order's sisterhood."

"Morgan Feynman," I replied and thrust out my hand while I walked for her to shake. "Friend of the sisters."

"More than that, from what I've been told." Filippa shook my hand. "You were instrumental in ferreting out corruption in the sisterhood last month. It was ill-advised for Rosemary to tell you the secrets of the order, but luckily you were trustworthy."

I kept my face impassive. I wasn't trustworthy. The Leaf burned a hole in my pocket. I wondered how much Filippa knew from her mother.

"All's well that ends well," I said blandly. "I was happy to help. Granted, Rosemary paid me, but I've grown fond of the sisterhood and am sympathetic to their goals. I hear you're training to be an archaeologist, and that you were one of the students at the dig when they found the Seed?"

Filippa nodded. She ran her hand along the front of my treadmill in an absentminded gesture.

"It was fascinating. Hot and dusty, of course." Her laugh tinkled lightly, and I could feel Jasmine listening hard while trying not to appear like she was. "But the evidence of the past was overwhelming. I must confess, I'm not a huge history buff. Some of my colleagues go weak-kneed when they spot a broken plinth or shard of pottery. I'm in it for the order, nothing more. But when we discovered a carving of the Tree of Life, well, even I felt a shiver go down my back."

"What a moment of history to be in the middle of." I let awe infuse my voice and hoped I wasn't laying it on too thickly.

"And now that the Seed is in the order's possession, what's the plan? How can you possibly protect such a valuable object?"

Filippa gave me a knowing smile. What did she think she knew?

"Don't worry. It will be well taken care of. We know the value of the Seed." Filippa patted the treadmill and stood straight. "It was nice meeting you, Morgan. If you'll excuse me, I should speak with Joy about the future of the sisterhood."

Filippa moved away and left me to fume at my ineptitude at getting information from the younger woman. How was I supposed to get the Seed if the motherhood and their minions were onto me?

During my morning toast and news—read on my phone because I couldn't justify splurging for a paper copy with my limited budget—ringing startled me. I pressed a button and held my phone to my ear.

"Hello?"

"Good morning, Ms. Feynman," a male voice said, his Lebanese accent familiar. "This is Amir Khoury. Would you come into the grocery today? I would like your opinion on my business plan if you are still offering your services."

"Yes." I put down my toast and let my grin lift my cheeks. "Yes, I'll be there shortly."

I raced through my morning routine and was out the door in twenty minutes. I walked briskly down Cormorant Drive, speeding with anticipation but careful to avoid walking so fast that I would sweat. The bitterly cold air aided me in my endeavors.

The grocery was quiet this early. It must have just opened. I entered through the glass door, and Amir beamed at me.

"Ms. Feynman! Please, come in. Can I get you something to drink, eat?"

"Please don't trouble yourself. I just came from breakfast."

"No trouble at all. Please, I insist."

I didn't want to offend Amir, so I accepted a chipped mug of strong black coffee. It was warm and heavily sweetened with a hint of cardamon, and I sniffed it with satisfaction as I followed Amir behind the counter and to a back storage room. The area wasn't any bigger than my bathroom at the condo, and in it was squeezed a tiny desk stuffed with papers facing a floor-to-ceiling shelf unit with extra inventory.

"I have it somewhere," Amir said.

He shuffled the papers on his desk, and I winced when a few drifted to the floor like falling snow. My tidy mind rebelled at the chaos, and I wanted desperately to take over and organize the madness.

"Ah, yes. Here it is." Amir brandished a paper at me, then held it out with more composure. "Here. I was writing down all the things we do to promote the store, and a few numbers of profit and expenses. Just the general figures so you could get a sense of what I'm working with."

"Wonderful." I scanned the paper. Amir's notes were scrawled over the page in black ballpoint pen. "And what are your goals for the grocery? Your short-term and long-term plans?"

Amir looked confused.

"Selling groceries, I guess."

"Yes, of course." I smiled indulgently. "But do you want to maintain status quo, or would you like to grow your business? Can your storefront here support more customers? Would you like to open another shop in a different part of the city? Are you interested in expanding to an online presence?"

With every question, Amir's eyes grew a little rounder. He cleared his throat once I finished speaking.

"I guess—hmm, I'm not sure." He shrugged with his hands out. "I guess that's why I was interested in your thoughts. How can you help me?"

"Here's what I can do." I scanned the paper again and nodded. "I'll take this information home with me, and I'll work out a few different future scenarios and what it might take to get your shop there. I'll also outline some strategies that you could adopt. If any interest you, we can delve into them further. Does that sound like a plan?"

Amir nodded fervently.

"Thank you, Ms. Feynman. This is very generous of you."

"Please, call me Morgan. And why don't you see what I come up with before you start praising me." I folded the paper and put it in my coat pocket. "But, of course, if you find me helpful, a testimonial wouldn't go amiss as I grow my own consultancy. We can speak about that later."

Amir grabbed my free hand and shook it vigorously.

"To new beginnings," he said with a grin.

I smiled back.

"To fresh starts."

I would have skipped home if my dignity weren't at stake. As it was, my steps were light and quick, and I darted around pedestrians without noticing the chill that caused them to hunch into their coats.

Once in my apartment, I stripped off my outer clothes and slapped a piece of paper and pencil on my table. For the next hour, I scribbled notes and ideas for the growth of the little grocery, aided frequently by searches on my phone. When I finally placed my pencil down with satisfaction, Caelus emerged from my arm with a grumpy expression.

"Too bad you need to work to maintain this body," he said. "It's a pain. Working eats up so much time. That's time you could be looking for artifacts."

"Caelus, we're doing really well. Artifacts are hard to find, and they don't grow on trees." I paused. "Well, apparently they do, but that's a new discovery. Do you think there's only one Tree of Life? I guess so, otherwise the order wouldn't be so excited to grow this one."

"We still don't know when the Seed is arriving in Vancouver, nor how you and Rosemary will steal it when it does. Have you talked to her? Does she have any ideas where the order will take the Seed?"

"I'll call her today, I promise. In the meantime, I heard about an exhibit opening in Los Angeles featuring ancient Mesopotamia. What do you bet there's an artifact in that collection?"

Caelus' eyes brightened with interest, as I had hoped they would.

"Yes, I'll bet you anything. When can we go?"

I was feeling hopeful and exultant after my work on the grocer, despite not earning any money from my efforts. Hope was a powerful thing, and my bank account didn't seem so dire with the promise of future money to come once I'd proved myself to Amir.

"Let's book a flight right now," I said grandly and opened a browser on my phone. "I know you wanted to go to Copenhagen, but I think this exhibit is a better bet. I'll arrange it for right after we get back from the Smithsonian. At this rate, we'll earn enough frequent flyer points to find our next artifact for free."

Caelus rubbed his thread-hands together in a gesture of glee, and I took a few minutes to book a flight to Los Angeles for next week. When that was complete, I sat back and looked at Caelus.

"What?" he said when he noticed my gaze. "Do I have a thread in my teeth?"

He chuckled to himself while I rolled my eyes at his terrible humor.

"No. I was wondering about the place where they found the Seed. The archaeology site."

"What about it?"

"How did they know it was a likely spot for the Seed to be? Were there signs? Did the Book of Souls give some indication?"

Caelus shrugged. I crossed my arms at his obtuseness, which made him sway in midair.

"It's important," I said with exaggerated slowness. "Because we need to find the Thorn before they do. Preferably soon. I don't know that finding it in a few decades will help you with gaining your superiors' trust."

Caelus' face fell.

"No, it wouldn't do." He sighed and narrowed his eyes. "How do we find out?"

"The only way we can," I said. "Research. The dig was a big deal, as far as I can tell. There should be news articles about it, at the very least. And our translator will hopefully come through for us."

I turned on my phone and searched for digs in Turkey. A few websites later, a profile picture of Filippa in the background of a dusty dig site caught my attention.

"Here it is," I said.

Caelus swooped closer to look, and I scanned the article.

"It looks like they were tipped off by an ancient manuscript detailing the location of a treasure," I said. "What do you bet that was the Book of Souls. Then they surveyed the ground, found some irregular indentations, then dug into a buried chamber. They think it was a temple for the goddess Aphrodite. They found priceless statues and jewelry. The archaeologists are over the moon, say it's the biggest find since Sutton Hoo, although the journalist seems skeptical."

"No mention of the Seed, though," said Caelus.

"I think the order whisked it away pretty quickly. In any event, I don't think the Seed looks like much. The Leaf certainly doesn't. An uninitiated archaeologist probably wouldn't look twice at it."

My phone pinged with an incoming email. I opened it, and my heart leaped.

"Our first translated page," I said aloud. "Ready to read the Book of Souls?"

Caelus' strands jolted as if with electricity.

"Yes," he breathed. "This whole Spirit elemental business is fascinating. I've never heard of her before, and I feel a little miffed that some humans know more about elementals than I do."

"Listen and learn, my friend." I read the graduate student's note. "She says that this is the first page I sent her from the section that the sisters don't know about. It has an image of three women holding hands and a thread-face in the center." I cleared my throat and began to read.

The Seed bursts forth with life only in the bosom of its mother Tree and watered from blood sacrifice of Thorn and the faithful. The Seed blossoms into the Tree, and Spirit flows forth from the Tree. So the great cycle of Spirit lives and dies and resurrects in the great wheel of life of which it is the source and the end.

The Tree grows heavily with fruit at maturation, then not again for a century. Remember death. Keep the Seed hidden in the most precious temple, for the Tree lives and dies as all life does, but will be eternal with careful preservation of the Seed.

I set the phone on the table and looked at Caelus' thoughtful face.

"What did we get from that?" I ask.

"The Spirit elemental is connected to the growth of this Tree," Caelus said slowly. "It needs all three parts to grow. We mostly knew that."

"The text did say to keep the Seed safe in a temple. That must be why the order joined this dig. It was to excavate what they think was a temple to the goddess Aphrodite. She was a commonly worshiped fertility goddess in the region during that time. It fits the female motif the order has going on. I guess it was a good place to look."

"We need more of this book translated to get clues for the Thorn."

Caelus' strands quivered with his excitement. I grinned and tapped my phone.

"They should be coming soon."

CHAPTER XIV

Jerome texted me the next day to ask if I wanted to meet after he finished work midafternoon. His message warmed my stomach with a pleasant heat. I'd missed him yesterday. I had plenty to tell him, and I couldn't wait to hear how his newest client was progressing. I texted back an affirmative then spent a few minutes in my closet. I needed to get dressed anyway—I'd spent all morning in my sleepwear like a heathen, working further on Amir's business plan—and I tried to convince myself that I wasn't spending longer at my task because I was meeting Jerome.

I settled for comfort, in the end. We were planning a walk, and my coat would be zipped up to my chin. Caelus whooshed out of my arm.

"Your emotions are leaking out," he said. "It's distracting. What are you going on about?"

"Nothing." I suppressed whatever Caelus was feeling. When I was sure I had controlled my youthful body, I continued, "I don't know what you're talking about."

"You like Jerome, don't you? Humans are so strange. What now? Do you sleep with him? Marry him? What's the plan?"

I heaved a long-suffering sigh. I usually enjoyed Caelus' constant companionship, but we would have to work on tact.

"There is no 'plan'. I am going for a walk with my friend. Honestly." I evaluated my words and decided I was ignoring the truth like a much younger person. Just because I looked twenty-eight didn't mean I couldn't act my true age. "Yes, my body is attracted to Jerome, because he is an attractive man and this body is young and prone to such displays. My mind enjoys his company because he is kind and we have enough in common to chat easily. Will this progress into something more? Maybe, but I'm in no rush for that. I would rather get to know him better before I jump into any rash decisions."

Caelus stared at me with a raised eyebrow, and I willed my body to match the calmness of my words.

"Sure," he said with a skeptical tone. "Whatever you say. Humans are so strange."

With that comment, he melted into my arm and took his accustomed place at my torso. I shook my head in the mirror and straightened my shirt. Then, figuring I'd spent enough time hemming and hawing over clothes, enough time that even my elemental companion was questioning me, I slammed the closet door shut and left the room.

Jerome was waiting for me outside Upper Crust when I arrived. His face lit up when he saw me, but the first thing he did was thrust out a napkin. Placed on it were three lemon tarts. I laughed aloud.

"You know, I enjoy your company even without these. If you turned up without them, I wouldn't be terribly offended."

"But do I want to risk it?"

His eyes twinkled, and I huffed another laugh. My hand reached out for the treats despite my words.

"Oh, give them here. Since you brought them. I wouldn't want to appear ungrateful."

"Always so polite."

We turned down Cormorant Drive and down a side street. The rain was holding off for now, although large, black clouds hung on the horizon with menacing weight. Snow was in the forecast, but I would believe it when I saw it.

After I insisted he share my lemon tarts, we chatted about Jerome's cake decorating business, now four clients strong and with more interested people on the way. I told him about my consulting plan, and he promised to give me a glowing testimonial.

Caelus' question at my closet made me want to open up a

little more with Jerome. What could I offer? Caelus was an awkward subject, and Jerome already knew about my air abilities.

"I've been training with the women I worked for last month," I said. "They're a really nice group, actually. It's been fun."

"What kind of training?"

"Mainly self-defense. They know about my air powers, so I use that, too. I'm getting pretty good."

"That's a challenge if I've ever heard one." Jerome took my arm and pulled me into a park that we were passing. The swing set moved with the wind, empty in this forbidding weather. He released my arm and faced me. "Go on. Let's see what you've got."

I laughed then realized Jerome was serious.

"You want me to beat you up?"

He grinned.

"I'd like to see you try."

I raised my eyebrow at his cockiness. Jerome had a way of speaking, a weight to his words that spoke of experience and trials in his past, and I often forgot that he was still a young man and prone to bravado. My mouth quirked upward.

"Come at me, then."

I placed my feet in a balanced stance and brought my hands up in preparation. Jerome lunged at me with his arms outstretched. I sidestepped and yanked air strands from near his feet as I passed. He toppled forward and landed with a graceful roll that he immediately sprang back from. I barely had time to admire his smooth moves for such a large man before he rushed forward again.

This time, he was quicker, and his hand grabbed my arm with a firm but not crushing grip. I twisted my wrist around in the way the sisters had taught me, and Jerome's thumb couldn't maintain its grasp. I darted back then threw a blast of air at him, heated to uncomfortable but not burning temperatures. I would make it hotter for a real attacker, but I didn't want to have to heal Jerome's second-degree burns.

His face flushed and his eyes widened at the attack, but he didn't hesitate. He sprang to the side then darted back at me in a surprise move. I found myself trapped in a bear hug from behind, my hands near my face and arms constrained.

I flushed all over at the sensation of his body pressed against mine. How could it switch from fighting to attraction in the blink of an eye? I forced my will to focus on the problem at hand. Desire would have to take a back seat to winning this battle. No one got the better of me if I could help it, even if I were fighting a friend.

I had a few options in this position—dropping like a deadweight sometimes worked—but I had more power than an average fighter. With my fingers, I twisted air strands flowing from Jerome's mouth and pulled them as far as I could manage with my trapped arm.

Jerome coughed with a terrible choking noise. His arms loosened, and I wriggled free, releasing my hold on his air threads as I went. I gave him a minute to catch his breath. When he finally straightened from his coughing fit, his eyes were streaming but bright with interest.

"Time to up my game," he wheezed.

With astonishing speed that could only be born of long practice, he drew out a switchblade and flicked it open. My eyes widened. What sort of background did Jerome come from, where wielding a knife like that was a necessary skill?

"You were serious." I glanced at the knife then at Jerome. His mouth twitched.

"I'd say I was coming on too strong, but you have literal magic powers, and you can heal yourself from injuries. Besides, I know how to handle my blade."

My stomach flopped at the innuendo I was certain he hadn't meant, but my fingers twisted their own counter blade. A smile fought to show itself on my face.

"I hope you're ready, boy."

Jerome feinted right then sliced left, but the air currents around his body alerted me to his movements almost before he made them. I spun away and sliced my own blade at his upper arm. It nicked his coat, and Jerome lurched backward in shock.

"Do you have an invisible weapon?" he gasped.

"Oops." I shrugged with pretend apology. "Didn't I mention?"

Jerome leaped forward again with incredible speed. His blade flashed a finger span away from my arm, but I dodged and grabbed a handful of air threads. I poured my intention into them, and Jerome slowed as frigid temperatures surrounded his body. I released my hold quickly—I didn't want to send his body into shock—and he turned wide eyes on me.

"You are something else, Morgan."

I threw back my head and laughed with delight at my power and his awe of it, but Jerome pounced when I was distracted. He threw his arms around me and pinned my hands to my sides. His heaving chest pressed against mine, and I was distracted again for an entirely different reason.

His pressure on my hands forced me to release my air blade. Pinned, helpless, I looked into his eyes with an expression of tragic vulnerability.

"You got me," I whispered.

His eyes changed from triumphant to something more, wild yet gentle. I knew what he wanted, and in that moment, my body wanted it too. My mind was on the fence, but I tilted my head up to his face and half closed my eyes.

Jerome slowly brought his lips close to mine until I could taste the sweet lemon on his breath. The scent only took me higher, and my body screamed for me to bridge the gap and feel his soft lips on mine.

My mind had other notions. I couldn't let my body rule me.

I parted my lips and allowed the strands of his breath to pass between my teeth. Jerome leaned closer. Our lips grazed.

With my tongue, I curled air strands around and around.

His lips touched mine. I jerked my tongue backward in my mouth.

Jerome's chest spasmed. He released my arms and stepped backward, his eyes bulging. He dropped his switchblade and brought his hands to his throat.

I swooped down and picked up the switchblade, only then releasing my hold on the air strands in my mouth. I examined the switchblade while I waited for Jerome to catch his breath again.

"You—" Jerome coughed then shook his head. "You…"

"I know, that was terribly cruel," I said.

"You were magnificent." He shook his head again and crossed his arms. "That was inspired. I don't think anyone on the street could get the better of you. I like knowing that. Although, I would like my knife back."

I passed the blade back to him, handle forward, and he folded it and slid it into his pocket. I wondered if I should say something about the kiss that almost was. I wasn't against bringing it up—I was old enough to not dance around awkward situations, instead meeting them head on—but I wasn't yet sure what my stance on the matter was. Did I want to kiss Jerome? My body gave an emphatic yes, but my mind wasn't sure. I was still reinventing myself as Morgan and figuring out how my mind and body connected. Involving myself with someone else didn't seem wise at this stage. Not to mention, my mind was twice Jerome's age. What did that mean for any future relationship? I didn't want a fling with a younger man, and I didn't want to ruin one of the few friendships in my new life. Until I figured out what I truly wanted, I was content to ignore the elephant in the room.

Jerome was apparently willing to do the same, for he didn't bring up the almost-kiss. He examined his arm with a rueful glance.

"I should have taken off my coat before getting the jump

on you. Now there's a gash in the sleeve."

I pursed my lips. Could I fix it? My fuzzy memories were certainly filled with visions of Merlin performing similar feats over the centuries.

"Here. Let me try something."

I drew close to Jerome, trying to ignore the warm scent of him, and bent to my task. I healed the bleeding scratch below his coat in a matter of moments, but the coat was a different beast.

Caelus flowed out of my arm and examined the gash.

"There are enough threads to patch it together," he said. "It might not be perfect, but it will keep out the rain."

I nodded and twisted strands until the hole was only a puckered scar in the waterproof fabric. Jerome ran his fingers over the seam.

"Incredible," he murmured.

When he glanced at me, I got distinct impression that he wasn't referring solely to my mending job. Adrenaline still coursed through my body from our fight, as well as other hormones from our intimate moment, and it made me want to share something about myself with him. I cast about for what to say. My true age and the body switching business was too much right now, and I should discuss with Caelus before I blurted out his secrets.

Now that I was certain the order was not as altruistic as they had first appeared, and I was currently in cahoots with Rosemary to steal the Seed, I was less concerned with spilling their secrets. In any event, I wasn't their employee any longer. I wasn't under any vows or contracts to maintain silence for them.

And collecting the Seed was a huge part of my life right now. It felt right to share that with Jerome. I threaded my arm through his and propelled him to the sidewalk to continue our stroll.

"Can I tell you something?" I said.

"Of course." He glanced down at me. "What's up?"

"You remember the security job I had last month? I'm not working for them anymore, so I can tell you about it now. The women are part of a decades-old secret order that is devoted to seeking out and protecting magical artifacts."

Jerome looked blown by this news.

"You have a far stranger life than anyone I've ever met." He tucked my arm more securely in his. "Is there a whole world of conspiracies that I don't know about? Should I be watching my back for magic hitmen?"

I squeezed his muscly arm. "I'll keep you safe. And as far as I know, this is the only secret order around. But secret is in the name, so who knows?"

I neglected to mention the secret society I used to run when I was March Feynman. That was a whole other can of worms that I wasn't ready to share with Jerome. Technically, it was disbanded, so I had no reason to count it.

Jerome gave a heartfelt sigh and blinked a few times as if taking my revelations in. Then he shook his head.

"What does an artifact do?" he said.

"The order wants three in particular. They're supposed to merge to bring about a utopia on Earth, apparently, but higher-ups in the order mainly want to up their magic game, which will also occur when the artifacts unite." I shrugged. "Who knows what the truth is? It's all prophecy at this point. What is undeniable is the power that each artifact has itself. The Leaf, which was the first artifact found, bestows a spell of protection on the holder. The Seed, artifact number two that the order recently discovered in an archaeological dig in Turkey, must have similar powers." I squeezed Jerome's arm with my enthusiasm. "I want to get that Seed. Think of what I could do with more power! There is so much potential for good. And no one would ever best me again."

"I think you've got self-defense already covered," Jerome said with a wry glance at his healed arm. "No one is taking you down against your will. You have magic powers already. Why do you need more?"

"I haven't told you what I've been doing at the women's center where I volunteer." Briefly, I described how I infused helpful magic into donated clothing. "But there's so much more I could do. Without extra power, my reach is limited."

"I guess." Jerome's voice was laced with doubt. He patted my hand and released his arm from mine. The removal of his warmth felt like a bereavement. "I should get going. I need to make some calls for that wedding next Saturday, make sure I know when they expect me with the cake."

"Of course."

I took sneaky glances at Jerome as we walked back to Cormorant Drive. His face was somber and thoughtful, and I wondered what was going through his mind. Something about my desire for the Seed bothered him, but I wasn't sure what it was. If his mood persisted the next time we met, I would inquire. Until then, I would let Jerome ruminate on his own.

We parted ways at Cormorant Drive, Jerome to the bakery and I to my condo. I wanted to clean up my notes for Amir so I could bring my findings to the grocery on Monday before my shift at the women's center. Caelus emerged from my arm halfway home.

"I can't get a read on your emotions," he said with a searching glance at me. "You're very confusing. Why did you almost kiss Jerome but then stop? You wanted to, but you wanted to win your battle as well. The flipflopping was hard to follow."

"I'm sorry my inner feelings are so difficult to parse," I said with a roll of my eyes. "I'll remember to feel clearly next time. Humans aren't simple creatures, most of the time. We have many motivations that pull us in different directions."

Caelus was silent as I strode toward my condo, and he didn't speak until we exited the elevator.

"Wait," he said. "Something's not right. There are new

threads on our doorhandle."

"Damn it, not again. Haven't the mothers already searched my place for artifacts? What do they think they'll find this time?"

"Be on your guard."

I fashioned an air blade, readied an air ball that would deliver a blast of freezing air to its unfortunate recipient, and quietly pushed the unlocked door open.

My limbs locked to my sides. Rough hands dragged me across the threshold, and the door slammed shut. Three figures wearing black balaclavas converged on me. One was slight, the same build as my burglar and covered with the same salmon-red. Another sported wide hips and an ample bosom under her black clothes and ruby strands. The third woman towered over the others, looming like a menacing tree with sage-green strands to match.

But I wasn't helpless. I'd been expecting this ambush, and my grip on my created weapons was firm. I twisted my wrist to awkwardly toss the air ball at the slight figure then threw myself sideways to slash at the tall woman with my blade. My body froze and then fell like a cut tree, but the tall figure howled with pain as my blade sliced her side.

Something interrupted the binding spell on me. As soon as my arms were free, I whipped them around to throw wind in my attackers' faces. With my left hand, I flung strands in undirected bundles that distracted the women from the workings of my right hand. When my weapon was ready, I threw it toward the three figures.

A massive barrier erupted between us. To them, it must have appeared as a roaring disturbance in the air, more sound than sight. To me, it was a boiling mass of silver threads that swarmed with disruptive intent. If any of the women tried to walk through the barrier, they would be instantly repelled by a barrage of gale-force winds.

I scrambled to my feet while the others were distracted and

planned my next move. The figures conferred, their voices indistinguishable over the howling of my wind barrier. I readied another specialized air ball.

As one, the figures raised their hands. Each held an amulet, strands writhing against their fingers and twining up their arms. They marched forward, and my wind barrier parted.

My jaw dropped. What sorcery was this? The mothers clearly had a more robust amulet stash than did the sisters. I threw my airball at the central figure and backed up while I spun another ball in my hands.

The curvy woman shrieked and batted at her body, trying to stop the burning sensation that spread across her torso from the ball's impact.

The slight woman tucked her amulet in her pocket and jumped toward me while I was still in the middle of forming my next ball. She swung hard, and I instinctually responded with a counterblow from my self-defense training with the sisters.

We traded blows a few times, but this woman had trained in the same style as the sisters and undoubtedly for longer than I had. I retreated until my back hit the wall then dodged her next blow and threw a desperate bout of air into her face. It distracted her, and I straightened with triumph.

A blow to my stomach doubled me over. I wheezed.

"Get the rope," a low voice commanded before cold metal pressed against my forehead. Multicolored threads snaked over my eyes, then darkness overtook me.

CHAPTER XV

I swam through a sea of mist. Shadows loomed on every side, and voices babbled without words. I tried to push the figures away, but my hands wouldn't move. I was trapped, but I couldn't work up the energy to do more than stumble through the fog in an ever-increasing pulse of terror.

I gasped, and my eyes flew open. Daylight whisked away the dream as if it had never been. I focused on the ceiling and frowned. My condo didn't have popcorn ceilings.

My head turned, and I examined my surroundings. I lay on a fluffy white duvet with crisp white pillowcases. A small vanity, white again, rested against the wall. Its surface was clear of clutter. A neutral-colored abstract painting hung on the opposite wall, but otherwise the room was empty. It looked like a guest bedroom in a minimalist's house.

I tried to move my arms to raise my torso from the bed, but they didn't move. My dream returned to me, and I panicked when my eyes rested on ropes binding my wrists together in front of me. I bucked against the bed, frightened further when my legs didn't respond to my movement. They were also bound with stout jute rope, and a strange coin with a hole in its center was tied around my waist. The protection bracelet that Rosemary had given me was no longer on my wrist, and a chill of fear settled in my bones. My entrapment highlighted my desperate need for a bathroom break. How long had I been trapped here, in this room, in my head? The light was dim. Was the sun setting?

"Caelus," I whispered harshly. "Get out here and talk to me. I need ideas."

Caelus didn't appear. I peered at my waist. No threads twined around my torso. When I glanced around the room to confirm, no threads wriggled around anything.

My blood ran cold. Had my captors somehow removed

Caelus from my body? The loss hit me like a blow to the stomach. Caelus was my constant companion, my confidant, the only one who knew everything about me. Losing him would rip a gaping hole in my life, the life I was only now creating anew.

And what did that mean for Caelus? Was he back in the elemental plane? We'd only destroyed one artifact so far. According to him, that wasn't nearly enough. Was he even now being sent into dormancy, by his estimation a fate worse than death?

Belatedly, I also recalled that without Caelus, I had no magical powers. I was simply Morgan, a young woman with no experience, no history, and no permanent place in the world.

The rage that my body often fought boiled over, and this time, I let it. I screamed loudly and thrashed on the bed like a trapped snake. My movements were so violent that I flopped onto the floor with a thump that rattled the room. My hip would have a mighty bruise tomorrow.

I continued to scream my rage into the air until the bedroom door swung open and slammed against the wall.

"Really!" Thea stood silhouetted against the lit hallway. "This is no way to behave. Stop that racket at once. The neighbors will be wondering."

"Get me the hell out of here," I said through gritted teeth. "Right now."

"There's no need to be upset," Thea said in a calm voice, as if she were soothing a rabid dog. "We'll work all this out, don't you worry. Here, let me help you onto the bed. I can't imagine the floor is a comfortable place to recline."

I allowed Thea to guide me onto the bed, although I made her do the heavy lifting. I wasn't about to help her in any way. My screaming, while mostly an opportunity for my body to vent, had served a purpose. Thea was here, and now I could get some answers.

"Tell me why I'm here," I said. "Why did you kidnap me?"

"Morgan." Thea shook her head in a patronizing way, and her carefully coifed hair brushed her cheeks. She had clearly been working with children for too long. Her charges must despise her. "Morgan, Morgan. We both know why you're here. You have something of ours, and we want it back. But first, I would like to have a calm conversation with you. Can we do that?"

"Over my dead body," I spat at her. "And I don't die easily." I opened my mouth and screamed at the top of my lungs. "Fire! Ambulance! Rape! Call the cops!"

I hoped the neighbors were nosy ones and would come to investigate. It was a slim chance, but I was out of options. Thea sighed and took a coin from the pocket of her beige cardigan.

"It always has to be this way," she muttered to herself. "No one can be trusted to conquer herself."

Thea rubbed the coin. My screams cut off mid-shout. A cooling numbness spread over my mind. I wondered vaguely why I'd been screaming, but it was too difficult to remember why, so I desisted. I turned languid eyes to Thea's smiling face. She was a sensible woman. She really did know best. It couldn't hurt to listen to her side of the story. This all probably had a perfectly rational explanation.

"Are you ready for our calm conversation now?" Thea asked pleasantly. I nodded and she smiled again. "Good. You can tell me everything, and it will all be fine. You'll be so much happier when you comply. People always are. They need someone to tell them what to do. No one really wants free will, as much as they bleat about it. You'll see how happy you are. Now, tell me about your powers. How can you manipulate air the way you do?"

"I'm possessed by an air elemental," I said in a dreamy tone. It felt good to tell someone about Caelus, and Thea was the perfect person to unburden myself upon. She would understand. "He lets me use his powers, and I let him stay in my body." I frowned. "At least, he used to be here. You stripped him away."

"Ah, not quite. I suppressed your magic. I expect your elemental is still in there, buried deep. An elemental, that's very interesting. Tell me, what is your relationship to and opinion of the sisterhood?"

"Rosemary hired me to protect them during the Starr debacle. I don't work for them anymore, but we're friends now. I join them for training, meet them for coffee, all that." I wriggled on the bed to get more comfortable, but even my bonds didn't chafe anymore. I knew that Thea had a good reason for my bonds, and that was enough for me. "They are definitely believers in the Book of Souls—the utopia coming when the three artifacts are united, every living thing connected—rather fanatically so."

"And do you know what their opinion of the motherhood is?" Thea asked gently.

"They don't talk about it much. Fine, I guess."

I wanted to tell Thea about Rosemary's recent disillusionment and rebellion, but a niggling feeling stopped me. Should I tell her? Would that be good for Rosemary? How could it not be, if Thea found out? She had our best interests at heart. But unease plagued me, so I compromised.

"One of the sisters isn't sure about the motherhood," I said. "But the rest are fine. I don't remember who it was."

Thea looked disappointed, and I almost opened my mouth to blurt out Rosemary's name, which reminded me of the protection bracelet she had given me, the one Thea had taken away. What was it for? A memory of strength and clarity wriggled into my mind, and I grabbed hold of the comforting feelings. I let the sensation fill me until my will asserted itself. It was my constant companion but somehow had been suppressed in the past few minutes. It grew in strength and slowly cleared the fog of compliance from my mind.

What had Thea done to me? My eyes flicked to the coin in

her hands, and a shiver ran down my spine. That amulet somehow made me a puppet for Thea's whims. With Rosemary's bracelet stolen from around my wrist, I had been vulnerable to attack. She had taken over my mind, and that I could not forgive.

I had to play along until I found a way to escape. My mind pushed aside the last of the fog and thought frantically.

"The Leaf." Thea leaned forward, her eyes intent. I sensed that her earlier questions had only been a warm-up for this one. "I know you have it. Where is it?"

I made my eyes large and innocent. Thea's compliance spell beat against me, but I resisted with all the iron will I'd mustered over my long life.

"What do you mean? One of the sisters has it. I don't know which one, though. Isn't that the point?"

While I spoke, I probed within myself. Surely Caelus was there, only buried deeply. I had to find him. Thea's eyes narrowed.

"Don't play dumb with me, girl," she snapped. "The Seed will be interred tomorrow night, but I need to ensure the safety of both artifacts. Where did you put the Leaf?"

I inwardly chuckled at her use of the word 'girl,' but my amusement didn't last long. Thea raised the amulet higher, and the compliance spell grew in intensity, beating at my mind like waves on a beach. I tried to keep my distress off my face as I fought off the compulsion and searched for Caelus.

There. Deep in the back of my mind, a foreign sensation of silvery light nestled. I didn't have time for niceties. Instead, I rammed my conscious into the glowing energy and hoped it would do something useful.

The light surrounded my conscious with a welcoming glow. The world beyond my physical eyes blossomed with threads. Thea's angry face swirled with navy blue strands, and silver threads drifted through the air. Caelus wasn't free, not yet, but he was present enough to help.

My fingers immediately crafted an air blade, and I sawed at my rope.

"I don't know what you mean," I repeated to Thea. I needed to keep her distracted long enough for my hands to be free. I forced my face into an expression of distress, which wasn't difficult in the circumstances. "I feel strange. What's happening to me?"

Thea frowned and glanced at the amulet in her hand. The rope binding my wrists snapped, and I whipped my arm around and hit the coin out of her hand. Thea gasped, but the pressure of the compliance spell cleared from my mind and I sighed in relief.

I didn't give up my advantage. From my position lying on the bed with my feet bound, I tossed a ball of air in Thea's face with my free hand to distract her. I fashioned an air blade while my other hand threw various unformed balls of threads at Thea. My control wasn't complete with Caelus bound.

Thea gasped and sputtered at the blasts, but they couldn't hold her back for long. Already, she was fumbling at her pockets for more amulets. My air blade finally did the trick, and my feet sprang apart. I ripped at the rope holding another amulet to my waist, and when it sprang free, Caelus whooshed out of my arm.

"Finally!" he shouted. "That was terrible. Get her!"

Thea stood until she was between me and the door. She brandished another amulet at me with a look of triumph on her face. With a jolt, my feet flew out from under me, and I fell to the ground on my side with a jarring thud. Flecks of light dazzled my eyes, and I shook my head to clear them.

"Get up," Caelus yelled at me. "She's coming!"

I flipped to get my feet under me and heaved myself upright. Thea grabbed another amulet from her pocket. How many did she have stashed in there?

I didn't wait to see what new horrors awaited me. Instead, I sent burning-hot air at her hand until she shrieked and dropped a glowing metal ring.

I whirled to the window. With fumbling fingers, I unlocked the latch and slid the panel open.

"What are you doing?" Thea screeched, her voice thick with pain. "Get back here!"

There was nothing for it. I would have to jump.

"Caelus," I said as I climbed through the narrow opening and perched on the window ledge. "This should work, right?"

"Yes. Most likely. It's pretty high. We'll see."

I grimaced. "Thanks for the vote of confidence."

I gathered air strands in my hands and weaved them hastily together to create a pillow under my body, forcing as much intention as I could muster into the strands. Thea's footsteps pounded across the floor. I took a deep breath and jumped.

The ground rushed to meet me, but not as quickly as it should have. I gritted my teeth and poured intention into my air cloud. My descent slowed marginally, and when I hit the ground, it was with a gentle tumble instead of a splat.

I scrambled to my feet, shaking with relief but keen to put distance between myself and the madwoman upstairs. Caelus whooped, but I put my head down and sprinted west, considering the events of the past few hours.

Thea knew I had the Leaf and was willing to kidnap me to get it back. She had an amulet that gave her incredible mind-control powers, powers that compelled me to comply with whatever she wanted. I'd encountered such amulets before, when Starr had used them against her fellow sisters, but this felt different, both stronger and more subtle. The other amulets were blunt force hammers, and this was a fine scalpel. If done with care, the compulsion might not be even noticeable to the victim. I remembered with a start Thea's students, with their incredible lack of bullying and mental health issues, then I recalled Starr's strange calm and lack of recognition. A shiver ran down my back. Was Thea controlling all those people?

What was more, the Seed would be beyond my reach by

tomorrow. I'd known that my time was limited, but my specific deadline was sobering. I needed to figure out where the blasted artifact was, but I had so little to go on.

First, I needed to escape Thea's clutches. I pounded along the pavement, my chest heaving with effort. Ahead was a major road. I hoped a bus would come quickly, or maybe even a taxi. Funds were tight, but the threat of Thea behind me was worse. I picked up speed.

"How did you get out of there?" Caelus asked. His body bobbed beside me, jostled by my movement. "You didn't have my air abilities."

I glanced at him in consideration. He was right. I'd freed myself using only my will and determination to not be controlled. Granted, I'd needed Caelus' magic to escape fully, but throwing off Thea's compliance spell was all me. A glow of pride grew in my chest, next to my gasping lungs and overtaxed heart. Magic was power, but maybe I didn't have to solely rely on it to get me out of scrapes.

"I have many talents," I said loftily. "Elemental powers aren't everything." I slowed my pace when I approached the main road and dropped the act. "I was worried when you were gone. What happened?"

"Whatever amulet Thea used was powerful," Caelus said with a scowl. "One minute, I was facing the masked mothers with you in our condo. The next, I was tucked in a ball at your center, unable to see or feel anything with our body. It was distressing, to say the least."

"I'm glad you're back."

We exchanged grins of relief, then I jogged to an approaching bus. I didn't know where it was going, but anywhere was better than here.

Three buses, a pit stop at a gas station, and an hour later, I flung the door to my condo open and collapsed on my couch. My legs ached from my sprint away from Thea's house, and adrenaline had drained out of me ages ago. I closed my eyes in relief.

"We can finally talk again," Caelus said beside me. "You're always surrounded by people. The bus is especially crowded."

"What do you want to talk about? I'm exhausted."

"Yes, I feel it too. But what about Thea's compliance amulet?"

I sighed as my brain revved into gear. Thea's power was worrisome. I'd succumbed far too easily to its lure of brainless ease and had only escaped by using my own tenacity and desire to stay in control of myself. How many others would possess the same strength of will?

"It was strong." I opened my heavy eyelids and focused on Caelus, who swayed next to me. "I don't know if others could escape it. It took everything I had."

"What does she do with that amulet normally?"

"Exactly. Who else is she using it on?" I wriggled upright with a groan, wishing I'd jumped in the shower before dropping onto my couch. "I can't imagine Thea sitting on that sort of power. Who else is she controlling?"

"What if she comes back for us?" Caelus' eyes were round with concern. "We know her secret, and she knows where we live. Do you think you can fend her off again?"

"I'm going to have to."

My condo, which had felt like a safe haven a few minutes ago, now felt like a trap. I shifted uneasily. Should I even stay here tonight? Surely, Thea would be here any minute. My heart raced.

"We can barricade the doors with threads," Caelus said in a firm voice. He must have been responding to my body's panic. "We'll be fine tonight. I'm more worried about when you're walking around, undefended."

I stood, my fingers flexing with their need to protect

myself. "Quick, show me how to protect the condo. I'm feeling itchy just thinking about Thea bursting in here, amulets blazing."

Caelus directed me in weaving a barrier across the front door and the patio for good measure. By the time we were finished, the entrance was covered in a spider web of silvery strands. My heart slowed to its normal rate.

"When I'm out," I said in a continuation of our previous conversation. "I need to activate the Leaf. That's the best way to combat Thea. Its defensive magic feels airtight."

"Artifacts are far more powerful than amulets," Caelus said thoughtfully. "It's a good idea."

"You're such an elemental snob."

"Don't be sore at me for being right. You'll have to practice, though. You only held the protection for seconds last time."

"I can practice." My shoulders straightened in my determination. If there was one thing I'd learned in my extended life, it was that almost anything was achievable with enough willpower, and I had that in spades. "I'll start now."

"Is there a human way you can come after Thea? She did kidnap you, after all. From your mind's outrage, I gather that's not an acceptable human practice."

"No, not acceptable. I'd rather not go to the police, though. There's too much I can't explain—you, for example, and the compliance amulet—and I also want to stay off the police's radar. My identity is still tenuous, and the authorities could poke holes in it. If we can do this your way, it would save me some hassle."

"Noted. You'd better get practicing with that Leaf." Caelus pointed at my pocket where the Leaf was. "Go on. Wait, speaking of artifacts, how are we going to get the Seed? Thea will be on the lookout for you now."

I tapped my foot in thought.

"We need to get it, more than ever. Even beyond your

mission, and the power it might give me to get you more artifacts, Thea is clearly not a worthy guardian of the Seed. She already misuses her amulets. What would she do with an artifact of power? No, we have to stop her from getting her grubby hands on it."

"Protect yourself with the Leaf," Caelus said, his hands on his nebulous hips. "Steal amulets from the sisterhood. Grab Rosemary, then go with all the power you can muster. Give Thea everything you've got and grab that Seed."

"Guns blazing?" I considered Caelus' eager face. "It does hold a certain appeal. I might have to gather all my forces against whatever amulets Thea and the mothers are wielding. Come on, let's get to work on this Leaf."

I practiced enveloping myself in the Leaf's protection for the next hour, steadily increasing the time I could hold it, but my mind frequently wandered. Was a magical onslaught the best way to achieve our artifact-stealing goals, or was there a smarter way?

By the time I could hold onto the Leaf's defensive spell for a full five minutes, I was beyond exhausted, but I wasn't done yet. According to Thea, the order would incarcerate the Seed tomorrow. If I wanted to claim it before it was hidden for good, I needed to steal it before the ceremony.

I sent a text to Rosemary, asking her to come over and citing urgent news. Within fifteen minutes, she knocked on my door. I confirmed it was Rosemary through the peephole, then I carefully swept away silver threads until I could swing open the door. Once Rosemary entered, her face quizzical at my summons, I reattached the strands.

"I was kidnapped by Thea," I said without greeting her. "Did you know she has an amulet that can compel people to do whatever she wants? I only escaped by the skin of my teeth."

Rosemary's already round eyes grew even rounder.

"What?" she gasped. Her gaze grew thunderous. "No, I did

not. Why doesn't it surprise me? Argh!"

She threw her hands up in the air and paced into my living room. I followed until Rosemary whirled around.

"We have to get the Seed," she said. "Tonight. Now."

CHAPTER XVI

"Hold on." Rosemary's frantic strands fizzled and jerked like a sparkler. Her agitation was far greater than I'd anticipated. "We need a plan."

"I knew the mothers weren't worthy to keep a priceless artifact." Rosemary paced around the room, oblivious to my words. "Thea wants the power of the Seed for herself. And what will she do with it? What horrors will she start? Morgan." She whirled around and stared at me with dismay. "Her students. She's renowned for her work as a counselor. Since she started, they haven't had any bullying issues, or mental health concerns, or acting out of any kind."

"That doesn't sound like a bad thing."

"But how is she doing it? Is she controlling all her students so they have no free will? Is that really better?"

A shiver raced down my spine at the memory of Thea's absolute control over my thoughts and actions. No, nothing justified the power Thea wielded.

"I can't let such a corrupt woman take the Seed," Rosemary ranted. "I'm dealing with it tonight. We know Thea is moving the Seed from her house to the secret location tonight. Her day planner said so. We can intercept it. Are you with me?"

I wavered. This was a decent chance to at least discover the secret location. I wasn't interested in a showdown tonight—not without a good plan—but intel gathering was never wasted. Now that the Seed was in Vancouver, it was tantalizingly close. Caelus stirred near my stomach with anticipation of getting another artifact, and I squared my shoulders in determination. For him—and for me, and for the women at the center I could help with more power—I would take steps toward finding the Seed.

"I'll come to find out where the Seed is going," I said. "That's all. Then we can decide how to best steal it before tomorrow's ceremony."

Rosemary nodded, the fire of passion still in her eyes. She checked the time on her phone.

"Good. Let's go. Thea wrote down that she would move the Seed in half an hour."

Once we hopped into Rosemary's little hatchback, she roared toward Thea's house. Within minutes, we were parked one street over. Rosemary turned off the car and we sat in silence, listening to the cooling engine tick.

"Now what?" I said eventually.

Rosemary worried her lower lip.

"Put your hood on," she instructed. "We'll walk by Thea's house and find a bush to watch from."

Privately, I doubted Thea's neighbors would leave prowlers to lurk in their bushes unmolested, but I kept my mouth shut. Rosemary was still wired too tightly to hear reason. I would reassess the situation when she found our hiding spot.

I followed Rosemary's brisk steps down the sidewalk with my hands tucked deeply in my pockets against the cold and my hood covering my head. The night air was frigid, and a few flakes of snow drifted from heavy clouds above without releasing their promised payload.

"Over here," Rosemary hissed.

She gestured toward a fence across the road from Thea's house. A manicured laurel hedge grew beside it, but there was a small gap between vegetation and the fence. After an incredulous glance at Rosemary, who waved me impatiently toward it, I wriggled into the gap with a quiet grumble. Rosemary squeezed in after me and turned to face the street.

"This is perfect," she whispered. "I can see Thea's front door and her garage. There's no way she's leaving without us noticing. And look, the lights are on in her living room. She's home and hasn't left on her errand yet. The Seed must be in the house now. Maybe we should run in there and grab it."

"That's a terrible idea. Thea is the head mother. Can you imagine how many amulets she has and how powerful they are? We wouldn't stand a chance, not without knowing where in the house she's keeping the Seed."

Rosemary's shoulders slumped, then she straightened.

"Then we watch and wait," she said and stared across the road.

Fifteen minutes passed, then half an hour. After forty-five minutes, my teeth were chattering, and I rubbed my hands together fruitlessly.

"She's changed her plans," I whispered. "She must have known someone looked at her day planner. It was inevitable, really. If I were her, I would have moved the Seed earlier."

Rosemary turned to me with a grimace.

"Then we'll have to find someone else to question. The Seed is somewhere in the city. We need to get it tonight."

"What we need is a plan," I protested. Rushing in without preparation was a recipe for disaster. I could only hold the Leaf's protection for five minutes, and I needed more practice. "We need amulets from the sisterhood's collection. And we don't know where the Seed is headed. We need a strategy."

"I can ask Joy," Rosemary said, fanaticism gleaming in her eyes. "She's going to the ceremony tomorrow, she'll know. Come on, Morgan. It has to be now."

"I'm not rushing into anything without a plan. You don't know what it's like under Thea's influence. That threat isn't one I take lightly, nor should you. Calm down and let's talk about what we should do tomorrow."

"Calm down?" Rosemary looked ready to explode. "Tomorrow is way too late. I need to intercept the Seed tonight. If you're not going to help me, then I'll do it on my own."

Rosemary pushed out of the hedge and marched toward her

car. I followed, shaking my head at her antics. When she reached her vehicle, she threw open the door and dropped inside. I followed more sedately, and Rosemary pulled away from the curb.

"Try to sleep on it, okay? The ceremony isn't until tomorrow night."

Rosemary threw me a withering glance as she turned toward my condo.

"Whatever. I thought you were on my side. I guess I'm on my own, as always."

I sighed, and we passed the rest of the trip in silence. Rosemary screeched to a stop in front of my condo and didn't reply when I said good night. I gently closed the passenger's door, then she took off into the night.

"She needs her own elemental to talk sense into her," Caelus said after he emerged from my arm.

I nodded. "She could use some sense. Do you think she would listen, though?"

"Perhaps not. She is rather volatile."

"I wonder if I should have gone after her. Are we missing our opportunity?"

"No," Caelus said. He nodded with decision. "You were right, we need a better plan than racing in unarmed. Call Rosemary in the morning after she's had a chance to calm down. I'm as eager to get the Seed as she is, but we have until the ceremony tomorrow night. That's plenty of time to get amulets and talk to Joy for directions."

"I hope Rosemary doesn't do anything stupid." I strolled to the front door while I considered Rosemary's state of mind, then the full weight of my day fell over me like a hot elephant in a cool river. I needed bed, and I needed it now.

"She might," Caelus said. "But that's on her. You're probably better off without that loose cannon."

The morning dawned clear and cold after a restless night of waking every half hour. I'd been convinced that every creak of the condo was footsteps of the motherhood despite my thread barricade. Caelus had finally promised to keep watch so I could sleep undisturbed.

Over breakfast I held the Leaf's protection for a solid fifteen minutes.

"That was impressive," I said to Caelus, elated. He sniffed.

"It's better. You still can't do anything with the threads while you're under the Leaf's defenses. You have a protective bubble but no way to attack."

"It's better than nothing. Stop being so negative."

"Keep practicing."

Once I stopped glaring at the unrepentant elemental, I tried calling Rosemary, but she didn't answer. Disquiet danced at the edge of my mood, but Rosemary might be sleeping in after a late night. I would catch up with her later to discuss plans for tonight.

I dressed in exercise clothes and left the condo for a run. The brisk air chilled my cheeks, but I pressed westward. Soon I would search for the Seed, but it wouldn't hurt to start the day in training. I held the Leaf protection over myself for a full twenty minutes while I ran, which pleased me. The sensation grew more natural every time I used the power.

My phone rang, and I wiggled it out of my coat pocket to answer it.

"Morgan," my friend Anna cried out with real fear in her voice. "Morgan, please help. We're trapped in a burning building!"

My heart lurched. Questions crowded my mind—how, why—but only the important one sprang to my lips.

"Where?"

"The end of Quimby Road, I think." She coughed. "I don't know what else to do. I called emergency, but they aren't here yet…"

"I'm coming," I said. "Stay strong."

I disconnected the call and sprinted west. A shudder underfoot almost tripped me. Was that an earthquake? I picked up my pace. I was grateful to whatever force had convinced me to take an early morning run in this direction. Anna's life hung in the balance. Would I arrive in time to save her?

I turned onto Quimby Road, my heart nearly pounding out of my chest. Smoke rose behind an unkempt, towering hedge. Caelus emerged from my arm as we approached our destination but didn't say anything to distract me from my mission, for which I was grateful. I sprinted toward the hedge and skidded through the driveway opening.

Flames licked the left side of a porch that hung off a dilapidated house. My fingers clenched in my palms, but my mind calmly assessed the situation. If Anna were stuck in there, I still had time to get her out. It wasn't too late.

I strode closer, then movement on the porch caught my attention. I narrowed my eyes at a familiar figure, who feebly pried at a board over the front window with a rock. It was a hopeless endeavor, as the board was covered with threads of the world that prevented it from moving. He should have known that.

"There are strands all over the board, holding it down," I said to Merry Lytton. "Why don't you move them first?"

He turned to me. His handsome, usually smug face was pale and drawn, and his hands trembled. What was wrong with him?

"What are you doing here?" he said in a hoarse voice. "Never mind, it doesn't matter. I can't see strands anymore."

That was a surprise. Merry without his powers? I wondered how that had happened. I hadn't even known it was possible.

"You're human now?" I glanced at Caelus for confirmation.

"Apparently," Caelus said with an appraising glance at

Merry's brown strands. "Half-elementals are a strange breed, but he's not one anymore."

I nodded at Caelus then shook myself. It didn't matter what Merry was. Anna was waiting for me.

"That's unexpected," I said shortly. "Here, move over. My friend Anna is in there, and I'm not leaving her to die."

Merry shuffled to the side. I stepped forward and pulled at the sticky strands that covered the boarded-up window. After a few sweeps, they all melted into the air.

"Okay, do your rock thing now," I said.

I stepped back and wiped my forehead as he set to work. Heat from the burning porch was intense. Shouting from inside gave me hope that Anna was still okay. I debated grabbing the rock from Merry and prying the board off myself, but it started to loosen. I moved to the side, anticipating the board flying back from the pressure of trapped victims inside.

Merry clearly hadn't anticipated the same thing. With a wrench, the board flung outward and smacked him on the head. He fell on his bottom, stunned, and the porch underneath him gave way. With a yell, he disappeared.

Anna and her friends climbed out of the window. I breathed a shallow sigh of relief when I saw Anna—the heat and smoke were too intense for anything deeper—and I reached my hand into the porch's jagged hole to help Merry. Once he was out of the hole, looking bewildered and sore, I turned to help Anna and the others out of the house and down the steps. The crackling of burning wood accompanied our efforts, but we skirted the encroaching flames and regrouped on sodden grass.

Anna dropped to her knees beside her unconscious boyfriend Wayne after his friend lowered him to the patchy lawn. The others murmured their consternation, and Merry told them with a shamed face that he couldn't heal anymore.

The ground shook again underfoot. After my heart stopped pounding from the adrenaline rush that the earthquake necessarily evoked, I knelt at Wayne's side. Once I'd cleared

Wayne's airways and healed his scorched lungs, Anna stepped toward me with teary eyes. I reached over to give her a swift hug. She clung to me, and my heart warmed with satisfaction. We might have drifted apart for now, but she was still important to me.

The others nattered about someone I didn't know. It didn't matter. Anna was safe now, and I wanted to leave before I came under too much scrutiny. These people were Merry's friends, with past lives of their own, and we were connected in ways I didn't care to remember. Morgan was my fresh start, and these people were relics of my past.

"If you're okay, Anna, I'll head off."

"Merry has the grail in his pocket," Caelus hissed at me. "We could grab it right now."

Caelus was frustrated, but I'd made a deal with Merry. My eyes sought Merry's face.

"When you're ready," I said to him. "You know how to find me."

I turned and walked slowly down the overgrown driveway. My body was still wired after my run and Anna's rescue, although I knew I would collapse later. I hoped my energy would last for my run home.

A deep groan filled my ears. The world jerked to one side, then everything shook. I dropped to my hands and knees. Terror filled my usually tidy mind until all I could do was hold on and wait for the tremor to cease. Trees creaked and snapped overhead, and the burning building popped and crackled with the motion and fire.

I couldn't abandon Anna now. What would be the point in saving her from the fire, only to watch her fall prey to an earthquake? At the very least, I could build a thread barrier to protect her from falling branches.

I stumbled to my feet and leaped over cracks forming in the pavement, landing with unsteady feet on the other side. Anna wasn't far away, and I skidded to a halt at her side, threw a few hastily woven air threads over us, and grabbed her hands. The ground heaved and buckled under us, and streamers of smoke writhed past our faces.

Finally, the trembling ceased. My heart took longer to settle. Anna squeezed my hands in gratitude.

"You came," she whispered. "You're always there for me. And you saved my life with the magic you've wanted for so long."

Warmth stole through me at Anna's praise, even as a part of me protested. My powers didn't do much this time. The thread barrier over the window had been an issue, but surely that could have been dealt with another way.

But still, I saved Anna and my abilities were key. I squeezed her hands then released them.

"I'm glad you're safe," I whispered back. "But I should get out of here before the others wonder who I am."

Anna nodded, and we rose from the ground. A thought struck me.

"Anna, could I borrow your car today?"

A set of wheels would make it easy to follow Joy to the ceremony's location. Anna shook her head regretfully.

"I'm sorry, it's in the shop. It needed new brake pads."

"It was worth a shot." I would have to find another way to tail Joy. A cab would do it, but I shuddered at the cost.

The others were chattering about finding whoever had locked them in the burning building, but I'd been in their company for too long. I waved at Anna, made a swift exit through the overgrown hedge, and picked my way along the ruined pavement. Cracks splintered through concrete like lightning bolts. I shook my head at the carnage and thought with fear about my condo. Was it still intact? I didn't have any possessions there that I cared about, but I would be sad to say goodbye to my first home as Morgan.

Sirens wailed in the distance, and I surveyed the streets with wide eyes. The earthquake had shaken shingles to the ground, strewn branches over the asphalt, and even toppled a chimney so that bricks scattered on the lawn. Nervous looking neighbors huddled together in the road.

I kept moving. The more space I put between myself and Merry's crew, the longer my secret remained hidden. I had things to do, anyway. I had to arrange a vehicle so I could follow Joy this evening, and I could use some practice with the Leaf. Jerome crossed my mind, and my stomach cramped. Was he okay after the tremors? I wanted to make sure.

My phone rang with serendipitous timing, and the caller ID squeezed my heart.

"Jerome," I gasped. "Are you okay?"

"Yeah." His deep voice was soothing. "Yeah, I'm fine. Just a little shake-up here. I heard that the west side took a beating, though. Something about a really shallow epicenter. Where are you?"

"I'm in the thick of it," I admitted. "But I'm okay. Heading toward Cormorant Drive now, actually."

"Good." Relief filtered through the connection. "Hey, while I have you here, I wanted to talk about you wanting the Seed. Just, be careful, okay? I've seen good people go bad with wanting too much power. I don't want to see you go down that path."

I frowned at the phone. What was Jerome saying? I wanted the powers of the Seed to help Caelus avoid dormancy, as well as to improve the lives of the women at my volunteering gig. My motives were entirely noble. How could that corrupt me?

"I'll keep it in mind," I said in a clipped tone. Being berated by a man half my age was galling. I had twice as much experience as he did—twenty times, if I counted my past lives—and I knew a thing or two about power. How else was I going to thwart Thea and her order, if not by gaining more power than they had? Jerome didn't know what he was talking about.

Shaking interrupted my thoughts. I dropped to my knees to

remain stable as the world jolted under me.

"I have to go," I said quickly. "It's another tremor. We'll talk later."

"Stay safe—" Jerome said, but I was already ending the call, still miffed at his presumption.

The shaking didn't last long, but it was strong enough to topple a few more chimneys. People screamed around me, then a cry of pain whipped my head around. That was a voice I knew.

Merry was on his knees under a tree, hugging his arm to his chest with an expression of agony. A sword crossed his back in a leather scabbard, and a huge branch lay in pieces beside him.

I sighed in exasperation. I kept trying to remove myself from Merry and his friends, and still they roped me in. I carefully picked my way through debris that lay scattered on the road and stopped in front of him. Merry's eyes were squeezed shut with pain, and his breath hissed through clenched teeth.

"You big baby," I said with a shake of my head. He might not have the power to heal himself anymore, but I did. A thread of pity snaked its way through my dislike. Besides, I needed him intact so he could give me the grail later. "Let me have a look."

I didn't wait for a reply. My fingers plucked at the knot above his wounded shoulder. Caelus swooped out of my arm.

"It will take ages to fully heal him," Caelus said. "Why don't you just stop his pain? Unknot that one, there, and that one. And while you're at it, grab the grail from his pocket."

I threw a withering glance at Caelus, although the thought had crossed my mind. That damn pity was still lodged in my heart. Merry was an arrogant thorn in my side, but we had plenty of history together. I would give him a chance to find whoever he waited for.

Merry gasped his thanks when the pain lessened.

"It's not healed," I said, straightening from my crouched position. "That would take too long, and I know you're on some grand mission. But you'll be able to think straight for now."

"I don't know what to do without my abilities," Merry said quietly to his hands.

I suppressed a sigh of exasperation and a chuckle of mirth, both of which threatened to burst out. Now Merry finally felt what it was like to be a powerless human. Throughout my many lifetimes, I'd striven to gain the awesome abilities that he'd shown me when we'd first met. Now, I had them, and he didn't.

But I understood how much one could rely on magic. Its uses were countless. If I lost Caelus' abilities, I would feel defenseless.

Merry's face was despondent, and his chocolate brown threads drooped. He needed some tough love, and I was happy to dish it out for him.

"Spare me the pity party. I doubt you're entirely useless without your magic. You still have eyes, two feet, mostly working hands. You have a sword on your back—do you know which end goes into the enemy? Magic is only one facet of your usefulness. Granted, it's a helpful one, but it's one that most people function just fine without. It's time to put on your big-boy pants and do what you set out to do."

Merry stared downward, but his threads slowly rose from their lackluster position of before. With a heave upward, he stumbled to his feet and looked around with confusion.

"Aren't you looking for someone?" I said to prompt him into action so that I could keep moving toward Cormorant Drive and my new life. I had things to do that didn't involve Merry and his injuries and quests.

"Yes." Merry visibly pulled himself together, although his face was still pale with whatever ailed him. "Yes. Thank you for your help. I have to keep looking."

I watched him walk east with unsteady steps. That was the direction I wanted to go as well, but I didn't want to give the impression that I joined him in his mission. I walked behind him, leaving enough room so that he wouldn't notice me. I doubted he would have. His distraction was absolute. Even when he rushed forward and saved a small child from falling debris, he barely seemed to notice other dangers.

"He almost got himself killed again," Caelus muttered beside me. "Get closer. He won't remember to give us the grail if he's dead."

I walked forward, torn between getting back to my old life and doing some minor gloating, since Merry had just proved to himself that he didn't need magic to function.

"I told you so," I said with a grin when I was close enough for Merry to hear me. "Oh, that's a very satisfying phrase to say."

The damn earth rolled again before Merry could reply. We were right underneath a tree, and its waving branches threatened to fall on our heads.

CHAPTER XVII

"Make a barrier," Caelus shouted. "Quickly."

I bent my knees to steady myself against the trembling ground and raised my hands. My fingers swiftly wove air threads into a tent over our heads, and none too soon. Branches cracked and fell onto my makeshift dome, but it held.

When I caught Merry's dumbfounded expression after the shaking stopped, I hid my smile. Now he knew what it felt like to be on the other side of magic abilities.

"Yes, it's a perk. You'll miss it, I have no doubt. But you've had your abilities for a good long while, I'm guessing. Time to pass the torch."

From Merry's pocket, a bubbling mass of silver threads burst forth and ballooned into a humanoid shape next to him. My eyes widened, and Caelus hissed.

"It's an elemental," he said.

"Merry," the other air elemental whispered.

Merry frowned in confusion and a hint of fear.

"Who's this bozo?" I said to Caelus while Merry and the other elemental spoke. "Some rogue?"

"I think so," Caelus said. He frowned at the elemental in distaste. "It happens."

"I guess Merry was getting in his way," I said thoughtfully, looking at Merry's pale face.

"He needs a swift kick into dormancy," Caelus said with finality. "I can feel the upset he created in the balance from here."

"So, he's working against what you stand for," I said quietly.

"Yes, you could say that."

"If you captured him, would that count toward your artifact quota, or at least give you bonus points?"

Caelus' mouth opened, then he snapped it shut as my words

sunk in.

"Maybe," he said thoughtfully. "We could try."

"Why didn't the elemental notice you, by the way?"

"I've hidden myself from elemental eyes." He sniffed delicately. "It's something higher-level elementals can do. That's why Merry couldn't see me earlier, as well. I'm on a secret mission, after all."

"Yes, you're very important."

The sarcasm in my voice wasn't lost on Caelus, but he merely glared before directing me on how to create a trap for the unsuspecting elemental. As I worked, I tuned into the others' conversation.

"If it's the last thing I do, I will take him down." Merry said.

"It might be the last thing you do," the elemental hissed. He reached his thread-formed hand toward Merry's mouth and pulled at the air threads there.

Merry gasped then clawed at his throat. The elemental grinned and yanked harder.

"Now," Caelus shouted. "Right over the top."

My woven threads acted like a drawstring bag. The elemental was so intent on his strangulation of Merry that he didn't notice the strands until they fell over him like a parachute. With a swift yank, I pulled the threads together to contain him.

"We got him!" Caelus crowed, but the other elemental hadn't given up yet. The air bag stretched and twisted in my hands. I clenched my fists together tightly.

"I've got him, but not forever," I said to Merry, who stared at me in alarm. "If you want to finish what you started without interference from this rogue, now's your chance."

Merry pushed to his feet and gazed at me with a frown. My arms were already tired, but I didn't release my grip on the threads. His confusion at my presence hit me with a burst of amusement, and my mouth twitched with mirth.

"Thank you," he said.

"You can thank me by bringing me that grail one day soon."

Merry turned on his heel and darted away. I gritted my teeth and glanced at Caelus.

"How long do you think this bag will hold?"

Caelus looked worried, but not at the strength of the bag.

"It will be fine for a few minutes, as long as you hold tightly."

"Says the person with no muscles to get tired," I muttered.

"But now I must contact others in the elemental plane to fetch the rogue." Caelus' strands shivered with apprehension. "I'm not supposed to interact with the other plane during my mission. And I've only destroyed one artifact so far. What if they think it's time to recall me?"

"Will your superiors necessarily know you're here? We can be quick."

"You're probably right."

He waffled for another moment. I blew air through my teeth in exasperation as I wrestled with the air bag.

"Any time you're ready. This elemental isn't making it easy for me."

Caelus nodded then closed his eyes. A few of his strands melted away until I couldn't see them anymore. I was curious—was he sending a part of himself into the other plane to fetch an elemental?—but I forbore questioning him while he worked.

A great rushing sound, of gales and hurricanes and tornadoes, filled my ears. I ducked in fear and clutched the wriggling bag tightly to my chest. When I looked up, another presence in a humanoid form floated next to Caelus, whose eyes were now open wide. His anxiety flooded my system from our connection.

"Air," Caelus croaked. "You're here."

I delved into Caelus' mind—easy to do when his emotions overwhelmed our shared body—and gathered that Air was the greatest elemental of Caelus' element. I swallowed. This was not good news. The upper echelons of the elemental plane were exactly whom Caelus had been hoping to avoid.

"You have a rogue?" Air whispered to Caelus.

Although the sound was quiet, the power behind the voice still ripped through me, and I gasped. Caelus nodded, his strands frozen. He pointed at the bag between my hands, and I held it out. Air considered it for a moment then wrapped threads around the package. I let go and took a step back, my heart hammering.

With a fluid motion, Air condensed the bag into a tiny ball of dense strands. Then, with a burst, the rogue elemental's threads flew outward and dispersed on the wind. One glance at Caelus' frozen expression of horror convinced me that I'd just witnessed an elemental entering dormancy. I swallowed as a chill of fear wriggled through our connection.

"Good," Air said. "We have been looking for this rogue. But why are you contacting the elemental plane? Have you completed your mission?"

"Not yet," Caelus whispered. "I have destroyed one artifact and have another in my keeping, but there are still more."

"And you are not in control of the body I sent you to possess."

Air gazed at him, and Caelus' mind exploded with incoherent thoughts that pushed into my brain like a swarm of angry bees. Foremost was an overwhelming fear of dormancy, swiftly followed by a consideration of Air's strength. Could Caelus beat the head elemental? Visions of Caelus besting the other and ruling the elemental plane chased through our shared mind. Fueling the vision was desperation. Caelus had no idea what else to do.

I pulled back from his overpowering thoughts. From what I could sense of Air's power, Caelus had no chance. We had to be smarter about this because we were severely outclassed.

"It's better this way," I said. Air turned to me slowly, as if surprised I had the intelligence to speak. "If Caelus had taken over completely, he would have been at a loss. Partnered with me, we're using my extensive knowledge of ancient objects and the spiritual world to hunt down artifacts with far more precision than he could have accomplished alone. We have found two artifacts, are currently collecting two more, and have clues for a fifth. Caelus is well on his way to annihilating the imbalances in this world, and he ought to be commended for his quick thinking in cooperating with a human to further his cause."

Through Caelus' mind now flowed a thread of hope at my words, amid the chaos of his desperate fear. I held my breath and waited for Air to speak. Another tremor shook my knees, and shouts rang out from people on the street.

"Very well," Air said once the shaking stopped. "I will allow you more time to complete your task."

"Thank you," Caelus forced out.

Air dissolved and flowed away until nothing remained of the silvery strands. Caelus draped himself over my arm like a tea towel on a rack. His relief throbbed in my head.

"You did it," he croaked from his inverted position. "You were great. Now I have a reprieve to find more artifacts."

"Dormancy is really that bad, isn't it? What did we subject that other elemental to?"

"He deserved it. Nothing gives an elemental the right to upset the balance." Caelus righted himself with a virtuous expression, but fear and doubt lingered in our connection. "Besides, he was going to kill Merry. I thought that would bother you."

"Yes, you're right. He shouldn't get away with unjustified murder." I looked around at people picking up the pieces of their lives, and I wanted to go home to do the same.

"Ready to get out of here?" I asked Caelus.

"I thought you'd never ask."

Jerome was right. The destruction was oddly confined to a twelve-block radius on the west side of Vancouver. Long before my tired legs jogged me to Cormorant Drive, the streets were merely dusted with small twigs instead of huge limbs, and no one wandered the streets with injuries.

I entered my condo with a sigh of relief at its intact state. After a shower, food, and a strong pot of coffee, I was ready to tackle the world once more. I left my building and dropped off my detailed plan for the grocery. While chatting to Amir about the plan, I held my Leaf defense for a full twenty minutes. I tried tweaking the strands of a draft while in the store through the defensive barrier but had no luck.

"Still," I said to Caelus once we'd exited the shop. "I can enact the barrier whenever I want. I can take a small break, throw an air ball at someone, then put the Leaf defense back up. Hopefully it will do the trick tonight."

"We'll see," Caelus said doubtfully.

My brain had been hatching a strategy while I fitfully slept last night, and I shared the finer details with Caelus as I walked toward Cut Right to find Rosemary.

"Okay, here's the plan. I wheedle the location out of Joy. I can pledge my undying loyalty to the cause, offer to join her for celebratory drinks after the event, whatever I can to get her to spill the beans. Let's be honest, it probably won't take much. Joy loves to talk. After I find out where the Seed is being held, I'll sneak down to the basement where the sisters keep their amulets. I'll grab the most useful ones, then I'll go to the Seed and liberate it."

"I guess that's as detailed a plan as we're going to get." Caelus' threads wiggled with unease. "We need to get this artifact, Morgan. Every day that passes is one day closer to my recall to the elemental plane. Air gave me more time, but I don't have forever."

"I know." I reached out and grabbed the threads of Caelus' hand. My fingers squeezed his briefly. "I'll do everything I can to get the Seed."

Joy was with a customer when I entered Cut Right, but she was the only hairdresser in sight. Her frazzled expression melted into relief at the sight of me.

"Hi, Morgan. I was worried it was a drop-in customer. Shu called in sick, and Rosemary never showed up. She won't answer her phone, either. So, it's just me this morning. And then the news about those earthquakes in the Kitsilano neighborhood—I don't know, the world is topsy-turvy today. I'm glad they seem to have settled down. So strange. Clean-up crews will be busy this week."

Merry must have solved whatever problem he and his friends had been in a tizzy about this morning. I hid a smile of satisfaction. He could get by fine without magic, just like I'd told him he could.

"Rosemary didn't answer for me, either." My concern was brewing into fear for the younger woman. Had she stormed over to Thea's house and gotten herself into hot water? As hotheaded as Rosemary had been last night, I'd still been counting on her support in stealing the artifact.

The phone rang, and Joy's weary expression returned.

"I don't have hands enough for this," she muttered.

I waved at her and walked to the phone.

"Let me help out for a bit." I picked up the phone. "Cut Right Salon. How can I help?"

I shoved my worries about Rosemary to the back of my mind while I helped Joy get a handle on her work. Sweeping and answering phones kept me busy while Joy trimmed and washed hair. Joy finally leaned against the wall with a sigh after setting up an elderly woman in the dryer. The lull gave me a chance to speak to Joy.

"I can't believe Shu and Rosemary didn't show up today." She wiped her forehead dramatically. "What a mess. And

Miranda is in class this morning, although she should be coming in soon. I was going to use my lunch break to buy supplies for the ceremony tonight—Thea wants pillar candles—but I don't know if I'll be able to get away. There's so much to do. I guess I can grab them after work. What a mess."

"What time is your ceremony?"

"Seven o'clock. That should give me two hours to go home, change, buy candles, and drive over there. It should be fine, but I hope traffic isn't too bad."

"Maybe I could help," I said, my mind thinking frantically. "I could buy candles for you and drop them off at the location. Where is it?"

"That's such a nice offer, but I can't tell you where it is, I'm sorry." Joy looked apologetic. "It's not that I don't trust you. But I made a vow to keep the location a secret."

"I understand." Inwardly I cursed Thea's tight grip on the order. "Maybe I could drop it off at wherever the Seed is now, and whoever is transporting it to the ceremony can take the candles with them?"

"I don't know where it is right now. Someone is keeping it safe, but I wasn't told who. Thanks for the offer, Morgan, but I should be good for time. I live really close to here—on the corner of Azalea and Fourteenth—so it won't take me long to get changed and get out of here."

It was too bad Joy wasn't more forthcoming. I could follow her tonight, but how? Again, frustration welled at my lack of wheels. I needed to up my business game to make more money, but that wouldn't happen today.

"Glad to hear it," I said. "How exciting, the Seed being put in its proper place tonight. You must be over the moon. What about the mothers? Thea must be happy now that the Seed has been found."

"I'm sure she is. She's pretty driven, a good thing for the head mother, but even more so since her son died, I think.

Hopefully this is a nice distraction for her."

"How did her son die, if I might ask?"

"Oh, yes, it was terrible. Early last year." Joy's voice took on a hushed cadence that still managed to carry over the hairdryer. "He committed suicide. It was a terrible shock. Thea was so strong, but I think she channels a lot of her energy into the order and her work at the school. The students really turned around after that. There were some bad eggs in a few of the grades, but now it's a model student body."

I pushed my broom around without looking at it. Thea, driven by the loss of her son, had made it her mission to eradicate similar mental health issues in the students she cared for. How could I fault her for trying to prevent another loss like what she had suffered?

The memory of the compliance spell returned to me, and I shuddered. There were better ways to improve the wellbeing of young people without taking control of their minds.

"I'm glad it's the ceremony tonight," Joy continued. "Otherwise it would be training night, and I'm tired of dealing with Filippa. She's insufferable. So bossy, and she thinks she's so much better than us." Joy made a face. "I don't know what happened. We used to have sleepovers together and braid each other's hair, and now she's too good for me. Don't get me wrong, Rosemary has her issues, but at least she treated us the same as she treated herself. Filippa locked down the amulet room, and no one can use them without special permission, and it has to be an ironclad reason. And the way she talks to us, ugh."

"I gather that Thea doesn't consider the sisters to have much chance at entering the motherhood one day," I said with as much delicacy as I could. "Maybe Filippa absorbed the sentiments."

"Yeah, well, that's nothing I didn't already know."

"Really? Rosemary was keen on joining the motherhood."

Joy shrugged and glanced at the hairdryer's timer.

"She deluded herself. But you only have to look at who the mothers are and what they do to know that a hairdresser doesn't stand a chance. Filippa is on track, that's for sure. And, who knows, now that Miranda is in the archaeology program, she might get there one day. But me? Or Rosemary? No, I never expected that. Being in the sisterhood is enough for me. I'm taking accounting classes just in case, but that's a skill I can use in the order or outside it. I was brought up with all this, and it's an honor to be involved in whatever way I can."

The timer beeped, and Joy bustled over to release the elderly woman from her noisy shackles. I finished sweeping and answered the phone until Miranda showed up, but I chafed at the delay. I needed to sneak into the basement. Amulets were waiting.

While Joy and Miranda were busy with customers, I slipped out the back door into the hallway that connected all the stores. It was quiet there, with a faint musty smell. I strode with confidence to a doorway that led to the stairwell. It was the same path I took every week to join the sisters at their training sessions.

At the bottom of the stairs, I didn't walk forward into the sisters' gym. Instead, I created a serrated air blade and crouched next to the rightmost door. It only took a minute to pick the lock, and I congratulated myself on my speed. Then I shook my head. What had I become, that being a better lockpick was cause for celebration?

I was Morgan, that was who. She was a vastly different person than March, and I enjoyed the contrast with my former self.

The door swung open, and I wandered through the sisters' hangout room. It was cheerless with a faded plaid loveseat and a bookcase with well-worn paperbacks on the bottom shelf. The Book of Souls—the few pages that the sisters were allowed to read—sat on the top shelf bound in a black hardcover. I didn't bother peeking inside. I had a copy of that and more, and Dr. Romanoff's student was currently translating pages for me.

A door at the end of the long, narrow room opened to an even mustier-smelling hallway of whitewashed walls and concrete floors that twisted and branched in a bewildering pattern. My footsteps echoed in the dimly lit warren, but my memory was keen. Before long, a familiar door appeared around a corner.

I picked up my pace and skidded to a halt at the amulet room's threshold. Another locked door stood in my way, but I'd already proven that it was no match for my skills. After creating another trusty air blade, the lock clicked, and I swung the door open.

Caelus whooshed out of my arm, and his interest was palpable. He peered into the impenetrable darkness while I fumbled for a light switch.

"I know they're only amulets," he said, his strands quivering with excitement. "But any way we can power you up is welcome."

My questing fingers finally encountered a toggle, and I flicked the switch in triumph. My eyes watered at the sudden brightness. Caelus cursed beside me.

I blinked rapidly. The room appeared through my slitted eyelids. It was a tiny place, no larger than a walk-in closet, and its walls were lined with shelving to house amulets.

Every shelf was empty.

CHAPTER XVIII

"No," I whispered. Caelus was right. I needed every advantage I could get against the motherhood. Strategy was all well and good, but I had to match their power with power of my own if I didn't want to be mowed down.

"Where did they all go?" said Caelus.

"Filippa," I said with grim resignation. "The new head sister. Joy said she was controlling. What do you bet she confiscated the amulets to better dole them out and keep them out of the hands of those she deemed less worthy?"

Caelus drooped, his eyes downcast and his shoulders slumped.

"Rosemary isn't answering your calls, we have no access to amulets… How are we supposed to get the Seed now?"

"We still have the Leaf," I reminded him. "And we still have you. None of the mothers, as far as we know, has an elemental on her side. Let's stop by Rosemary's house right now to find her. We can do this."

Caelus straightened and met my determined gaze with one of his own.

"You're right. We can get this artifact."

Miranda stopped me in the hallway at the top of the stairs. My heart leaped at the surprise, but I kept my expression calm. She didn't need to know I was sneaking around trying to steal amulets.

"Morgan, I wanted to ask you something." Miranda wrung her hands and stared past me, down the hall. Her strands twisted in agitation.

"Ask away."

"You aren't part of the order, but you know a lot about it.

You're objective, is what I'm trying to say. What do you think of our mission?"

I paused and wracked my brain for what to say. The truth might not endear me to a follower of this artifact search, and I wanted to stay in their good graces to aid my own quest. But Miranda clearly had something on her mind, so I didn't want to brush over her concerns.

"I didn't grow up reading the Book of Souls, so the story is all new to me," I said, carefully watching Miranda's face. "I'm a naturally skeptical person, and I like to think critically of every piece of information I receive, whether it's gossip, a news article, or a belief system. I think the story of the Leaf, Seed, and Thorn likely has some basis in fact—most legends do—but is the Book of Souls meant to be taken literally, word for word? That, I don't know."

Miranda nodded slowly, her eyes raking my face.

"Thanks," she said at last. "Food for thought. I'd better get back to Joy before she throws a fit."

I shook my head when Miranda walked through Cut Right's back doorway. At this rate, the order wouldn't have many sisters left to guard their Leaf. I snorted softly and patted my pocket, where the Leaf rested in its beaver keychain. They had nothing to protect. Maybe the sisterhood wasn't necessary anymore.

I was fired up to find Rosemary after discovering the loss of the amulets, but woman does not survive on fire alone, so I exited the building and directed my steps toward Upper Crust for my daily fix of coffee and lemon tarts.

As luck would have it, Jerome was washing his hands for his break when I entered. His warm smile made my stomach flop. I sternly told it to behave, but my mouth answered with a smile of my own. I'd been worried that our terse phone call during the earth tremors would create awkwardness between us, but Jerome looked like he was ready to forgive and forget.

He waited for me at an available table until my order was

ready. I slid into my seat with a happy sigh and sniffed my coffee in appreciation.

"Glad to see you're okay after those freak earthquakes," he said.

"It was bizarre. But I escaped unscathed. Can't say the same for the buildings in Kitsilano." I nodded at the napkin before me that held two sunny yellow desserts. "Are those for me?"

"I tried a touch of cardamom in the tarts today. See what you think."

"I will. But first, how was your client meeting yesterday? Did you sort out the decorative direction?"

"It will be amazing. If I can pull it off." Jerome flashed me a self-deprecating grin, then he sobered. "I don't know how long I can keep using the bakery's kitchen, though. The new manager is still riding me hard. I leave the counters cleaner than I find them, but he always picks out something. Today, he found a dirty spatula that the sandwich cook left under the sink. It wasn't even mine, but I took the blame."

"Can you find a new kitchen to work in?"

"Where? And with what money? It's touch-and-go whether I will even keep this job. He's really got it out for me." Jerome's strands drooped with his despair, and he rested his forearms on the table. "I don't know, Morgan, this might be the end of Butter and Scotch."

I reached out and grabbed his hand with an impulsive gesture.

"There are kitchens for rent around town," I said. "And this is not the only bakery that's hiring. We'll brush up your resumé so that you can hunt for other jobs if this one becomes unbearable. We'll figure this out."

"I don't know who else would hire me," he said in a broken whisper. "I'm—my background—well, the old manager here took a chance on me. I was lucky to get a position."

I searched his face for answers, but Jerome didn't meet my

gaze. Why would he not be a good hire? What sort of history would affect a bakery employing him? A few ideas crossed my mind, but I shut them down quickly. I refused to speculate without evidence, but I might weasel out answers out of him sooner rather than later. Maybe when I was ready to dish on some secrets of my own.

Jerome stared at our clasped hands, and I pulled mine away after a quick squeeze. He gave me a swift smile.

"Thanks for being in my court, Morgan."

I nodded briskly.

"If your business fails, let it not be from lack of funds or effort. I wanted to ask, how are you doing? After your parents' anniversary the other day?"

Jerome waved his hand.

"I'm fine. It's been so long, I hardly remember them anymore."

His voice was nonchalant, but his threads twisted at the words. I tightened my lips with sympathy.

"If you ever want to talk, I'm happy to listen."

"My past is murky waters. You don't want to dive in there."

"Like where you learned your fighting skills?"

I snuck the words into our conversation to gauge Jerome's reaction, and he didn't disappoint. His strands froze, and his eyes flicked to mine then back to the table.

"That's a story for another time."

I leaned back at his dismissive tone, but I wasn't offended. Jerome didn't want me to know something now, but that could change. I was a patient woman, and now that I had a younger body, I could afford to wait for things. Not too long, though.

"Trust me, I know all about complicated pasts."

Jerome's mouth lifted in a mirthless grin.

"You think you do."

"Try me sometime." I checked myself. Was I ready to tell Jerome about my body-switching past? Why was I being so impulsive? I mentally shook my head at my body and said hastily, "But it doesn't have to be today. Today, I need to steal an artifact from the motherhood."

"Today?" Jerome raised his eyebrow. I nodded.

"They're having a ceremony to hide it away in some vault. I assume it will be well protected after that, so today is my last chance. The motherhood can't be trusted with something of that power. The head mother, Thea Diamanto, kidnapped me yesterday."

"What?"

Jerome half rose in his seat, as if he would run out the door and hunt Thea down right now. I waved him to a seated position.

"I escaped, and it's fine. I have protections in place." I checked my barrier from the Leaf's power, and it was still sound. I was proud of myself for mastering it so quickly. Too bad I couldn't use Caelus' abilities at the same time. "But I need to take the Seed from Thea and the others. Who knows what she'll do with it?"

Quickly, I gave Jerome a rundown of Thea's tight control of her students via an amulet, and Jerome's face darkened.

"No, she shouldn't have any more power," he said. "No one should have that."

"It's all about what you do with the power." I thought of infusing magic into donated clothing, and my plans to increase my reach with another artifact. "When I get the Seed—well, it will depend on what powers the Seed bestows—I'll use it for helping at the women's center. Can you imagine the good I could do? In the right hands, directed in the right way, power can be a godsend."

Jerome's strands squirmed, although his face stayed impassive.

"I should get back to work." He stood and pushed in his chair. "I'll see you later."

I stared at Jerome's back in astonishment. Why had he left so abruptly? Had I said something? I combed through my words. Something about using power for good… I shook my head. I didn't know what Jerome's problem was, and if he didn't tell me, I wasn't going to waste time guessing. I had artifacts to steal, and time was marching on.

I walked the few blocks to Rosemary's little house. It was the shabbiest bungalow on an already shabby street, but the door was freshly painted red, and a hose was neatly coiled at the corner, waiting for warmer weather. Rosemary's tiny hatchback ticked in the driveway, cooling from a recent trip. I frowned. I'd fully expected this to be a wasted journey. Was Rosemary at home?

I knocked on the front door, and my eyes widened in surprise when the latch clicked. Rosemary swung the door open.

"Morgan," she said with a smile of welcome. "Please, come in."

"You weren't answering your phone," I said as I squeezed past her into the tiny living room. "And you didn't come into work. I wanted to make sure you were okay."

"How sweet of you. Yes, I'm fine. I just arrived home."

"Well, good."

I scanned Rosemary with a critical eye. She looked tired, but far calmer than last night. Her strands flowed smoothly and slowly around her body, and her countenance was serene.

"Did you get the Seed last night?" I asked. Maybe my work was done for me. Then I could relieve Rosemary of her burden without involving the motherhood.

Rosemary shook her head with a rueful smile.

"I tried. Then I had an epiphany. The Seed is best where it is. Thea and the others won't use it if it's locked in a vault. And we're probably mistaken about Thea's motives. She really does have our best interests at heart."

My eyes narrowed. Rosemary had been beside herself with righteous fury last night. Why the sudden turnaround?

"It's good the Seed will be protected," Rosemary continued. "We should make sure the Leaf is, too. We should put it in a vault with the Seed instead of draping it around a sister's neck. Why don't you give the Leaf to me, and I'll keep it safe until tonight?"

I took a step back. Rosemary wasn't just calm, she was under Thea's compliance spell. I shivered. How powerful was Thea's amulet that it could affect the former sister from a distance?

My ally was compromised. I was on my own.

"I don't know what you're talking about." I took another step back. "I'm glad to hear you're okay. I should get going now. Lots to do."

"I don't think so," Rosemary said sweetly. "I'll need that Leaf. Do you have it here?"

I reactivated the Leaf's protection, and a barrier of multicolored strands twined around me. Caelus emerged from my arm.

"Make a run for it," he said, his eyes on Rosemary. "Quick, before she whips out an amulet."

Rosemary's hand shoved into her pocket, although her face still wore an expression of placid unconcern. I pawed at the door handle, desperate to escape Rosemary's influence. I still wasn't sure how to fight with Caelus' powers and maintain my Leaf protection at the same time. When the door refused to open under my fumbling fingers, my mind whirled frantically.

"Incoming," Caelus shouted.

I turned around. Something hit my Leaf barrier. Instead of reaching my body to perform whatever devious attack Rosemary had intended, the spell dissipated into multicolored threads and shivered the barrier with a rainbow deluge of sparks.

My mouth opened in a grin of relief.

"It works," I hissed to Caelus.

"Yes, but keep it up," he said. "She's got more."

Rosemary's eyes were still calm while she drew out another amulet and aimed it at me. Again, the barrier erupted in rainbow sparks, leaving me untouched.

Defensive measures were excellent, but no one ever won a fight by hunkering down and hoping their opponent would go away. I needed to fight back.

While Rosemary rummaged in her pocket for another amulet to try, I released my hold on the Leaf's protection.

"What are you doing?" Caelus asked, his voice husky with fear. "Put it back!"

I didn't answer with words. Instead, my fingers swiftly rolled an air ball. I threw it with perfect aim.

It hit the other woman squarely on her chest. Rosemary's brows contracted slightly with the only indication that she was concerned about the blow. Then, the air ball exploded outward.

It enveloped Rosemary in a dusty cloud of itching particles that stung her skin and irritated her eyes. It was the perfect getaway device, and while she thrashed at her arms and wiped her streaming eyes, I walked with unhurried steps out her front door.

"That was a risk," Caelus said once we'd turned a corner on our way to Cormorant Drive.

"No risk, no reward. Besides, I had to find a way to gain the offensive, otherwise I was a turtle waiting for a predator to leave it alone. I'd rather be the powerful predator in control of the fight. Think, this way I can keep the Leaf protection on me while I'm preparing air balls, then let it go for the second that I throw my missiles. It's an almost perfect plan."

"It's clever," Caelus admitted. "You're using strategy to its fullest. That will help, especially since we don't have the ammunition of extra amulets. You'll have to use everything you have to gain an advantage over the mothers."

"Especially since Rosemary isn't on our side anymore."

My heart dropped as the full weight of Rosemary's predicament sank in. "Thea got her claws in her. I'd really hoped that she could drive us to the site, or that she would have more amulets, or something. That's an ally down, and it's also a reminder of how powerful Thea is. We need to be vigilant when we get the Seed. Rosemary charged in, guns blazing, and look where it got her."

Caelus gave an exaggerated shiver.

"I don't want to be trapped like that again. Keep that Leaf barrier up."

I strengthened my will, and more multicolored strands leaped around me.

"Agreed."

Rosemary wouldn't be much help now, but I wasn't defenseless. The power of the Leaf hummed around me like a force field, and Caelus and his air abilities nestled at my stomach with a comforting glow. I might not have an ally or any amulets, but I was far from helpless. All I needed was a way to follow Joy after she finished work, and she would lead me directly to the ceremony's site. A taxi would do, although I shuddered at the cost of traveling to an unknown destination. Maybe a ride share would be cheaper, although since I'd never tried one before, I was hesitant testing out a new mode of transport during such a vital mission. Sometimes I felt my mind's age keenly.

"What's that?"

Caelus pointed at my shoulder with a frown. I peered at it. Clinging to my coat was a pale pink thread that clashed with the burgundy, green, and silver threads of our body.

"I must have picked it up from somewhere."

I shrugged and lifted my hand to brush it away, but Caelus swooped closer.

"Wait. It feels strange. Let me check it out."

Caelus melted from his human form into a bundle of silver strands and darted around the pink thread that waved feebly from my shoulder. After a moment, he emerged again.

"It has the stink of a human-worked amulet about it," he said with a shake of his head. "I'm not sure what it does, but I think you should remove it. Who knows when it might activate and cause trouble?"

I plucked the offending thread off my coat and dropped it with a shudder.

"I wonder how it got there and what it does."

"It helped me find you," a familiar voice said behind me.

CHAPTER XIX

I whirled around. Filippa Diamanto stood on the pavement, her beautiful face smug with satisfaction. Caelus drew closer to me.

"The thread must have allowed her to follow you," he said in a loud voice. "What does she want?"

"You were tracking me?" I said to Filippa. "Why?"

"I track anyone who tries to get an amulet," she said. Her lips pursed at my obtuseness. "The sisters were running rampant before, totally out of control, using amulets for frivolous purposes. I needed to clean up the order, starting from the bottom. And you." She shook her head and took a step forward. "You should never have been brought into the fold. Rosemary made a huge mistake trusting you. You're not welcome at training anymore. You need to forget the order, amulets, artifacts, all of it. Stop looking for them, and back off. If you don't, I'll have to get a memory morph amulet and use it on you. It's not very precise, though, so I wouldn't recommend that option."

I centered myself in a balanced stance. I didn't know what was coming next, but Filippa's words were inflammatory. Things could get messy, and soon.

"I don't owe you any promises," I said. My chin tilted up in defiance. "You can keep your amulets, but you can't stop me from being friends with the sisters."

"You can give me the Leaf," Filippa said with a knowing look. She stepped closer again, and a trickle of fear traveled down my spine. Filippa's lips twisted with chilling menace, and her hand slid into her pocket. What sort of amulet did she keep in there?

"That's what this is about," Caelus said. He cursed. "Get ready for an attack."

"I have nothing to give you," I said to Filippa. "And even

if I did, do you really think I would carry around an artifact of such value on my person? I've always considered your order's strategy of the lockets to be ridiculous. Powerful artifacts should be treated with the care they deserve."

Filippa's eyes raked over my body as if searching for the Leaf, but her shoulders sagged with my words.

"She bought it," Caelus whispered.

"This isn't over," Filippa said with a glare that promised retribution when I least expected it. "If you have the Leaf, we will get it back. I don't care what sort of powers you have, they are no match for the order."

With that parting shot, she turned and strode away on long legs. I breathed a sigh of relief.

"That was close," I said as we continued on our way. "They're onto us, though. I'm glad I have the Leaf's protection. Who knows when I'll be ambushed next?"

A notification pinged on my phone, distracting me from my ruminations on the order and their mission. I pulled it out of my coat pocket and scanned the email. My heart leaped. Caelus leaned forward at the spike of my emotion.

"Look." I brandished the phone at him. "We have another translation."

"Read it," he said breathlessly.

I slowed my walking speed to avoid collisions and peered at the small screen.

"Keep an eye out for obstacles," I said to Caelus absently. "Looks like our student translated something about the Seed. See, here's the image for the page. It's a dot rising out of a purple fruit. I wonder what it tastes like."

"Or what powers the fruit's flesh would bestow."

Caelus and I glanced at each other, our desire for the fruit mirrored in each other's eyes. I shook my head to focus.

"Never mind that. We need all three artifacts before that happens."

"And we're destroying them before the Tree of Life can

grow."

"Of course," I said quickly. "Now, do you want to hear the translation or not?"

Caelus responded with silence, and I read the translation aloud.

On its own, the Seed brings life, and life constructs, not destructs. With the bounty of its life, healing flows from the Seed in abundance. Each Seed has the power to heal most ailments, even those near death. It is a precious gift of the Tree of Life.

To bring about the new world, the Seed must be planted alone, in soil from the Leaf, and watered with blood from the Thorn. If purity is not ensured, the Seed will never grow.

"Healing would be handy," Caelus said eventually. "Our human body is so feeble."

"Watch it," I said, but without heat. Healing powers would never go amiss. I was already competent at healing myself using threads, but the Seed sounded like it was a whole other level of healing. "Those near death" could even benefit. With the Leaf as protection and the Seed as insurance, I would be invincible. Could I create amulets with healing powers from the Seed? Each person who passed through the women's center could leave with an amulet that would heal any wound. I shivered at the possibilities.

"We can't use it until we have it," I said, trying to inject some practicality into my longing. "Let's focus on tonight, then we can talk about healing powers."

My phone rang, but I didn't recognize the number. I answered with hesitation.

"Is this Morgan Feynman?" a male voice answered.

"Speaking."

"This is Yevgeny Romanoff. Did you receive my student's latest translation work?"

"Yes, it was fascinating. Thank him for me, please."

"Fascinating is the right word. Did you find any

information on the history behind your text?"

His eagerness broke through the restraint he was trying to maintain. I didn't have any information for him, and I didn't want to tell him about the order, magic, elementals, any of it. Hopefully, he wouldn't be too persistent. I would have to disseminate.

"Not yet," I said, allowing regret to color my voice. I turned a corner and continued walking in the direction of my condo. "There may be a connection to Turkey, although I can't confirm that yet."

"Are we talking Ottoman empire-era? But then, why would the text be in medieval Latin? Or is it older than that, Byzantine perhaps, and then translated over the years?"

"I don't know."

"It might help us with the translations if we understand the content better. Please, if you find anything out, let me know. This text might be the start of a new discovery."

I didn't believe him—Latin was Latin, at least for the level of translation his student was doing—and Yevgeny's insistence bothered me. Had I been wrong to take the book to him? I'd been hoping for an impartial translator, not an invested historian.

"If I find anything out, I'll pass the info on," I promised with my fingers crossed.

I signed off and looked at Caelus.

"Will he be a problem?" Caelus asked.

"He'll have to be a problem for another day. We have enough on our plates for now."

A cooing broke me out of my preoccupation, and I stopped at the corner of Twelfth and Magnolia. Was I here already? The cooing returned, more insistent this time, and I looked around for the bird.

A rust-colored pigeon peered at me from a leafless branch beside the sidewalk. I narrowed my eyes.

"Beaky?"

The pigeon cooed again. My face broke into a smile, despite the stern expression I tried to force upon it.

"Taking over my balcony wasn't enough? Now you're following me? Honestly, Beaky, you're a menace."

"Now you're talking to birds," Caelus said beside me. "As if talking to yourself wasn't bad enough."

"Who do I have to impress?" I shrugged. "If I appear eccentric, so be it. There are worse traits."

I turned up Twelfth. Before I took two more steps, a flapping sound made me duck. Beaky landed with an awkward stumble then strutted in a circle as if to maintain her dignity. I frowned.

"Shoo, you flying rat. I want to go home. Go on, off to the balcony that you've claimed."

Beaky fixed me with one beady eye and cooed again with force. She strutted back and forth on the sidewalk.

"Do birds usually act like this?" Caelus asked, eyeing the pigeon with mistrust. "She looks like she has a message for you but can't communicate."

"She probably wants food. I don't have any for you, Beaky. Out of here!"

I walked forward with deliberate steps. Beaky held her ground for a moment. Then, with a noisy flapping of her rust-colored wings, she took off and landed on the railing of a nearby balcony.

I shook my head at her antics, but my skin prickled. Filippa's parting glare crossed my mind. What if Beaky were trying to warn me of something? Surely, a pigeon didn't have the brains for planning of that complexity. But what would it hurt to be cautious?

"Do you see anything out of the ordinary?" I asked Caelus when we were halfway down the block.

"Beaky made you nervous, too? Make sure the Leaf's protection is on."

I reactivated the Leaf—without my constant vigilance, the

defenses slackened—and held an air ball at the ready, this one designed to cover the recipient with stinging hot needles of pain. It was a distracting attack, to say the least. I still had marks on my arm where I'd tested the effect on myself.

I cautiously stepped forward, my body on high alert.

Rainbow sparks exploded from an empty alley on my right side, and I whirled to face my attacker. Starr, the young former sister, stared at me with a calm expression that was growing uncomfortably familiar. She held up her amulet again, as did the tall mother beside her, whose sage-green threads I recognized from my kidnapping.

"We're here to get the Leaf," the mother said in an even, reassuring voice. "Hand it over, and no one needs to get hurt."

Another blast of rainbow sparks showered around me from behind. I turned my head. The curvy mother from my kidnapping approached from the street, arm extended and a look of surprise on her face. Despite my confidence in the Leaf's protection, my feet backed me into the alley with involuntary steps.

"And if I don't hand it over?" I said. It was too late to deny my possession of the Leaf. I'd told them I didn't have it before, and they hadn't believed me.

"Then we will extract the location from you by any means necessary," the tall mother said.

"They'd better not hurt this body," Caelus muttered. "Not before we get the Seed, anyhow. Go on, Morgan. Show them what you've got. But keep that Leaf protection up as much as you can."

I tuned out Caelus' well-meaning but distracting instructions and readied my air ball. Having three opponents was tricky, but I had the advantage that they couldn't see the Leaf's protection and wouldn't know when it was down.

I released the Leaf's defenses, lobbed my air ball at the tall mother, then snapped the Leaf into place once more. My fingers twirled another air ball while I watched the mother writhe in sudden pain. When Starr turned with concern to her companion, I released the Leaf and threw my second ball of stinging heat at the girl.

Something hit me while my defenses were down, and every muscle in my body cramped. The torturous tightness dropped me to my knees, and I gasped. It was like having a Charlie horse in every limb of my body. I needed to stretch my muscles out, but I didn't know where to start.

"It's all in your mind," Caelus shouted at me, his tone fearful. "Shake it off. Your Leaf protection is down, and the other mother is coming!"

Footsteps thudded on the asphalt. Starr and the tall mother still writhed in pain, but the curvy mother was coming to finish what she'd started.

CHAPTER XX

Anger flared in me, and this time, I welcomed it. No one should take over my mind without my consent, whether it was to make me compliant or to torture me. I grabbed onto that rage and channeled it into the pain in my muscles. I gasped again, but my imagination pushed the pain out from my body into the surrounding air.

Threads lifted from my limbs like a rainbow fog of yarn. My eyes watered, but the pain was already leaving me. I narrowed my eyes and pushed harder. Threads flowed faster away from my body until only a faint trembling remained in my legs.

I pushed myself upright and swung around to face my attacker. There was no time for finesse. I gathered strands as my hand passed through the air, and whatever I collected, I tossed at the surprised mother.

She stumbled backward, and I didn't stop to evaluate further. I brushed past a mewling Starr and burst onto Twelfth Street. My final attack on the curvy mother had been weak to the point of uselessness, and I didn't want to hang around.

My feet thundered down the sidewalk. Caelus flowed beside me, his face grim, but for once he didn't have any commentary to add. He didn't speak until I sprinted down Magnolia Road and tucked myself behind a nearby fence on Thirteenth Street.

"Why did you stop?" he asked. "They'll be after you soon. You know those air balls don't last for long."

"I can't keep running away," I panted, my hand on my beating heart. "They know where I live. Besides, they might be my ticket to tonight's show. What if I can get one of them to talk?"

Caelus nodded in consideration.

"Good idea. It's too exposed here, though." He waved at a

person on the opposite side of the street, who was climbing into his car with a confused glance at me. "You'll have to follow her somewhere quieter."

I nodded and maintained my vigil, willing my heart to calm. My body still pulsed with anger, but I used that emotion to funnel energy into my Leaf protection and my next attack. If I had excess emotion floating around my body, I might as well use it for my benefit.

Four long minutes passed, then Starr and the tall mother emerged from around the corner and walked swiftly to a car parked on the road out front. I edged behind the fence to avoid detection and waited some more. By the time the two had pulled into traffic and sped away, the curvy mother had turned onto the sidewalk and strode away from me.

I straightened and walked on silent feet behind the mother. She never looked back, not until she turned into an alley where a minivan was parked. By the time her key was in the lock, I had pressed her against the van.

"Scream and I will make sure you never scream again," I hissed.

I wasn't planning on murdering anyone, but my rage had chosen the words. They sounded appropriately threatening, so I let them be. The mother's eyes widened and then narrowed.

Fingers jabbed into my waist, and I coughed. The mother whispered words in a frantic undertone, but I pressed her harder against the car and grinned. The rainbow threads of my protection bubble remained intact.

"Nice try. You'll have to do better than that to get the jump on me. Now, tell me where the Seed is."

"It's at its final location now," she spat. "Waiting for our leader to begin the ceremony. There it will lie, protected, until the Thorn is found. And I wouldn't tell you the address in a million years. You think I've been in the order my whole life and taken multiple vows only to bend at your paltry efforts? Hardly. I will never break. Do your worst."

The mother tossed her head in defiance. I managed not to snort at her theatrics, although it was a near thing. I wasn't interested in torture, no matter what words flowed out of my mouth. Instead, I thrust my hands into her coat pockets and rummaged around until my fingers closed on a few metal objects. I pulled them out and held them up.

"I'm taking your amulets. And I'm not letting you leave scot-free. Caelus, help me out here."

"Memory modification?" Caelus looked interested. "Let's try it out. What's the worst that can happen?"

I shuddered at the memory of the man whose ability to talk straight I had stolen from him last month. My anger reminded me that this woman had been ready to torture me to gain knowledge of the Leaf's whereabouts, and I doubted she was under a compliance spell. I would do my best to leave her relatively intact, but I couldn't afford to have her follow me and attack again.

I dropped my Leaf barrier, since the woman had no amulets to threaten me with, and my left-hand fingers waved above her head. The mother looked apprehensive at my invisible work, but my right hand held her ruby strands firmly no matter how hard she wriggled.

When the mother's squirming slowed then stopped, I released my hold on her strands and stepped back. She blinked and looked at me in confusion.

"I'm sorry. Do I know you?"

"You came over faint," I said in a firm, compassionate tone. "I was walking by and helped. Do you feel better now?"

"Yes," she murmured. "I think so."

"You still look woozy. Do you know how to get home from here?"

The question was a test to make sure I hadn't removed too many of her memories. To my relief, she nodded firmly, and her eyes cleared.

"Yes. Thank you for the help. I can drive home from here."

She climbed into the minivan. I let her drive away, then I jogged in the direction of Cormorant Drive.

"That was useless," Caelus said as he floated beside me. "We still don't know where the Seed will be tonight."

"But we removed one mother from the equation," I panted. "That has to count for something. And I have a few amulets now that should ramp up my offensive game. Can we use them without the magic words?"

"You've got me, baby," Caelus said with a grin. "No sweat."

I snorted at his words.

"Since when have you been using human vernacular? Are you watching videos on my phone while I'm asleep?"

"I'm observant. But, yes, we can use the amulets. I'll check them out right now."

He disappeared into my pocket. I focused on my steps. Time was running out, and I needed backup. Rosemary was out of the picture and the sisters' amulets had disappeared. My only other ally who knew about the situation and my part in it was Jerome.

He didn't have any magic abilities, but he was good in a tight spot. What was more, the thought of him made my heart sigh in relief, and that had to count for something. I didn't trust easily, but Jerome was carving out a space in my life.

He also had a vehicle. I could really use a ride tonight.

Upper Crust was warm and scented with delicious bread as always, but the kitchen was conspicuously empty of Jerome.

"He left for the day," the girl behind the counter told me. "Try calling him, maybe?"

I thanked her and walked out of the bakery, dialing as I exited. On the third ring, Jerome picked up.

"Hello?"

"Jerome." I took a deep breath. "You were a bit strange the last time we talked, and I want to clear the air."

Silence reigned on the other end of the line.

"Was I strange?" he said finally, although his tone clearly understood what I meant.

"Yes. And I think I figured it out. Every time I mentioned getting the Seed to get more power for myself, you shut down."

One of the many benefits of having a fifty-something mind was the ability to analyze situations with the backdrop of experience. Another was dealing with situations as they arose without unnecessary delicacy.

"I guess so."

Jerome seemed surprised at my astuteness. I smiled grimly, although he couldn't see my face.

"You have history with someone power-hungry in your life, and it worried you to see me talking in the same way. But I wanted to let you know that I don't just rely on my newfound powers." My mind recalled my kidnapping by Thea, and how I released my bonds without Caelus' help, using only my brains and iron will. "I am much more than that, and I don't rely on magic to solve all my problems. Powers certainly help—I'd be lying if I said I wouldn't miss them if they left— but that's not all I have. I honestly do have the intent to use any power I gain for a good purpose, but I plan to pair that with good sense as well. And, if you're willing to continue being my friend, you could keep me honest with my powers."

I waited with held breath for Jerome to speak. When he did, his voice held more warmth than before.

"I'll keep you honest. Anytime."

"Good. That's settled. Also, if it makes a difference, I found out what the Seed does. It's a power I think you'll approve of. As far as I could discover, it has the power to heal. There isn't too much evil I could accomplish with that."

"Unless you bring a tyrant back to life," he said, but a grin was in his voice. "That's true, it's a helpful power. How are you going to get it?"

"That depends. Are you free tonight?"

"I could be, if you're asking."

"Don't say I never take you anywhere. If you're up for crashing a party, I have just the place." An idea lanced through my brain, so brilliant and sharp it almost hurt. I wouldn't pretend that my motives weren't a tiny bit petty—Filippa had been on her high horse for long enough with me and the other sisters—but I hoped my plan would prove helpful this evening. "Oh, if you have time to bake cupcakes, that would be great. A party without cake is just a meeting."

"Cupcakes." Jerome sounded both amused and puzzled. "Any particular flavor?"

"Whatever you like. They're not for me. Nine, please, and don't ice them until I get there. I have a special ingredient for one of them."

After I signed off, I jogged to the nearest pharmacy and bought my ingredient. I tried not to grin as I handed over my cash to the bored cashier. Mission accomplished, I jogged back to Upper Crust, whose doors were closed for the day, although one of the servers swept under tables.

At Jerome's wave, the woman opened the door for me. I tiptoed past her dirt pile with a smile and walked into the kitchen. Jerome pulled out a baking tray from the oven, where eleven chocolate cakes puffed from their cups. I sniffed the air with appreciation.

"You're amazing," I said. "Thanks."

Jerome's mouth twitched from my praise. As he carefully extracted each cake from the pan, he nodded at the paper bag in my hand.

"What's the secret ingredient?"

I stole a glance at the server, but she was shaking the front mat outside.

"It's a laxative," I whispered. "For the head sister. She's a royal pain in the ass, so I thought I'd return the favor. Hopefully, it will take her out of the running tonight."

Jerome snorted with mirth.

"You have a cruel streak," he said with a shake of his head.

"I like it. But how will you get her to eat the right one?"

"Can you pipe initials onto each cupcake? Then we can literally label the correct one for her."

Jerome nodded with a grin and turned to a bowl filled with butter.

"Let me get the icing ready while the cupcakes cool."

I grabbed a bowl from a shelf and carefully emptied three capsules into it while Jerome beat the butter and added icing sugar. By the time he was done, the cakes had cooled. I watched while he expertly filled icing bags and piped large creamy white swirls on ten cupcakes. With a finer tip, he carefully traced a letter on each with chocolate icing at my direction. I stirred leftover white icing into my bowl of medication, then Jerome piped it onto the final cupcake and labeled it with a "F".

"There," he said finally. "Let me put them in a box."

"But we made too many. What will we do with the extras?"

"I have no idea," he said with mock wonder. "Who could possibly eat two cupcakes right now?"

I laughed and whipped my hand out to grab an unlabeled cake. Jerome grinned and swiped the other one. With conspiratorial glances, we bit into our treats.

"Mmm," I said then swallowed. "Delicious, as usual. Here, let me run over to Cut Right to deliver these, then I'll help you clean up before we go. I don't want to give your manager a reason to sack you."

I slid my arms into my coat, grabbed the box, and flew out the door. It was almost five o'clock. Would Joy still be at the salon?

Luck was on my side. Joy was turning her key in the front door when I skidded to a stop beside her, panting from exertion.

"Joy. I had these cupcakes made for you and the sisters. To celebrate tonight. I thought you'd like them before your ceremony."

"That is so thoughtful." Joy took the box and peeked inside. Her face lit up. "And look, they have our initials on them. You're so good to us, Morgan. Thank you. I will pass them around. Not all the sisters will be there tonight, but I'll save theirs for tomorrow."

"Oh? Who was invited to the ceremony tonight?" Was my ploy unneeded?

"The more senior sisters, that's all. Amanda, Jasmine, and Sarah won't be coming. The rest will be there, though, and they'll love these."

I sighed with relief. Filippa still had a good chance of getting her cupcake.

"I think Filippa said she liked chocolate," I improvised. It was a good guess—I didn't know many women who didn't adore chocolate. "I hope she likes these."

"I'm sure she will. I'll make sure to give her one first, I promise." Joy smiled and tucked the box firmly under her arm. "You're a true friend, Morgan."

I watched Joy walk away, her words churning in my mind. I hoped Joy still felt that way after tonight, but I doubted it. The full weight of what I was planning sank on my shoulders. Life would be different after tonight, one way or other. It was too bad—I'd enjoyed the companionship of the sisters over the past month or so—but it couldn't be helped. Caelus needed me, and I needed to stop Thea from her plans of controlling everyone in her grasp.

Still, the price would be heavy.

CHAPTER XXI

I walked back to the bakery and helped Jerome wipe the counters after sneaking a slice of his bread to munch on for my dinner. He shooed me out after he caught crumbs falling on his clean floor, so I absconded to the window ledge outside the door and quietly conversed with Caelus while I ate.

"I figured out what your amulets do," he said with pride. "They're pretty inventive. There's one that pulls all the strength from one leg and funnels it into the other. Makes you hop around in circles, I guess. As long as we work together, you won't need a secret word to unlock them."

"Good." I swallowed my mouthful and sighed happily at the flavor of Jerome's excellent sourdough. "I like having as many tools in my kit as I can. The sisters were bad enough last month, but these mothers don't hold their punches. Their amulets pack a wallop."

"You'll love these ones. One instantly knocks out your opponent and makes them snore like a thunderstorm."

"An odd detail, but useful overall. Good. Those will come in handy."

I rolled up the paper bag of my sandwich and shoved it in my coat pocket, then lifted my lemon tart with delicate fingers to transport it to my waiting mouth. Caelus looked at me with amusement.

"Bodies are so strange, obliged to fulfill all sorts of whims and desires."

"Welcome to being human," I said after I'd fully savored my bite and swallowed it. "It's a wild ride."

"Back to business. We need to enter this ceremony location without hesitation. Guns blazing, as you said. You have the new amulets, you have the element of surprise, you have the Leaf's protection, and you have me."

"I agree, we'll need to use all of the above to defeat the

order. But that won't be enough. We need a good plan as well, otherwise all this power will be wasted if they get the jump on me immediately. What are ways we can confuse them, or isolate them so I can combat each woman one by one?"

"Fog is always helpful," Caelus said after a moment's pondering. "Humans mostly use their eyes."

"Good one. That will allow me to pick them off one by one. I don't really want to hurt anybody—well, I don't care about Thea, and the other mothers are bad apples too, but the sisters are my friends—so I'll do my best to render them unconscious or tie them up."

"Removing air from their lungs has worked in the past."

I took the last bite of my bread, then a rusty pickup truck rolled into the bakery's loading zone with Jerome at the wheel. He must have exited out the back alley and fetched his truck. I stood and dusted off my hands.

"That's not much of a plan," I said. "But it will have to do. I'll think more on the way over."

When I slid into the passenger's seat, Jerome gave me a smile that made my stomach flop. I pushed on it with my hand in annoyance. Jerome's eyes glanced down.

"You feeling okay?"

"Yes, thanks." He didn't need to know how my body reacted to him.

"What's the plan?"

I pointed forward.

"We're going to Joy's house and waiting until she leaves, then following her to the ceremony location. I hope you can keep up."

Jerome's mouth twitched with amusement, although he didn't share the joke.

"I'll do my best."

It was late enough that we didn't have to wait long at the end of Joy's block. When she emerged from her apartment wearing black jeans that hugged her curves, her hair long and bouncy as always, I gripped Jerome's arm.

"There she is," I whispered. "Let's go."

Jerome started the truck without a word, and we rolled into the street behind Joy's sedan when she drove away. Jerome's fingers were loose on the steering wheel, but his sandy threads were tight and indicated his focus. My fingers fidgeted together until I sat on them. It was a bad habit of my new body—one I had trained out of my old body decades ago—and it irritated me to have to reteach myself that control.

"Where is she taking us?" I said aloud twenty minutes later. We'd followed Joy onto the highway heading east, and after many minutes of driving in busy traffic, she'd signaled at an exit after the nearby city of Maple Ridge.

"What kind of spot would be right to hide an ancient magical artifact?" Jerome muttered. "Your guess is as good as mine. Probably better, actually."

The land around us transformed from houses and shops into farmland. I gazed at trees lining the road illuminated by streetlights in the darkness of a wintery night, and I shook my head.

"It's a Seed," I said. "Maybe the order thought it was best suited to somewhere it can grow?"

"I thought it wouldn't sprout until all three artifacts were together."

"Yes, but at least it will be in the right place when they find the Thorn." I drummed my fingers on my knee then pointed forward when Joy's car flicked on its signal. "There. She's turning."

It was a driveway, so Jerome cruised past while my neck craned to look at the property. A large farmhouse, lights in its windows, sprawled next to a huge hunk of bedrock that sprang out of the ground next to it. Beyond, a tidy orchard was nearly invisible in the inky blackness except for what looked like tiki torches in the center.

"The ceremony is in the trees," I hissed. "Don't go too far."

"First rule of following someone." Jerome pulled over against a ditch behind a drooping willow. Occasional trees graced the roadway, but our surroundings were mainly sloping fields, fallow at this time of year. "Never let them guess they're being followed. This should do the trick."

Once outside, my breath formed clouds in front of my face, so I zipped up my coat and tucked in my chin against the cold. We trekked to the driveway, walking behind trees when possible, ever observant for other headlights approaching, but it appeared that Joy was a latecomer. A row of cars lined the driveway right up to the expensive-looking house. I wondered who lived here. Was it one of the mothers? Someone else in the order?

Jerome's hand clamped on my shoulder, and he drew me behind the nearest minivan.

"There are two women at the trunk of that car," he hissed. "What's the plan?"

I thought wildly. This was our first chance to take down some of the order, and these two were helpfully isolated from the rest. What should we do?

"Do the fog trick," Caelus said from beside me. "Then each of you takes an opponent. Can you put the Leaf's protection on Jerome?"

I nodded. It was worth a try. I didn't like him without a defense against magic.

"I'm going to try putting a protection around you," I said to Jerome. "So magic will roll off you. I don't know if it will work, but I need to try."

Jerome looked doubtful about tampering with magic, but he submitted to my ministrations. I activated the Leaf then pulled strands of it away from my body and draped it over Jerome's. They held, surprisingly, but their coverage was less than ideal.

"It might help," Caelus said. "But only until you release it to throw an air ball. And you can't test it without taking off the

Leaf's protection yourself."

"We'll give it a try," I said to Jerome with more conviction than I felt. "But try to dodge magical attacks if you can, okay?"

Jerome nodded, a wry smile on his mouth.

"This isn't my first dirty fight. Don't worry about me."

I did worry—male bravado always made me shake my head with the wisdom of age—but there wasn't much else I could do. The amulets I'd taken from that mother near my condo wouldn't work without Caelus, so I couldn't give one to Jerome. The best I could do was what I had already done and provide cover with fog.

To that end, I raised my hands.

"Nice and thick," Caelus murmured beside me.

I glared at him and his less-than-helpful remarks, then I focused on my task. Before long, a billowing cloud formed in the air before us and drifted in a thick bank toward the two figures at their trunk.

"Now," I whispered to Jerome, and we stole from behind our shelter and into the cover of the mist.

Fog blanketed cars, trees, and even the gravel at our feet, but it couldn't hide threads. I took Jerome's hand and led him unerringly toward the two figures, who exclaimed at the encompassing mist that flowed around them. One thread cluster was Shu—I recognized her tomato-red strands—and the other's salmon-red cluster looked familiar. They bent over a glowing mass of multicolored threads at waist-height. Did they have a stash of amulets? My mouth nearly watered from the power available.

"It's the burglar mother from your condo," Caelus said.

My eyes narrowed. I wouldn't have to hold my punches with this one. She'd been one of my kidnappers.

"I'll take the right, and you take left, okay?" I breathed in Jerome's ear once I had drawn his head down to mine.

When my lips accidentally brushed his earlobe, he shivered. I wondered if it were from me or the fog, and my body thrilled to imagine it was me. I schooled it to focus on the task at hand. Jerome nodded silently at my words.

"Don't hurt Shu too much, if you can," I whispered. "She's a friend. I'm going to give the other woman everything I have, though."

Jerome's brows contracted at my words, and I regretted how they must have sounded to the man who was already concerned about my ability to corral my use of power. I would explain later how the woman had threatened me. Hopefully, that would alleviate Jerome's concerns. Until then, I couldn't risk saying more for fear of being overheard.

When we were only five steps away, yet still invisible in the fog, I gave Jerome a gentle push toward Shu and leaped toward my own target. My aim was true, thanks to my elemental-sight, and the mother shrieked her dismay before I tackled her to the ground.

She was no slouch, though, and she immediately kneed me in the side and whipped out an amulet. With one hand she smacked the side of my face, and with the other she pressed a fountain pen against my head and shouted a word that I didn't catch.

My barrier sparked and sizzled but held firm. I grinned and leaped back, then momentarily dropped my barrier and shoved an air ball in her face. It immediately sucked oxygen from her lungs in a swirling funnel, and she fell back, gasping. I scrambled forward and grabbed her legs while she was distracted. Thumps and cries from the fog nearby alerted me to Jerome's battle, and I hoped with a squeeze of my heart that he was triumphing. The cries were feminine, which gave me comfort.

The mother kicked wildly, undoing the few strands I'd managed to twist together to secure her in place while my barrier had been down. I growled and let my rage out. This woman had kidnapped me, and her fellows had threatened to torture me. She didn't deserve my mercy. What was more, I needed to defeat her to access the hoard of amulets in her trunk. With Caelus' help and that treasure trove of power, I would be unstoppable. What had been a faint hope of success would turn into a certainty with those amulets on my side. How could anyone stand in my way?

Jerome and Shu were silhouettes in the fog now. Jerome was still on his feet, although he favored one leg, but Shu didn't seem too steady herself. She clutched one arm as if in pain, and I remembered Jerome's switchblade. I hoped he was making good use of it, but not hurting Shu too badly. At least I could heal her later if necessary. The important thing was to get to the stash of amulets and steal the Seed with them.

The mother's foot contacted my neck with a well-placed kick, and I choked long enough for her to wriggle away. The air ball I'd smothered her with dissipated, and she scrambled to her feet.

My reflexes were swift after a month of training and my new-found youth. I leaped to my feet then punched her in the stomach. The mother doubled over, winded. While she was distracted, I kicked her knee. She fell to the ground with a silent grimace of pain, curled around her injured joint.

A twinge of consternation rippled through me at my actions. I needed to get the amulets to carry out my task, but I wondered how Jerome would react at my ruthlessness for more power. It was for a good cause—retrieving the Seed would remove the artifact from Thea's grasp as well as help save Caelus from dormancy—but every power-grab could be justified by the grabber, I was sure.

Still, I couldn't stop now. I relaxed my Leaf barrier and twisted the woman's own threads with the air strands that flew in and out of her mouth. She choked, her eyes wide, then she thrust another amulet my way. Just in time, I triggered my barrier. This amulet must not have needed a word to activate it, for the rainbow sparks of my protection were quite dazzling. I grinned at her.

"Nice try, but you'll have to do better than that."

Her eyes rolled in her head from the lack of oxygen, and she slumped to the ground. With a few swift knots, I tied her legs together with her own strands. It wouldn't last long, maybe an hour, but that would be more than enough time to invade the ceremony and get the Seed. If I could take her down without much trouble, how much more could I achieve with the amulet hoard? I had this task in the bag. I had my ammunition, and I was ready to storm the castle.

My mind registered the quiet my ears had been hearing for a while. I peered through the mist and saw two stationary clusters, Jerome's and Shu's. My heart seized at Jerome's unmoving strands, then I saw them shift, and I relaxed. My hands lifted to remove the fog.

"Don't," Caelus said. "Leave it. It will be useful to isolate the others with."

"Does it matter now?" I pointed at the outline of the open trunk where amulets glowed through the mist. "I have more power than I know how to use. How can they stop me?"

"Weren't you the one moaning about needing a plan? Leave the mist. It will come in handy."

"Fine."

I walked to the trunk and grabbed handfuls of pens, eyeliner, tubes of lipstick, and keys. Apparently, the mothers were cut from a practical cloth, and every item could be easily concealed in a purse without comment. My pockets rapidly filled, then I draped the necklaces over my head. With every glowing amulet that I tucked against my body, my confidence grew. The power locked in these small objects was immense and mine for the taking. With it, I couldn't lose. Why would I need a plan when I could run in, guns blazing? The Seed would be mine. These amulets were definitely coming home with me afterward.

"Jerome," I called softly. "Are you okay? Come get some of these amulets. I bet we can find some that don't need a password, so you can use them."

When Jerome didn't answer, I frowned and turned from my amulet gathering. With steady feet, I tracked his sandy cluster until I stood over him. He looked up at me with eyes glazed from pain, and my heart stopped. Why was he still seated on the ground? What was wrong with him?

My eyes fell to Jerome's stomach. He gripped it tightly, and although his hands were large, they didn't cover the terrible wound that pulsed blood with every heartbeat. A mighty gash sliced from his left ribcage to the right side of his pelvis. I couldn't tell how deep it went, but with the amount of blood he was losing every moment, it didn't matter.

I dropped to my knees, my breath coming in sharp bursts.

"Jerome," I squeaked, then my head cleared. I could heal him. My fingers darted out and grabbed the knots that nearly obscured his injury.

"It would take an hour or more," Caelus said gently beside me. "He doesn't have an hour. And the ceremony is starting now, I can feel it. You'll have to leave him."

"What?" I stared, open-mouthed, at Caelus. My mind refused to comprehend his words. "You want me to walk away and leave him to die? I don't accept that."

"There's no other way. Even your human doctors couldn't fix him now. Look at him."

Caelus swept his arm toward Jerome, whose eyes were now closed in his pale face. His grimace of pain twisted my heart.

"There's nothing more we can do for him," Caelus continued. "You can't save Jerome from death, but you can make his sacrifice count for something by getting the Seed."

I stared at Jerome, who gasped with shallow breaths to avoid moving his stomach. He was beyond hearing my conversation with Caelus. His focus was entirely on his pain.

But even that would cease soon. I couldn't let that happen. But how could I prevent it?

An idea came to me, a wild, insane idea that filled me with

fearful hope.

"Caelus. You healed our new body when it was near death. That's how you prepared it for possession."

"Yes." Caelus looked confused. I pressed my point.

"Then you can heal Jerome. Hop over to his body, heal him, and come back."

"It's not that quick," he protested. "And not that easy. Do you really think that if I'd been able to body hop, I would have stayed with you in the beginning when you were suppressing me?"

"But can it be done?" I asked, my heart bracing itself for Caelus' answer.

His mouth twisted in thought. "If you transfer me yourself," he finally answered. "Pull me over with your hands and your intention. I'll still have a connection to you, so I'll jump back to our body when you're close enough." He sighed. "But his wound is beyond my capabilities to fully heal. I can keep him alive for a while, but no more than that. I can only return a body from the brink of death with certain types of injuries. If you had the Seed, its healing powers might be enough for Jerome, but if you leave me with him, you won't have any powers to get the Seed. You can't control the amulets on your own, and without me you can't activate the Leaf or see threads or use any powers at all. You'll be a helpless human, and there's no way you'll get the Seed like that."

Caelus' words hit me hard. Something inside me shrank and shriveled at the reminder of how small and helpless I was without him and the abilities he brought to my life. Without his powers, I was weak and useless. Caelus was right. How would I ever stand a chance against the might of a magical order?

But I still had my wits. They might not be much, but they'd released me from Thea's hold, and I'd escaped with little else than my willpower and brainpower. I wasn't helpless. Magic brought a whole new level of might to my life, but the core of my being was still strong. If I could escape Thea, I had a chance to steal the Seed. I just had to be smart about it.

And if I didn't give up my powers, Jerome would die. I nearly stopped breathing at that thought. I glanced at his pale face again and reached out my hands in time to lower his torso to the ground. His eyes rolled until I could see the whites, and his hands dropped to the ground. Without their pressure, his wound oozed blood even faster. I pressed my own hands over the sticky mess and looked at Caelus with wild eyes.

"Go to Jerome right now," I said through gritted teeth. "You're going to keep him from dying, and I will get the Seed while you do."

CHAPTER XXII

"What?" Caelus looked shocked, "We only stand a chance of getting the Seed with our full combined might."

"Either you get in there and stabilize him, or I stay and try my best. One way gets us a chance at the Seed, the other is hopeless for both of us."

Caelus glared at me. "You'll never get it," he said, his threads shivering with anger and fear. "How will you make it three steps without me?"

He wasn't saying anything that my fearful inner self wasn't already wailing, but I stood firm against him as I had against myself.

"Magic isn't everything. If you want the Seed, you'll have to take a chance on me."

"Fine," he said, his threads drooping with despair. Caelus' confidence in me was underwhelming. "I'll stabilize Jerome."

"Good," I said. "I'll get the Seed. You'll see."

Without further warning, I unceremoniously grabbed Caelus' threads. He squawked then melted against my fist. I shoved his silver cluster into Jerome's chest until it mingled with the sandy strands there and then faded. I looked around, and the mist pressed against me with no relief of glowing threads in the blank grayness. I shivered. I was alone. Alone and powerless.

Jerome's blood wasn't leaking out of his wound anymore, but Caelus' progress was slow. I wiped my hands on my jeans then stood and hugged myself for a moment, watching the injury. It felt wrong for Jerome to be splayed on the ground, hurt and cold. It felt even worse to leave him in that state.

Caelus would keep him warm, though, and he would close Jerome's wounds enough to keep him from death. It was time for me to fulfill my part of our bargain. The ceremony to hide the Seed was happening now, and I had to stop it. Just me and my wits against an order with magical powers.

I wanted a plan, but I had no information. I would have to charge forward and think on the spot. I hoped my faith in myself wasn't misguided.

I shook my head. Doubt was my enemy now. All I could do was to take every opportunity that presented itself and use it to my best advantage. That was something I was good at.

I creeped in the direction I thought the house was in. Everything was indistinct in the cloying mist, but occasional cars loomed out of the darkness and guided my feet. Before long, a porch swing emerged from the dimness and a light glimmered through the fog.

I tiptoed up the steps, every sense on high alert. I counted in my head how many adversaries I might encounter, but I had no idea who had been invited to this event. Was the entire order here? Only a select few? I could discount two of the five mothers, and Joy had said that only six of the sisters would be present, but I didn't know.

I squared my shoulders. My minimal plan was still solid, despite my lack of magic. Isolate each order member, incapacitate, move to the next. If any sisters or mothers were in the house, they could be isolated in rooms. Outside, my fog still clung to the orchard. I would use my last magical feat to my best advantage.

And I was no slouch in the physical department. I'd taken my training with the sisters seriously, and my youthful body had responded quickly. I was strong, quick, and smart.

That would have to do.

The front door, solid wood with beveled glass inserts in an old-fashioned pattern, was unlocked and mercifully silent on well-oiled hinges. I slid through the narrow gap into a spacious hallway with a carpeted staircase against one wall that led to a shadowy upstairs. Wooden floors were well-kept but rustic in appearance, and a row of boots sat beside the door. This was a farmhouse, albeit a pricey one. Lights glowed from an opening on the opposite side of the staircase, and I held my breath to sense the presence of others. I didn't have to wait long.

"This fog is so creepy." Denise's voice carried from the lit doorway. "If I didn't know better, I'd say Agatha had created it for effect."

"It would be just like her," Miranda's voice giggled. "She loves theatrics."

"Like these robes." Wanda's no-nonsense voice was unamused. "I feel like some ancient druid when I'm actually a tennis coach. I don't see why the order has to be so mysterious and backward. Just because we have magic and amulets doesn't mean we can't use them in a modern manner."

"I don't mind," Denise said. I crept closer to the doorway, debating my next move. "It makes all this feel more special. Not that it isn't already, but it gives some weight to it."

"It's only for an evening," Miranda said.

Wanda huffed. "I know. Just don't you dare take a picture."

There was nothing for it. I had an opportunity to deal with three of the sisters without others around. If I could incapacitate these woman, my path would be that much easier. But what could I do?

I had the element of surprise. I also had greater mobility, from what Wanda had said about robes. I would use that if I could. They were in a kitchen, from the glimpse of granite counter I could see from my position pressed against the wall. Kitchens had knives, fruit to throw, and water. Oil and flame? I dismissed that notion as soon as it entered my mind. I wanted to stop these women, not maim or kill them. They were some of the few friends I had, even if they were misguided.

I couldn't wait any longer. The three sisters were rustling their robes and making noises about going outside to the ceremony. It was now or never.

I raced into the kitchen and didn't hesitate. Wanda was the closest, on my side of an expansive granite island, and I kicked her in the back of the knees. The long black robe she wore impeded my aim—I had to guess where her legs were—but I made enough of an impact to send her crashing to the floor with a screech.

Denise and Miranda whirled around, their faces wearing identical masks of shock.

"Morgan?" Miranda breathed. "What are you doing here?"

I vaulted over the island, slid on my hip, and landed in front of Denise. With my elbow, I smashed her in the face. She brought her hands to her nose with a grunt of pain. Miranda backed away.

"Thea kidnapped me and tried to control my mind," I said quickly. Something in Miranda's eyes flickered. Should I have contacted the sisters before now, got some of them on my side? But how would I have known who would join me and who would snitch? "The mothers only want the power that comes with the Leaf, Seed, and Thorn, not the utopia you strive for. The mother's version of the Book of Souls says it all. I've read it."

Miranda's eyes were wide, and she bit her lip.

"Don't listen to Morgan," Denise cried. Her eyes glared at me with hatred from above the hands she clutched to her nose. "She's here to get the Seed for herself, I bet. Thea and the mothers have sworn the same oaths we have. They're our family in the order. Don't turn your back on us now."

Denise swung at me, and I dodged her fist. It was only a distraction from her other hand, which grabbed my hair and yanked my neck to the side. I cried out with pain, and Miranda gasped.

"No more fighting! We can talk about this."

I kicked Denise's knee, and she let go of my hair with a gasp then threw herself at me. Her tackle brought both of us to the floor, and my elbow smacked against the tiles with a tremendous jolt. I hoped I hadn't broken anything, but it certainly felt like a bone bruise at the very least.

A scuffle and a cry from Miranda drifted past my ears, but

I didn't have time to listen to anything other than my own battle. Denise pushed her fist into my stomach and said a few words in Latin. A clunky gold ring was on her middle finger.

The blow winded me, and I doubled over, wheezing. Worse still was the malaise in my limbs. Denise had attacked me with the magic in her ring, and I couldn't activate the Leaf to protect myself anymore. I melted into the floor like a boneless jellyfish. Denise stood over me, panting.

"I got her," she called out to the others, then her voice grew exasperated. "Miranda, what did you do to Wanda? Whose side are you on, anyway?"

"I wanted to hear Morgan out," Miranda said, her shaking voice carrying a hint of defiance. "You can't tell me you've never had doubts about the order. What did Morgan find out? I want to know."

"You made vows." Denise grated out each word with emphasis. "Doesn't that mean anything to you?"

"The truth is important, too."

I wasn't idle while the sisters debated. The amulets affected me, but was this particular one working on my body or my mind? I fervently hoped it was the latter, otherwise all my hopes were pegged on Miranda.

I gathered my mind's will, powered by my body's rage at my helpless state, and forced my limbs to move. They twitched and slid across cold tiles with glacial speed at first, but as they gained momentum and I got the hang of pushing with my mind, they sped up. When the dreadful heaviness had lessened enough for me to be confident that my legs would support me, I made my move.

From a crouched position on the floor, I swung my leg around and kicked at Denise's knee while she argued with Miranda. Her locked leg, now that she wasn't in a proper fighting stance, was not in her favor. With a popping noise that made me wince, her leg buckled, and she crashed to the floor with a yell.

I leaped up, holding onto the counter for stability, and looked around for ammunition. Something cold pressed against the leg of my pants, and I looked down in horror. Denise pressed a keychain against my calf with vindictive glee. The spot went from cold to fiery heat, and I kicked her arm away.

But the damage was done. An angry red welt appeared through the new hole in my pants, and my legs grew weak again from pain.

Denise had to be stopped. Not only was she maiming me and surviving like a cockroach, but she'd also ruined a pair of my favorite jeans. I wasn't exactly rolling in cash these days.

I grabbed the first item I saw on the counter. It was a jar of sugar, and I flung it into Denise's face. She shrieked again and clawed at the crystals irritating her eyes. Quickly, while she was distracted, I kneeled on the floor and grabbed her in a chokehold.

She flailed and wheezed, but I only squeezed tighter. Miranda gasped.

"Don't hurt her too much," she said.

I shook my head but didn't let go.

"I need her unconscious so I can tie her up. That's all. Although I confess, I'm not feeling too charitable at the moment. Thank you for not attacking me, by the way. And taking care of Wanda."

"Everything you said was only repeating what's been running through my mind in the past year," Miranda said with a queasy eye on the slowing movements of Denise. "I've wanted to see the mothers' Book of Souls for ages, but there's no way they would let a sister read it. Why is that? And the mothers are always so secretive without good reason. What are they hiding? Without knowing more, I couldn't justify attacking you."

"But knocking Wanda out was okay?"

Miranda gulped and looked down at Wanda, lying next to

a rolling pin and sporting a lump on her forehead.

"I needed answers," she said. "And I trust you."

I didn't know what I'd done to deserve Miranda's unshaking trust—I had healed her heart condition, but still—but I would take whatever allies I could get.

"I'm here to get the Seed," I said, throwing caution to the wind. "I want it out of the hands of the order. Thea's actions proved to me that she and the others are not worthy custodians of such immense power. Once I collect all three artifacts, I plan to destroy them."

Miranda's eyes grew large in her thin face.

"Destroy—you really meant—" she gulped again and nodded. "Yeah, I can see how that might be best. Especially if our utopia is a lie. Just—let's find the full Book of Souls before you do anything drastic, okay?"

"Sure," I said, unwilling to quibble. I had more important tasks than negotiating with Miranda over something that hadn't happened yet. We could discuss finer details later. Now, I had a Seed to steal.

"The others are in the orchard," she said, a no-nonsense tone coming over her voice. "There's a gazebo in the center. After an elaborate ceremony—candles, chanting, ritual words, our leader Agatha is big into that sort of thing—they plan to place the Seed in the center of the floor and cover the whole thing with concrete. The only way the Seed is getting out is with a jackhammer once we find the Thorn. I think Thea managed to convince Agatha of this plan after the Leaf was stolen. Wait, was that you?"

"Yes, keep up. Who else is here? How many people do I have to get through?"

Miranda blew air out through pursed lips and counted on her fingers. "There's Joy, Rosemary, Shu, and Filippa here, of the sisters. Thea and three mothers are also present, along with Agatha. I don't know where the other mother is."

"I've already taken care of Shu and a mother. So that leaves three sisters and three mothers, plus Agatha."

"Agatha is over ninety, and frail." Miranda waved a dismissive hand. "She might have an amulet or two, but I can't imagine she'll be a problem."

"Okay." I ran a hand over my hair and hobbled to the patio door then turned. "Can I leave you to tie up these two so they don't join the party?"

Miranda nodded.

"Of course. I wish I had an amulet to give you, but Filippa is so stingy with them. Apparently, the mothers brought a whole stash to use in the ceremony, but Filippa refuses to pass them out to the sisters. She has a soft spot for Denise, which is why she gave her a few. At least you have your powers."

"Not at the moment." I grimaced at Miranda's shocked expression. "I'll do what I can. Wish me luck."

I didn't hang around to listen to Miranda's fear and pity. I had enough of that rattling around in my own head. Doubt was now my biggest enemy. That and the group of magically charged women between me and my target.

French doors from the kitchen led to a large patio made of slate. A dim porchlight bathed the stones and highlighted covered patio furniture, tucked away for winter. A trellis jutted from the house and partially obscured a dark orchard beyond. Thick grapevines, leafless at this time of year, wove through the wooden slats and hid me from view.

Footsteps and quiet chatter alerted me to company, and I flattened myself against the back side of the trellis. My heart pounded. What could I do? Chatter meant more than one person approached, and I felt my lack of magic keenly. The burn on my leg throbbed incessantly, and my elbow sent jabs of pain whenever I moved it. I gritted my teeth and held my breath.

Shapes grew more distinct as they approached the patio light. The two figures stopped at the end of the trellis where a coiled hose hung.

"How much does she want?" Joy's voice rang out clearly. An unfamiliar voice answered her. It must have been one of the mothers.

"Just these two buckets, I think. The cement is a touch too thick."

A creak of a turning faucet preceded the splash of water in a plastic bucket. Joy wandered onto the patio, whistling. I shrank into the shadows with nowhere to hide.

Joy's whistle dried up when she saw me. With a glance at the mother behind the trellis, filling their buckets, she wandered with jerky motions closer to me.

"You shouldn't be here," she hissed at me. Fear danced in her eyes. For me? "You're persona non grata to Thea. If she catches you here, you're done for."

I took a shuddering breath. Joy wasn't going to rat me out, but neither did it seem she would help me. I opened my mouth to reply, but the sound of splashing stopped.

The mother peeked around the corner to find Joy. Instead, my anxious face greeted her, and her expression grew grim. I felt like a minor celebrity among the order.

Joy backed away, clearly unwilling to be drawn to either side. I was on my own, but at least it was single combat. I raised my hands in a fighting stance, and the mother grabbed an amulet from her pocket.

Damn. They had way too many of those.

I ducked the motion of her hand, but not quickly enough. An invisible force sliced my shoulder deeply, and I suppressed my scream of pain with difficulty.

The mother tossed her amulet—apparently, it was a single-use item—and grabbed a nearby shovel. She was the tall woman I recognized from the attacks at my condo, and I had the sense that while magic was handy for her, she preferred to get physical.

My eyes widened. It would be ironic to set myself against a magical order, only to be brained by a garden shovel. I wished suddenly for Caelus beside me. It was lonely meeting my demise without his yells of fear and encouragement.

The mother swung the shovel with a punishingly strong arc toward my head. The metal whistled through the air.

CHAPTER XXIII

I ducked then looked up. The mother's eyes gazed at something behind me with a horrified expression. I whipped around.

Joy lay sprawled on the slate, a wound on her temple inflicted by the mother's misplaced shovel blow bleeding profusely and a bruise already forming. I swallowed in fear for her life, but I had no way of helping her now. I had no healing powers, and my own life was on the line. If I survived this, I would call emergency services. If Joy were lucky, Miranda would come to investigate shortly.

I turned back to the mother. She bared her teeth at me, her younger order member already pushed from her mind. She ripped off a necklace and pointed it at me. Her mouth opened to form words that would activate the amulet.

My eyes cast about for anything to help me. On a table to my left, gardening implements were scattered over its surface. I grabbed the closest item and pointed it at the mother.

"Stop or I'll shoot," I said fiercely.

The mother froze, her eyes intent on mine. I stepped closer, trying to keep my arms steady. The gun in my hands was cold and damp, but it gave me a perverse sense of security.

She glanced at the weapon, and her shoulders relaxed. She scoffed.

"That's a water spray nozzle," she said with derision. "I'm not afraid to get wet."

She spoke the words to activate her amulet, but since I was close enough to hit her, I swung my makeshift weapon at her head.

Pain erupted over my body, shooting jabs of agony that pierced every bit of skin and dived deep into my muscles. I dropped the nozzle just before the pain died, but I couldn't stop my body's trembling with the aftermath of shock. Dimly, I noticed the mother lying on the ground. My swing of the heavy-duty metal spray nozzle must have made contact after all.

The hose was near, so I limped to it and wrapped it around the mother's wrists. It was a pitiful excuse for a binding, but it was the best I could manage with the weakness in my arms that wouldn't quit. Hopefully, it would slow her down if she woke up.

I pulled myself to the trellis and found a clear spot to peer through. The darkness of a winter's night was heavier with my unnatural fog. It had started to dissipate, but wisps of mist still floated over the grass and clung to orchard trees. Amid the branches, fire illuminated the roofline of a gazebo.

Now that the patio was quiet, a tremulous voice drifted in my direction.

"This day has been long in coming, but our time of triumph approaches…"

The voice must belong to Agatha, the leader of the order. This speech must be part of her ceremony. It had a ring of pompous announcement.

I counted quickly in my head to determine who else I had to conquer. Agatha, but Miranda assured me she was ancient and would provide little opposition. Thea remained, of course, as well as her daughter Filippa. The controlled Rosemary was likely present, and another mother must also lurk. Was that it?

I scoffed at my overconfidence. Five magic users was quite enough to be going on with. Too much of my success so far had been down to luck, although I could credit quick thinking as well. Miranda and Joy's goodwill toward me hadn't hurt, either.

I clutched the trellis and willed my body to pull itself together. The wound on my shoulder stung and wept a slow trickle of blood that soaked into my coat, my burned leg ached and throbbed, and my body trembled from the aftershock of the mother's last amulet.

I couldn't attack all five order members, not even if I were whole and unharmed. I didn't have any advantage except my wits. It was time to put my brain to work.

I needed to pick the sisters and mothers off one by one. Single combat was the only way I had a hope of prevailing. Even better was the element of surprise. So far, no one at the ceremony was aware that half of their group was incapacitated at the house. They would figure it out soon—they were waiting for Joy and the mother to return with buckets of water—but I had a small slice of opportunity that I didn't intend on squandering. I glanced around the patio, tallied up my assets, then assembled my trap.

"Help!" I called out a few minutes later in a passable version of Joy's voice. "We could use a hand. These buckets are heavy!"

I peered through the trellis, my heart pounding. A murmur of exasperated voices spoke together, then a figure emerged through the mists. It was a dark-haired mother I didn't know, but in the dim light filtering from the house's lit windows, her resemblance to Shu was uncanny. This must be Shu's own mother. Her face was twisted with annoyance, and she stomped toward the trellis with her robe swishing around her legs.

I waited silently in my place. My shoulder throbbed, but I held myself steady. Timing was everything with this maneuver. The mother kicked a hose aside then marched directly into my trap.

I flung the tarp in a wide arc and covered the mother with it as soon as she rounded the corner. The crinkly blue plastic muffled her curses, but I didn't wait for her to struggle out of her confines. I grabbed my shovel and raised it over my head.

My body froze solid. I couldn't move a single muscle. My horrified eyes were fixed on the flailing tarp, then my view changed. The tarp rushed toward me as I fell forward. An accompanying jolt against the mother underneath confirmed my suspicions.

The mother had used an amulet against me through the tarp. I admired her quick-thinking. However, my frozen body's momentum had continued even though everything else had stopped, and I'd landed directly on the struggling woman.

I rolled off the tarp and leap to my feet. The blow from my body must have broken the mother's concentration. I scrambled for the shovel once more.

"She's here!" the mother bellowed as she extricated herself from the tarp. "Morgan is here!"

I swung my shovel with narrowed eyes. The heavy metal end contacted the back of the mother's head. She dropped to the ground, stunned.

It was too late to silence her. Shouts from the orchard alerted me to danger. Staying on this patio wouldn't do me any favors, and I didn't want to get backed against a wall. Speed and confusion would be my friends from this point on.

I burst into a sprint into the darkness of the orchard. Figures ran toward the patio, but one shouted when she saw me and turned to follow. I put my head down and ran faster through the rows of leafless trees, trying desperately to ignore the weakness in my limbs and pain from my injuries.

A thicker patch of mist loomed ahead, and I dived in gratefully. Pounding footsteps followed then stopped.

"Morgan," Filippa's voice said. "I know you're here. Come out and we'll talk. *Moderor*."

It was clear from her tone that she had no intention of talking. Before I could formulate a plan to take advantage of her confusion in the fog, something took hold of my mind.

It was a familiar feeling of compliance and peace, and I smiled with dreamy unconcern. My feet took two steps in Filippa's direction.

Then I stopped. Something was wrong. The sensation was different than the last time—I was aware enough to know that there had been another time I'd felt like this—and my mind weaseled through the differences. My mind was not my own, and through growing outrage that I used to fuel my struggle for release, I recognized the weakness behind the compulsion. Thea's control through her amulet had been smooth and almost absolute. Filippa's was unpracticed and rough.

I flung the compulsion off and threw myself forward. Filippa's form materialized in the mist. I tackled her to the ground. Her pretty mouth formed an 'o' of surprise, but she quickly flipped me over and straddled me. Her arm pressed against my throat. I scrabbled at Filippa's coin in her hand, wrenched it away, and pointed it at her.

"*Moderor*," I croaked.

Her expression of anger melted into calm. She sat up.

"Get off me," I said. "Then run west for an hour."

Filippa nodded and swung her legs off me then stood. I pushed to my feet and watched her lope gracefully through the trees and into the darkness. I had no idea how long her amulet's influence would last, but hopefully the midnight jog would keep her out of my hair for long enough.

"Filippa?" Rosemary's voice called out. "Do you see her?"

I dropped Filippa's compliance coin at the sound of Rosemary's voice. It disappeared into the long grass, and I bent to search for it.

"Filippa?"

Rosemary's voice was close. Too close. I gave up my hunt for the amulet and sprinted to my left.

"Morgan, wait!"

Rosemary must have seen me once I left my bank of fog. I ran faster, nearly tripping over a rake in my haste. The torches at the gazebo loomed ahead, but my goal was the bedrock on the far side. There were plenty of nooks and crannies to provide hiding places and traps.

"Wait! It doesn't have to be like this," Rosemary cried. "Just stop. I'm your friend. I only want to talk, I swear!"

I slowed with only a few trees between me and the gazebo.

Rosemary certainly sounded in control of herself. But she'd been coherent at her house, too. Thea's compliance spell was far more nuanced and longer lasting than the control amulet Starr had used last month.

"Join us," Rosemary pleaded when she emerged from the thick mist. "I don't want to see you get hurt. And think of the benefits if you join us. Remember the power that the mothers will get? Maybe you could train to become a mother, too. You and I, we're destined for great things. Imagine what we could do with that power."

I stared at Rosemary's earnest face. My mind wandered to the power that the Book of Souls described. My lack of magic tonight was more than hampering. My body was on fire with its injuries, and I still didn't see how I could defeat the rest of the order, no matter how hard I thought of a plan. Maybe my wits weren't enough to prevail. Without magic, what was I?

My shoulders straightened. I refused to use magic as a crutch. It was a useful tool when I could get it, but no more than that. I was Morgan Leigh Feynman, and no one could take that away from me.

"Keep your power and your cult," I called to Rosemary. "You'll snap out of it when Thea reminds you of how little she values you."

I turned, but my pause had cost me. Thea approached from the direction of the gazebo, her dark bob without a hair out of place, and her robe immaculately pressed. I would have laughed at her composure if the situation hadn't been so dire.

I gathered myself into a sprint. I must have been fast enough to dodge the thread tendrils of whatever amulet Thea was pointing at me, because nothing impeded my escape. Footfalls pounded on the sodden grass behind me, and Rosemary's panting breath grew closer. I put on a desperate burst of speed, too aware of my failing body. If I could make it to bedrock, I had a few more options.

The rock loomed ahead, impassive and forbidding. I

reached its almost sheer face and crawled up it like a lame spider. With every pull upward, my sliced shoulder and burned leg screamed at me.

I threw myself over the rounded top of the rock and rolled out of the line of fire. I didn't know what sort of amulets Rosemary had on her—not many, from what Miranda had said—but I didn't want to take the risk. She was right behind me, and I needed to use this rock as an opportunity to waylay her.

I surveyed the top of the bedrock. It was jagged shale, with pointed edges and crevasses that yawned with inky depth. Dim light from the house hardly made a dent in the misty darkness, but reflected lights of the nearby city cast a faint orange glow over the surrounds. It was enough to formulate my plan. I only hoped I was nimble enough in my injured state to pull it off.

Rosemary pulled herself over the top of the rock. I leaned over with my hands on my knees, pretending to be winded by the climb. When I saw her, I took off across the rock. She pulled herself to her feet and leaped after me.

A deep crack was half-hidden in the gloom. I saw it, but only because I had scouted the area before Rosemary appeared. In the dark, on the run, it was almost impossible to see.

To further put Rosemary off the scent, I pushed off hard with my left foot, pretended to take a midair step with my right, then landed again with my left. To Rosemary's eyes, I hoped it looked like I took a step in the darkness.

A shrill cry whipped my head around. Rosemary lay half in the crack, her eyes squeezed tightly with pain. My heart squeezed for her anguish, but I nodded in grim satisfaction. Only Thea and Agatha to go. I would get that Seed, with or without magic.

"I'm sorry, Rosemary," I said. "You'll understand once you stop drinking the Kool-Aid."

I slid and scrabbled down the side of the rock nearest the house. Mist still drifted in eerie streamers through the deserted orchard. I frowned. Where was Thea?

I slowed as figures surrounded me in the darkness. I squinted. Was that Filippa?

Wait. All the women striding closer and closer to me looked like Filippa. Why was she here? I'd sent her running west. Had my compulsion not stuck?

More importantly, why were there dozens of her?

Low laughter filled my ears from every angle. I spun around. Filippas approached from behind me as well. I froze and forced my beleaguered mind to concoct a plan.

"You think you're so clever," she sneered. "But you have nothing on the order. You can't even imagine the strength of our amulets. When we gain the powers promised to us by the Tree of Life, you will be first on the list of practice targets."

The Filippas paced forward. I had only seconds before the circle closed and they all attacked. What could I do?

My eyes narrowed. Filippa hadn't suddenly cloned herself. It was a mind game. I didn't need to fight off dozens of my foe. I simply needed to determine which one was the real Filippa.

When she finished her little speech, I bent to the ground and grabbed two handfuls of mud, dead leaves, and branches. With my arms flailing in a circle, I released my cargo.

Mud and detritus flew in all directions. The muck sailed through every Filippa except one. They all shrieked with disgust, but only one wiped off mud when they all raised their hands to wipe their cheeks. I leaped forward and swept my leg toward the real Filippa's ankles.

With a yelp, Filippa flipped onto her back, her feet flying above her head. I pressed my advantage and jumped on the other woman. I had no magic, no amulets, and little strength left. My best hope was to wrest Filippa's amulets from her and hope I could overpower her in hand-to-hand combat.

But Filippa had been training her whole life, and my month of self-defense practice was no match for her quick reflexes. Before I could make contact, she rolled away and rose to her feet.

I switched tactics and ran into the mists.

"Come back, you coward!" Filippa screamed. Her feet pounded behind me on the grass. "You're not getting the Seed!"

Trees loomed out of the mist in rows on either side, barren of leaves and spooky in the darkness. An abandoned wheelbarrow next to a stepladder caught my eye, and I whirled around to grab it. Someone must have been doing some early pruning, for the wheelbarrow was filled with cut twigs and a pair of secateurs.

I heaved the wheelbarrow onto its single wheel and raced back the way I'd come. Three steps brought me to Filippa who charged toward me with the determination of a rampaging rhinoceros.

CLANG.

The barrow was wrenched from my grasp, but it had done the trick. Filippa lay sprawled on the grass with her face creased with pain and her hands clutched to her thighs. That would leave a bruise tomorrow.

I turned in the direction of the gazebo—a glimmer of firelight peeked through the mist now and again—but Filippa hissed behind me.

I turned my head while I ran. She hobbled after me, murder in her eyes. She was tenacious to a fault. I wish I'd inspired this sort of devotion while leading my businesses as March Feynman. I would have ruled the world.

A cut twig whipped against my burned leg, and I screamed from the pain. I stumbled and nearly fell on the ground. Wetness dripped down my arm from the slice on my shoulder. What was I doing? Even if I reached the gazebo, I was in no condition to fight anyone for the Seed.

The stepladder appeared at my side, and I climbed up the rungs. A half-baked notion of jumping onto Filippa from above flashed through my mind. Maybe the advantage of height would outweigh the ridiculousness of my idea.

I made it three rungs up before Filippa was on me. I threw myself at her, and her surprise at my insanity worked to my advantage. We tumbled to the ground. A gasp ripped out of me as the thud of impact ripped at my shoulder wound.

Filippa punched my gut, and I doubled over, wheezing. She followed up with a knee to my side, then she flipped around until she straddled me from above. Her arm pressed against my throat. I gasped for breath like a landed fish. She bared her teeth in triumph.

"Give up, Morgan," she hissed. "We've been searching for artifacts for seventy years. You're not going to stop us now."

An expression of concern rippled across her face. My lungs heaved without the relief of sweet oxygen. A terrible gurgling noise came from Filippa's abdomen, and horror filled her eyes.

Without another word, she leaped up and ran toward the house. I lay on my back, coughing with the influx of air. When I stopped heaving for breath, I chuckled weakly. I might not have magic, but I had smarts. My longshot cupcake plan had paid dividends.

I pushed my throbbing body to my feet and stood there, wobbling, while I took stock. My leg barely held me, my shoulder was on fire, and my throat felt like it was in the wrong shape.

But I didn't have time to ponder. Who knew what Agatha would do with the Seed if under duress? I needed to take it off her hands before she did something drastic. With no impediments in sight, I hobbled quietly toward the flickering glow of the torches.

The mists parted. Tiki torches surrounded an octagonal gazebo, and white pillar candles encircled a hole in the wooden floor. Before the gazebo, wrapped in a white robe that dwarfed her frail form, stood Agatha. Snowy white hair covered her scalp in a smooth cap. Her hooded eyes scanned the orchard with intensity. Her shoulders were stooped, but she held herself proudly with the help of a metal cane. When she saw me approach, she stamped her cane on the soggy dirt. Someone had recently prepared the area in front of the gazebo for reseeding the lawn, and bare dirt was sprinkled with copious amounts of grass seed.

"Intruder," she screamed hoarsely. "You must be punished for interrupting our great work."

She fumbled at her neck, but I was too quick for her. Before she had fully pulled out a necklace from her robe, I snatched the chain and ripped it off her neck. The flimsy chain snapped, and I tossed it to the ground. Without the right word, it was useless to me.

Agatha's face wrinkled in outrage. I snatched a small box from her claw-like hands and stepped back.

"Is this it?" I asked. "The Seed we're all fussing over?"

I glanced at the box in my hands. It was no larger than my palm and made entirely of gold. Its rounded corners fit snuggly in my fingers. In the torchlight, it gleamed warm and orange.

"Take your foul hands off it, desecrator," the old woman gasped. She clutched her cane, as if the effort of upbraiding me was too much for her. I raised an eyebrow.

"Finders, keepers."

I cracked open the lid. The velvet-lined box was empty except for a slender white seed, smaller than a grain of rice.

"Give the Seed to Agatha," Thea's voice said behind me. "Or your friend will suffer."

CHAPTER XXIV

My heart sank, and I whirled around. Thea stood, her hair still miraculously neat, holding a disheveled Miranda by the arm. Miranda gazed at me calmly despite the large kitchen knife at her throat. Thea looked pleased with herself. The mother who must be related to Shu that I'd dispatched at the patio limped behind her, glaring at me with dark eyes. Filippa looked wan and clutched her stomach as if it pained her, but she stood behind Thea, ready for action.

"You used a compliance amulet on her," I whispered. "Why the knife?"

Thea shrugged.

"It would be a waste of a competent sister, but it's more important to the cause to have the Seed. While we're at it, hand over the Leaf. Let's tidy up this debacle. You're interfering in things you can't possibly understand, girl."

I barked a short laugh. Thea had no idea.

"I can't let you get the Seed, *lady*," I said with emphasis. "You would be the worst recipient of extra powers of anyone I know. Look what you do to your students and everyone around you. Controlling their very thoughts? That crosses the line. Your son killed himself, and I sympathize. Taking away free will to prevent the same thing happening to another isn't the answer."

Thea's face was livid. She gripped Miranda's arm with fingers that dug into the younger woman's flesh, but Miranda maintained her calm.

"You know nothing," Thea exploded. "The pain of losing a child? You would never understand unless it happened to you. If I could have helped him by controlling him, I would have done it in a heartbeat. If the students knew what I was doing for them, they would thank me on bended knee once they were old enough to understand."

"I doubt it. No one likes to be controlled. You may think I'm young, but I have enough experience to know that." I glanced at Agatha, who breathed heavily and clutched her cane. Thea continued to glare at me with murder in her eyes. I decided to steer the conversation away from her dead son. No good would come of poking her wounds. "This utopia the sisters talk about, the one that is supposed to come about when the three artifacts join. You don't care about it, do you? All you want is the power that comes with it. You can create utopia in your own fashion, with everyone under your thumb."

Thea's face twisted. She pushed Miranda aside, whipped out her own amulet coin, and whispered a word.

"You can shake off the compliance spell eventually," she said through the hypnotic calm of compulsion that draped over me like a fluffy blanket. "But by then, the Seed will be mine. Hand it over."

Thea spoke good sense. What did I want with a tiny seed, anyway? I could go to the plant nursery tomorrow and buy myself a whole packet of similar seeds. That was a wonderful idea. I held the box out with a smile, and Thea lunged forward.

Her sudden movement triggered my own forceful will to the surface. In a flash, I recalled everything that had led to this point, and exactly why I didn't want to give Thea the box. I snatched it back and leaped to the side. Thea howled with rage, the primal sound bizarre from her normally pristine self.

I was cornered and outnumbered. With my wounds, and the order's magic, I had no chance of escaping with the Seed. Only one option remained. With fumbling fingers, I opened the box.

"I know I can't get away with the Seed. But I can stop you from getting it."

I tipped the box upside down. With a fluttering fall, the Seed drifted to the ground and landed in the middle of the freshly planted lawn. For good measure, I scuffed my foot over the spot to mix the Seed among the grass seeds.

"No!" Thea wailed. She dropped her amulet, fell to her

knees, and began scrabbling at the dirt. Agatha toppled sideways in a faint, and Filippa rushed for her before she hit the ground. Her own face was frozen in horror. The other mother joined Thea in her desperate search. Thea's face was flecked with mud and her eyes were crazed.

I scooped up Thea's coin in a smooth motion and quietly limped away. No one stopped me. No one noticed me. I'd just dumped their life's work in the ground, and the chances of them finding it again were slim. Even if they scooped up the dirt in a box, how would they discover the Seed among so many others? The Book of Souls was clear about the need for purity—if the Seed wasn't isolated and planted in the Leaf's mulch directly, it wouldn't grow. They should have stopped me—I still knew where the Leaf was, after all—but no one had attention to spare.

Once I was out of sight, I broke into a stumbling jog. I didn't want anyone to come to their senses and chase after me. My body was done, and all I wanted to do was to rejoin Caelus and Jerome.

From out of the darkness, a figure hurled itself at me. I cried out and hit the cold ground with a thud that snapped my teeth together painfully. Thea's voice hissed in my ear as her hands groped for my pockets.

"Give me the Leaf," she panted, her eyes crazed and her once-immaculate hair disheveled. "I won't allow you to ruin decades of planning, the years I've devoted to the cause. You will give me the Leaf."

I thrashed my knees and arms in a wild attempt to shift Thea off me. I was injured and she was fresh, but my knee gouged her stomach in a lucky hit. She wheezed and jolted backward. I scrabbled away and stood with shaking legs.

"Everything I've seen today only cements my resolve to keep the artifacts out of your hands. Stay away from me, or I will ruin more than your plans. I have too much ammunition against you—kidnapping, for one—and a keen understanding of the legal system. If you threaten me again, it will be the last free move you make."

With those parting words, I left Thea kneeling in the mud, hatred etched on her face. She didn't attempt to follow me. I hoped she would take my words to heart, but the devotion of a lifetime of searching for artifacts wouldn't fade easily. I hadn't seen the last of Thea Diamanto, but if I could escape tonight to live another day, I would be content.

I quickened my pace into a stumbling run to leave the accursed orchard behind. My heart squeezed when I recalled Jerome's fatal wound. Had Caelus managed to heal him? I didn't know how it was possible, but this new body had been at death's door, and yet here I was. I jogged faster, anxious to return.

A quiet voice calling my name interrupted my gloomy thoughts. My heart leaped at the familiar sound.

"Jerome!" I skidded to a halt in the shadow of a copper beech and grabbed his hand. It was too cool for my liking. "You're alive and talking."

Light was scarce, but his teeth glinted in a brief smile.

"So far," he wheezed. "I'm not out of the woods yet."

Sandy threads blossomed around Jerome, and I dropped his hand with a start.

"I can't do any more than that," Caelus' familiar voice said in my ear. "He was at death's door, far worse than our body was. He'll need more healing than I can provide."

"Can I do it?"

I reached toward the knots on Jerome's chest, but Caelus shook his head.

"If I can't, you certainly can't." When I gave him a look, he shrugged. "That's not me being arrogant. It's just the truth."

"It's okay," Jerome said. He found my hand in the dark and patted it. "If it's my time, so be it."

"Don't be ridiculous," I spat. My body's anger was rising rapidly, and I didn't check it. "You are not dying today. I forbid it. Caelus, will he survive on his own for a few minutes?”

“Yes. But what if the order comes out?” He looked at me with dawning excitement. “Wait, your mission. You’re still alive, too. Did you get the Seed?”

“No.” I shook my head with impatience at Caelus’ dejection and burgeoning anger. “Come on, we’re not done yet. Jerome, I’ll be right back. Just give me your keys. Everything will be fine, do you hear me?”

“Yes, ma’am,” he murmured, his eyes half-closed. He dug around in his pocket with languid movements until a jingling emerged. I grabbed them, still anxious that his hands were icy, then hastily threw some air threads over Jerome and tweaked them until they resembled the gravel Jerome lay on. It wasn’t a great disguise, but it would do in this light. As long as no one tripped over him, he would remain undetected.

With a worried glance at the house, I crept down the driveway. Voices shouted within, but no one looked out the windows. Once I reached the main road, I bullied my body into action. It picked up pace with groans of protest.

“Can you run and fix your shoulder at the same time?” Caelus asked. “I can feel the hurt from here. Bodies are so inconvenient.”

“I can try,” I puffed. My fingers crawled up my sweater and massaged the knots above my cut. Caelus stared at me for a moment.

“What’s the plan?” he asked once it was clear I wasn’t going to speak.

“We get the car, bundle Jerome into it, and drive a safe distance away. I heal myself more, then when the orchard has calmed down, we’ll sneak back and get the Seed.”

“How do you even know where it is?” Caelus’ voice dripped with skepticism. “Your first attempt failed, after all. Excuse me if I don’t bubble over with confidence.”

“I dropped it in the dirt,” I said. At Caelus’ horrified

expression, I snorted. "Come on, I thought you of all people would understand. The order has no idea which speck of seed the real one is. But with your thread-vision, it will be obvious to us."

Caelus' stormy face cleared. He chuckled.

"Good thinking. I guess I keep you around for a reason."

"I keep you around, you mean."

We grinned at each other, then I turned my attention to my feet. The distance to the truck stretched like a funhouse mirror, but eventually my tired eyes spotted Jerome's truck behind a willow. I picked up the pace, despite my body screaming at me to stop.

I threw open the driver's door, slid inside, and started the engine. I had to adjust the seat so my feet could reach the pedals. Once driving was a possibility, I made a tight U-turn and roared back to the farmhouse.

No one was outside yet, but I didn't want to take chances that someone would notice a strange vehicle in the driveway. I parked out of sight on the road then ran to where I'd left Jerome. With a sweep of my hand, I removed the strands covering him.

His breathing was shallow and his forehead clammy when I touched it. My chest tightened.

"Come on," I whispered. My hands braced themselves around his torso. "Let's get you to the car."

Jerome didn't speak, but he used my support to push painfully to his feet. It took all my strength to help him upright. I slung his arm over my shoulder, and we hobbled down the driveway.

"Keep an eye on the house," I whispered to Caelus. There was no way I could crane my neck over Jerome's large shoulder, and all my focus was on keeping my feet under me with my burden.

"On it," he said in a louder voice since only I could hear him. Jerome twitched at the sound—Caelus must have allowed him to hear—but kept walking. Caelus peered with his thready eyes. "No sign yet."

"You let Jerome hear you?" I asked in surprise.

Caelus shrugged. "He felt like one of the team. I figured it was time to tell him about me."

I snuck a glance at Jerome in the darkness. His eyes flashed toward me.

"I'll be on your team any day," he said hoarsely. His mouth quirked upward. "But Caelus will take some getting used to."

It took what felt like an hour to get to the truck, although it couldn't have been more than two minutes. Finally, I eased Jerome into the passenger's side and pushed the seat back as far as it would go. Jerome's face was pinched with pain.

I hopped into the driver's seat and tore off to our previous parking spot. Once the engine stopped, I turned to my patient.

"I'll try to make you comfortable until we get the Seed," I said.

My hand stroked his in reassurance—his or mine, I didn't know—and his eyes opened a crack.

"I trust you," he said, then his eyes closed.

My chest tightened again. I didn't know what I'd done to deserve his trust, but I appreciated it all the same.

"Come on," I said softly to Caelus. "Help me out here."

With Caelus' direction, I smoothed the knots over Jerome's torso that were responsible for pain. Slowly, the creases on his face relaxed and his breathing deepened into sleep. I sat back, wishing I could join him in rest. My own body screamed at me to stop.

"How long do we have to wait to get the Seed?" Caelus asked. "We can't fully heal Jerome. I don't know if it's the amulet he was attacked with, or if his wounds are too great, but my skills aren't enough. The Seed is his only chance. Plus, I really need it."

"I know." I shot him a half-hearted smile. "Dormancy is the worst. I want to give the order time to calm down and hopefully leave the orchard alone. Let me stop the pain in my own injuries, then we'll sneak back."

Moving out of the car was the last thing I felt like doing, but too much rode on getting the Seed. Jerome's pale face in the streetlight haunted me, and Caelus' uncharacteristic gloominess reminded me of the stakes. I set my fingers to work.

When I was done, I felt a thousand times better, although the burn was still raw and my slice an angry red welt. It would do for now.

"What's in your pocket?" Caelus asked suddenly. "Do you have an amulet?"

Threads spilled from the opening. I drew out a coin.

"It's Thea's compliance amulet. I forgot I stole that."

"Nicely done." Caelus nodded with satisfaction. "Now you can destroy it."

"You love that word, don't you?" I held the coin in front of me. "It could be useful, you know."

I threw a sideways glance at Caelus, who looked as horrified as I'd expected. I burst into laughter which I stifled with my hand.

"Of course I'm not going to use it. Honestly. But that look was priceless." I gave one last snicker. "So, how do we destroy an amulet?"

"Allow me," Caelus said with a huffy sniff.

He melted into my arm, and his silver threads snaked over the necklace. After a minute of writhing around, the multicolored threads faded into blackness. Caelus reemerged, looking pleased with himself.

"And that's done," he said. "Now, can we please get the Seed? I really don't want to take over your body to force the issue."

I chuckled at Caelus' empty threat.

"As if you could. Come on, let's get this done."

The familiar trek back to the farmhouse was getting

tiresome, and I hoped this would be the last trip. Enough time had passed that only two cars were in the driveway, and the lights were off in the house. I heaved a sigh of relief and carefully walked around the side of the house. I had to climb over a section of bedrock to reach the orchard out of sight of the blank windows, but before long, I stood in front of the dark gazebo.

The world looked so different from before. The mist had finally cleared, but the biggest difference was my own vision. Threads wriggled and writhed over everything, and although they didn't cast light on their surroundings, they themselves glowed softly and surrounded the objects they were associated with.

A tarp lay on the ground before the gazebo, weighed down with rocks at each corner.

"See, I told you," I whispered. "They marked the spot so they could look when it's light out. The Seed is almost impossible to see in the dark, especially among the freshly planted lawn. Grass seeds are everywhere. My best guess is that they'll collect every seed from the area and examine each one for differences."

I folded back the tarp and smiled. Caelus squirmed next to me.

"There it is," he said loudly. "It's an artifact for sure. Pick it up, come on!"

I bent and brushed away dirt until the epicenter of rainbow threads emerged. Gently, I plucked the tiny white Seed out of the soil and held it up.

"How do we activate it, I wonder?" I said quietly.

"The same way you did the Leaf, I bet. Intention is everything. Come on, let's get out of here before the order comes back."

It was good advice that I was happy to heed. I slid the beaver keychain from my pocket, tucked the Seed next to the Leaf, then wrapped protective air threads around the whole package. Then I stole away into the night and back to Jerome.

He was still asleep when I arrived, huffing, at the car. I closed the door behind me as quietly as I could then gazed at his face for a long moment, resisting the urge to run my fingers over his cheek and along his jawline.

Caelus rolled his eyes at me.

"For pity's sake. Yes, you like him. Get on with the healing."

Beads of sweat dripped down Jerome's forehead, and his breathing was shallow again. I swallowed.

"He's getting worse." I pulled the keychain out and stared at it. "Should I test it on myself first? I don't want to hurt Jerome by accident."

"I guess so." Caelus looked worried. "Be careful, though."

Caelus' worry cemented my decision. I wasn't testing an unknown magical procedure on Jerome without learning about it first. I closed my eyes and poured angry intention into it, just as I'd done when I first tried out the Leaf.

Resistance met my efforts. My eyes popped open, and I stared at Caelus in fear.

"It didn't work. What do I do?"

"Try a different emotion," he suggested, although his voice was tight with anxiety. "Maybe it doesn't respond to anger. It has healing properties, after all, not protection ones."

I drew in a shuddering breath and closed my eyes again. What might a healing artifact respond to? I took another deep breath and released my fear and anger. It wasn't an easy task. Slowly, calm loosened my shoulders. Healing came from a place of hope, of light, of life.

I thought about Jerome's rare dazzling smile, and my stomach flopped. I didn't try to suppress the feeling this time. Instead, I used it to probe my intention into the Seed and connect it with myself.

Threads exploded from the keychain and latched onto every part of my body. My head rocked backward with shock. My skin tingled, then burned, then splintered into shards of agony. My throat was too tight to scream.

Then, it was over. I hung my head, panting with relief now that the pain was gone. Caelus lay draped over the dashboard, looking as winded as I felt.

"That was intense," he said finally. "But did it work?"

I glanced at my leg, now covered with fresh pink skin, and my shoulder sporting more of the same. I sighed happily.

"It sure did." I glanced at Jerome. "Do you think I should warn him first?"

"What good would that do?" Caelus sounded genuinely perplexed. "Then he'll fret about it. No, get it done, and he'll thank you later."

I shook my head at Caelus' elemental viewpoint then glanced at Jerome again. My heart lurched. His limbs were twitching, and the whites of his eyes were showing.

"Damn it." I pressed my hands against his shoulders in a vain attempt to calm the seizure. "Hold on, Jerome."

I closed my eyes and reached delicately into the Seed. I wanted to pull its power out with more finesse that I'd done on myself to spare Jerome the agony of healing.

"You don't have time for that," Caelus said in my ear. "We're losing him. Give him the full blast."

I grimaced, but Caelus was right. If I wanted him to survive, I had to give him some tough love. I took a deep breath and activated the Seed fully.

CHAPTER XXV

Power filled my body and poured out of my arms into Jerome. I hadn't noticed the sheer magnitude of the power when I'd healed myself, but now that I had no pain to distract me, I marveled at the energy contained in such a tiny Seed.

But I wasn't in control of it, not really. The Seed was using me as a conduit to work. The power in the artifact scared me, and it was the first time I'd felt that there should be a limit to the power a human could wield. I didn't know if that were a natural reaction to feeling the Seed's energy, or whether my triumph without magic this evening had changed me, but I no longer desired to add artifacts to my arsenal of tricks. I had Caelus for now, and that was enough power to be getting on with.

Jerome bucked under my hands and I pressed down harder. His knees bashed against the glove compartment, and I grimly hoped that the Seed would take care of new bruises caused by its healing.

It took far too long to my anxious mind, but Jerome finally quieted, and the Seed withdrew its tendrils until the keychain was calm once more. Jerome's eyelids fluttered open, and he focused on my face with a confused expression.

"Morgan?" he murmured.

"How do you feel?" I asked, my voice tremulous with emotion. He patted his chest with bemusement.

"Fine. Better than fine. What happened?"

I opened my mouth, but words didn't come forth. I hovered over him, my mind a racing turmoil of feelings—relief, pain, desire, exhilaration—and I had no way of expressing them verbally.

So, I kissed him.

My head dipped down with swift decision, and I pressed my lips to his. He didn't react at first, maybe surprised by my action, then he responded eagerly. His arms wrapped around me and crushed me tightly to his chest. I touched his healed chest, his face, ran my fingers through his hair with desperate relief. I didn't know how much of my reaction was my body's attraction or my mind's desires, and I found that I didn't care. This body was mine now, and it was time to make body and mind act with one accord. I was not two separate entities in one form. I was Morgan, whole and new.

Long before I was ready to stop, Jerome broke away from my lips and loosened his grip on me.

"I really don't want to stop," he said breathlessly. "But I'm weirded out by your spirit companion. I can't see him. Is he watching us right now?"

"I don't care what you humans are getting up to," Caelus said from his perch on the dashboard. Jerome stiffened, so I knew he could hear Caelus. "It holds no interest to me as an elemental. Well, I do feel whatever Morgan feels, so there's that. Is that strange?" He looked thoughtful. "Maybe you humans think it is. Anyway, it was high time Morgan took the plunge. She's been waffling about kissing you for ages."

I burst into laughter at Jerome's expression of distaste and slid back to the driver's seat. I was old enough to not be embarrassed by Caelus' impertinent remarks, but Jerome clearly felt that three was a crowd. He pulled his seatback up, still looking disconcerted. I placed my hand on his thigh, enjoying the firmness of his muscle and the swoop of my stomach when I touched him.

"We'll figure something out," I said. "Make sure Caelus is tucked away somewhere when we want privacy."

His eyes looked at me with smoldering intensity at my words.

"That sounds like a promise."

I rubbed my hand on his thigh slowly before drawing away. "Maybe it is."

I turned the car on and pulled onto the road. Jerome leaned

back against his headrest.

"I feel like there's a lot that you could tell me about Caelus and your powers," he said eventually. "When you're ready."

"I'd like that," I said softly. "Maybe you could help me find a safe place for the artifacts. I don't want to use them, but I don't want to lose them, either."

Jerome's eyes burned a hole in the side of my head, but I kept my eyes on the road. His threads reached out to me, and I suppressed a smile. My admission that I didn't want the powers of the artifacts had struck a chord in Jerome, and that made the inevitable loss of them even more worthwhile.

"Then you won't be able to use the artifacts," Caelus said with a sigh. "Oh, well, I guess we're going to destroy them anyway. And you managed okay without powers tonight, somehow. It was probably all luck. If I'd been with you, we could have got the Seed in half the time."

I dropped Jerome at his shabby apartment as the sky was lightening. It was too late for him to sleep—a baker rose early for work—but his eyes were bright and alert. I felt similar after my bout with the Seed, as if I could run for days.

The feeling wore off by mid-morning, and I collapsed in bed and slept until my phone's alarm sang in a disgustingly chipper tune. My bleary eyes cracked open.

"It's time for your volunteering, I think," Caelus's voice said from my other side.

I groaned.

"You could always tell them you're not coming," he said. "It's not like they give you money, or that artifacts are stored there. It's a waste of time, really."

"You might understand if you were human." I yawned and crawled out of bed toward the bathroom. "The women's center is important to me. And you can't bellyache about artifacts today, not after we got the Seed last night. Surely, that will satisfy you for a few days. Then we'll go on our next trip soon to find another artifact, just like I promised."

"What about the money?"

This was too much thinking for my bleary head, but I tried to pull myself together for Caelus' sake.

"I'll get a reference from Amir at the grocery tomorrow and ask him for job ideas in the neighborhood to earn a little cash until I can ramp up my consulting business." I nodded resolutely.

Caelus harumphed but melted into my arm without further comment. I dressed and performed my toiletries in record time. When my phone said three o'clock, I entered the women's center as promised.

"Good, Morgan, you're here," Greta said. She looked frazzled, and there were women in every seat waiting for her help. "Can you take Lia here to the back and find her some spare clothes? We're swamped."

A girl with bright pink hair, brown roots emerging at her scalp, shuffled over to me. She shivered, and rightly so, as she had no coat over her ripped long-sleeved shirt and torn jeans. She looked sullen, but her threads were tight with fear.

"Hi, Lia," I said gently. "We have lots of coats to choose from. I don't know how fashionable they are, but they're warm."

I led her into the back storage room. While she pawed through the coats, I considered my options. She was clearly running from something—a bad family situation, an abusive boyfriend, maybe even a life on the street—and it would be simple to learn her details and follow up with my magical abilities. Now that I could attach magic to clothing, I could tailor a solution to suit the girl's situation.

But was magic the best answer? Magical help might smooth things over for the short-term, but maybe it was a Band-Aid for a greater hurt. How could I help Lia heal on her own?

"Do you want to talk about it?" I said gently. "We've all been through something here. Whatever happened, I understand."

Lia's shoulders stiffened and her threads froze. Then like the rapid melting of an ice cube in the sun, her strands flowed freely, and she turned with tears in her eyes. She threw herself at me and buried her sobbing face in my neck.

I gathered her in my arms and held her while she cried. This wasn't Caelus's abilities, but there was a certain magic in being present for someone. I didn't need the power of the wind to make a difference.

After Greta and I took care of Lia and the other women at the center, I walked home, tired but satisfied. Maybe I was starting to figure out Morgan's place in the world. Finding the right balance of power was tricky, and I was a work in progress. Still, I was making strides.

Rosemary called me as I exited the elevator. According to my phone, which I hadn't checked all afternoon, it wasn't the first time today. I juggled keys and phone at my door and finally answered, my shoulder clutching the device.

"Morgan." Rosemary's voice was anguished. "I tried to call earlier but I couldn't get you. I'm sorry for last night. Not that I was in control, but still. I was trying to hurt you!"

Her voice caught on a sob, and I sighed. My key slid into the lock, and I pushed my door open.

"Thea had her claws in you. I understand, you weren't in control. Don't beat yourself up about it. All's well that ends well."

"But the Seed," she said in a hushed tone, her voice still thick with unshed tears. "The Seed is gone. What will we do? How can we bring about the promised utopia?"

I pushed the door shut behind me.

"It's a shame," I said with as much sincerity as I could manage. The Seed burned a hole in my pocket at my deception. "But better to bring about no change than to allow Thea to wield that sort of power."

"I guess." Rosemary didn't sound convinced. "Anyway, I'm sorry again about last night, and I'm glad you're okay."

She signed off, and I dropped my keys and phone on my hall table, relieved to have successfully closed the door on Rosemary's fascination with the three artifacts. With any luck, she and the rest of the order would never know that I now held the Seed.

After changing into pajamas and feeding myself a dinner of sandwiches—I couldn't muster the energy for anything more—the buzzer for my door rang. I stumbled to the intercom button.

"Hello?" My voice came out husky with tiredness.

"Can I come up?" Jerome's voice spoke through the speaker.

My eyes widened, sleep leaving my body in a rush. I buzzed him in and raced to my bedroom. While I didn't feel the need of a younger woman to make myself look more than I was, I still didn't want to greet Jerome in my pajamas and no bra.

When he knocked on the door, my teeth were brushed, and I was dressed in the clothes I'd discarded a few minutes ago. Jerome looked tired—his energy from the Seed healing must have run out like mine had—but he thrust a box toward me.

"It's a thank you," he said.

His eyes flicked to the box and mine followed. My hands reached out of their own accord.

"I'll never refuse something baked," I said. "Come on in."

As I closed the door behind Jerome and he stood awkwardly in the entryway, I realized that he'd never been in my condo. Every other meeting had been on a walk or in the bakery. It felt strange to have him there, but also pleasant. Very few people entered my abode, but Jerome felt right there.

I slid my fingernail along the tape holding the box closed and lifted the lid. The scent of lemon drifted out, and I inhaled deeply. Inside was a cake covered in pale yellow buttercream frosting and garnished with candied lemons.

"It's gorgeous," I breathed. "When did you find time to bake this?"

"My manager was away sick today, and Jodi and Kylie, the girls at the front, don't tell tales. It's to say thank you for healing me."

I carefully placed the box on a side table and turned to him.

"No thanks are necessary. You were only hurt because I dragged you into that mess. I should be the one thanking you." I chuckled. "But don't get me wrong, I'm keeping the cake."

Jerome grinned. My feet stepped forward on their own, and my arms decided to reach out and wrap my fingers around Jerome's neck. His breath hitched.

"Your bird is pecking on the window," Caelus said. He pointed at my patio door, where Beaky was tapping her beak against the glass. Jerome stepped back at Caelus' words, and my arms slid away from him.

"I forgot about your spirit," he murmured.

I sighed then chuckled. We would definitely have to figure something out with Caelus. He was a real mood-breaker.

"We'll deal with him soon."

"Hey," Caelus protested. "I'm right here."

"Yes, that's the problem." I waved Jerome into the living room. "Have a seat. Let's dig into this cake of yours. I just have to feed Beaky first."

"You have a pet pigeon?"

"She's a nuisance, but she's my nuisance. And she helped me out in a tight spot once, so she earned her bits of crust."

Jerome shook his head but didn't ask further questions. He sank onto the couch with a sigh of contentment, and I gazed at him for a moment while his eyes were on Beaky. I'd dithered about my feelings for Jerome for weeks, but now that my body and mind were aligned, a peace had stolen over me. Maybe I did want this.

I walked into the kitchen to find plates, forks, and a crust of bread for Beaky. A ping emerged from my pocket, and I opened my email. I scanned the document from my translating student, and my eyes widened.

"This page talks about the Thorn," I whispered to Caelus. My fevered eyes skimmed over the words, hardly daring to believe what I was reading.

"What does it say?"

I looked up at Caelus, my heart pounding.

"I think I know where to find it."

ALSO BY EMMA SHELFORD

Magical Morgan
Daughters of Dusk
Mothers of Mist
Elders of Ether

Immortal Merlin
Ignition
Winded
Floodgates
Buried
Possessed
Unleashed
Worshiped
Unraveled

Nautilus Legends
Free Dive
Caught
Surfacing
Hooked

Breenan Series
Mark of the Breenan
Garden of Last Hope
Realm of the Forgotten

ACKNOWLEDGEMENTS

A big thank you to those who read *Mothers of Mist* first and helped turn it into a worthy story: Wendy Callendar, Danielle Tatsakron, Nadene du Plooy, Bettina Luna, and Steven Shelford. Thanks to Deranged Doctor Design for an exciting cover.

ABOUT THE AUTHOR

Emma Shelford feels that life is only complete with healthy doses of magic, history, and science. Since these aren't often found in the same place, she creates her own worlds where they happily coexist. If you catch her in person, she will eagerly discuss Lord of the Rings ad nauseam, why the ancient Sumerians are so cool, and the important role of phytoplankton in the ocean.

Emma is the author of multiple urban fantasy series, including Magical Morgan, Immortal Merlin, Nautilus Legends, and the Breenan Series.

www.ingramcontent.com/pod-product-compliance
Lightning Source LLC
Chambersburg PA
CBHW030819210726
48290CB00002B/662